ALSO BY TERRIE NOVAK

Decision Dexterity:
How to Overcome the Agony of Indecision

Doodle and Decide:
Coloring Meditation to Awaken Intuition

Joy Centered HPV Healing:
Flower of Life Decision Guide

Jules Fae

A Story of *Adoption and Reunion*

TERRIE NOVAK

JULES FAE, A STORY OF ADOPTION AND REUNION
Copyright ©2022 by Terrie Novak
All rights reserved.

ISBN: 978-1-7331588-7-9

Developmental editing by Natalie Serber
Line editing by Brooks Becker
Cover design by Mila Book Covers
Custom book production by JW Manus

Published by Concept Bridges
Tigard, Oregon 97224

This is a work of fiction. Names, characters, places, and incidents either are the product of the author's imagination or are used fictitiously.

CONCEPT BRIDGES

for my family

Cast of Characters

Claire Jordan: First Mother

Claire's always been intuitive. They say she gets it from her Oma, who, according to family lore, continues to leave handwritten messages for loved ones, even though she passed over a decade ago. Claire is popular at high school, not only because of her natural Scandinavian beauty and fashion sense, but for her inner power and an uncanny ability to read photographs. She sees into the subject's past with just enough accuracy everyone suspects she is receiving insider information from teachers or parents. In her free time, Claire prefers to be alone in her room reading spy novels. She is fascinated by the power of secrets and how they can be used in both good and harmful ways.

Johanka "Jo" Černý Tischler: Adoptive Mother

Jo is the middle child and the only person in her family with head-to-toe freckles and red hair. She embraces her family's traditions and always knew she'd be a teacher, just like her mother and her grandmother who taught in Czechoslovakia. Jo dedicates her life to the belief that every child deserves to feel like they belong and has the opportunity to achieve their full potential. When Jo fell in love with a local farmer, her folks immediately prepared for their next grandchild. Jo's older sister married at seventeen and had her first baby just after turning eighteen. That's just how things are. Marriage and babies are an unspoken expectation of Cerny women.

Julia "Jules" Fae Tischler: Adoptee

Before she was legally named by Jo, Jules was known as "Sarah" by her first mother, "Baby Girl" by the Nebraska University Medical Center, "the said child" by Child Horizons Adoption Agency, and "Blank" by Douglas County and the State of Nebraska. Because it's the 1960s, Jules has no right to her original birth certificate and it's illegal for her to have knowledge of her birth parents or any subsequent siblings. Though prohibited from knowing her own ethnic and religious background, Jules assumes her adopted family's traditions. Jules will grow to discover the circumstances of her conception are a state secret, the conditions of her birth a rare miracle, and the color of her eyes is not the only trait that runs in the family.

Primal Wound

Claire always imagined there'd be sunshine the day she became a mother. She'd be wearing a yellow maternity gown and her husband would drive them to the hospital in a green Chevy Impala. But the January afternoon sky is grey. No sun. No husband. Not even a front door, since girls from the maternity home enter the hospital through the back door . . . to protect their identity.

"I'm here to check in Claire. Margaret Claire Jordan. One of the Franklin girls," says Lilli.

Claire has never liked being called a "Franklin girl," but at this point it doesn't matter. Her time with the work home will soon be over. Labor three weeks early, came as a surprise, but Lilli says that's still in the normal range and is nothing to worry about. Claire gently rubs her belly and reassures the child inside of her: *It's grey now, Sarah, but dark clouds always lift.*

If only Claire believed that herself. As the next contraction sets in, Claire braces herself on the counter and puffs through the wave of pain.

Lilli pulls a wheelchair from around the side of the counter and guides Claire to sit down.

Thank goodness for Lilli, the only one who makes Claire feel safe.

Head Nurse Ader looks over her glasses at Lilli, then down at Claire, disapproving of everything. Claire is used to on-the-spot disapproval, that's just part of the package of being a pregnant teen. The nurse clucks with agitation as she fingers through the rack of medical records and pulls out the one with the green label. "You're early,"

Nurse Ader states the only thing that feels obvious. "We may send you back with false labor."

"She didn't look right when she came in for work this morning . . ." begins Lilli. There wasn't a day that Lilli didn't make the pointed effort to ask Claire how she was feeling. Even when Claire responded "fine," not wanting to share the pitiful truth about her state of being, Lilli would grab Claire's hand and assess her wellness before moving on with the day's agenda.

Nurse Ader grabs Claire by the wrists, inspecting her swollen hands.

Hysterical cries from a few doors down ring through the hallway, creating a spine-chilling interruption. "Pleee-hee-heez . . . help me." The quivering voice projects a combination of pain and fear and youth.

Claire's head jerks around, her eyes wide. The sudden movement triggers a sickening headache. She winces and takes back her hand to rub the heel of her palm on her forehead.

Nurse Ader ignores the screams and Lilli's comment entirely as she takes back Claire's hand and clips on the hospital bracelet. Claire reads the birthdate of her first born, 01/03/1966 and wonders if the bracelet displays some indicator alerting the staff she's to receive the same ill treatment as the screaming girl.

Claire looks up at Lilli, searching her face for reassurance.

Lilli puts a steadying hand on Claire's shoulder and continues to debrief Nurse Ader on a concerning condition. "Her legs are swollen too, and the vomiting started along with the contractions."

Nurse Ader gets right up in Claire's face. "Wouldn't it be nice if all you girls had University sponsors to speak up for you?" The heat of Nurse Ader's breath on her neck brings Claire's nausea up a notch.

Actually, yes. Yes, it would be. Lilli created her a job in the library, which got her out of the usual work-home cleaning duties and away from the non-stop indoctrination of shame the other girls endured all day long. Lilli even allowed Claire to borrow her car once a week so she could spend some time with friends on a girls' night out. Yes, all the pregnant teens at Franklin could use someone providing them emotional support, resources, and real choices.

"Your color's off," says Nurse Ader as though she's scolding. She scans Claire top down, starting at Claire's favorite bright-orange head scarf all the way down to her stylish orange mid-calf PVC boots. Claire squints back at the nurse, wondering what she's looking for.

Nurse Ader clucks with continued disapproval as she removes Claire's scarf without ceremony and holds it out in Lilli's direction while simultaneously signaling her to remove the boots. "Aren't these fabulous?" she says with a condescending sneer. "What've you got to be joyful about? You're here to have a baby, not to become a mother."

Lilli purses her lips as she bends down to unzip Claire's boots for her. "I'll take care of your pretty things," she reassures Claire.

Heavy footfall approaches with a confident pace. Dr. Walter Greene comes around the corner smelling of greased hair and Wrigley's Doublemint Gum. The old man scribbles on his clipboard and glances at his watch. He barks orders in the direction of no one in particular.

"Nurse, why isn't room 8 silenced by now? Those who are morally bankrupt must not be heard." He glances at Lilli and looks like he's going to give her an order too.

Claire's body hardens as if he ordered a contraction. To push through the pain and steady her nausea, Claire keeps her eyes to the white tiles of the institution floor and follows Dr. Greene's shoes as he continues on down the corridor and steps into room 8. A young nurse with a medication tray scurries past them and enters room 8 just behind him. The screams from the girl quickly fade to a haunting silence. "I'm going to throw up . . ." Claire grabs the arms of the wheelchair and looks around for a container.

Nurse Ader expertly slides a nearby kidney dish into Claire's hands just in time, then gives a dismissive wave to Lilli, "You may go now." She positions herself to push Claire across the hall toward room 11.

Claire grabs onto Lilli's arm, "Lilli—" There is desperation in her voice.

Lilli steps into their path and leans down to allow Claire to look directly into her eyes, "Do as Nurse Ader says." Lilli looks up at Nurse Ader, making clear who she'd hold accountable. "She'll make sure you're both taken care of."

Claire nods and swallows the sour taste in her mouth. As they enter the room, Claire considers its similarity to a torture chamber. The hospital bed is equipped with straps and stirrups, a single folded sheet in the center. A metal cabinet with glass doors hangs on the wall and has two shelves stocked with towels and a few simple supplies. There's a sink in the corner and a metal bassinet with wheels next to it.

"Clothes off." Nurse Ader points to the hook on the wall and then the hospital bed. "Lay down."

Claire takes off her clothes and hangs them up as she's told. As a contraction takes over, she steadies herself against the bed, groaning and crying out loudly.

Nurse Ader peers outside the door and down the hall, then exhales in relief. Agitated, she closes the door behind her. "Look at me."

Claire musters her attention as best she can with the contraction subsiding.

"From this minute forward, you'll be absolutely silent."

Claire wrinkles her forehead in confusion.

"No more whining. No crying or moaning. No sound. We clear?"

Claire hesitantly nods once.

With the next contraction coming on, she purses her lips, leans into the hospital bed, and physically holds her mouth shut, as the waves of the pain of labor come over her. The sound of her breath and rapid heartbeat takes over her entire head. The room spins. She manages to hold in everything except a stream of hot tears.

Nurse Ader watches with satisfaction. "That's right. If you ever want to see that baby, not another sound."

In a breath of recovery, Claire grabs hold of Nurse Ader's sleeve, pulling her close to whisper her one and only demand: "I will see my baby."

Nurse Ader jerks her arm away, "It's not your baby," and proceeds to push Claire onto the table and buckle Claire's bloated limbs into the straps. "Your voluntary surrender is the basis for admission to Franklin."

Claire understands that Franklin is in partnership with Child Horizons Adoption Agency, and she knows she's expected to sign relinquishment documents soon after delivery. But as it stands right now, this is her baby. Claire squints from the fluorescent lighting as Nurse Ader positions her legs into the stirrups.

"You've made your bed, now lie in it and shut up."

Claire looks down at her belly and calms herself, determined to see her baby girl.

A young nurse opens the door, holding a med tray. Nurse Ader stops her from entering.

"Not here. The med order was only for room 8."

Dr. Greene, who was walking by writing on his clipboard, overhears this instruction and pauses outside the door to look up and see who dare contradict his orders.

Nurse Ader explains herself. "I promise you, this one will feel everything *and* be quiet about it. With God's help, the pain will teach her a lesson."

Dr. Greene tilts his head and huffs out his nose in agreement. He glances over his glasses at the young nurse and nods, confirming his approval of the head nurse's approach, then continues on his way.

Claire is left to labor alone. Though she makes no sounds, it's far from silent. The pounding of her heart is so loud she's sure it must be echoing off the sterile white walls. Or is that echo really Sarah's heart? She's not sure, but it reminds Claire to breathe, as oxygen is all she has left to offer her baby.

After an eternity of suffering, Nurse Ader enters the room and manually checks Claire's cervix. "It's time to push," she commands.

The pressure of probing fingers sends an electric shock through Claire's body, leaving a metallic taste in her mouth. Claire tries to create tension on the straps to support pushing, but her hands are frozen. She can't feel her legs and watches her disembodied knees shake until her vision blurs. Greyness sets in and engulfs her entire body like a thick fog.

The vibration from her legs continues to intensify until she's shaken clean out of her body. Released from the restraints of the birthing table, Claire looks up and sees star-filled darkness beyond the hospital ceiling. She looks down and sees the seizing body of a young woman about to give birth. Claire drifts into a hazy dream, comforted by knowing her daughter will be beside her soon.

Nurse Ader ignites the room with urgency, calling in Dr. Greene, who bursts in barking orders. Nurse Ader runs out. Two other nurses enter, one carrying a surgical tray with large metal forceps and a scalpel. Dr. Greene directs the nurses with hand gestures. The young nurse climbs onto the mother's convulsing body and performs brutal fundal pushing. The mother's limbs continue to jerk and jolt against the restraints. Dr. Greene lays down a broad slashing episiotomy. The nurse passes the forceps to the doctor.

"No!" he shouts as he brushes the instrument out of his way, knocking it out of the nurse's hand. Time shifts into slow motion as the metal instrument clangs on the tiled floor.

The seizing stops, and the mother's hands and legs go limp in the straps. The room is filled with silence as the membrane balloons out and the fetus emerges fully enclosed in the amniotic sac. Claire continues her dream from above as everyone freezes in awe of witnessing the miracle of an en caul birth.

Resting silent and calm in the warm fluid, the baby is completely at peace, her head and arm shifting about in the familiar limitations of the protective membranes. Though detached from the scene, a chill comes over Claire with the baby no longer in her body. Sarah is out of her reach, but Claire remains aware of their connection.

"Incredible," mouths the doctor as he holds the baby, fully contained in the transparent bag. He gently rubs the baby through the sac, adjusting the position of her arm. His voice barely a whisper, he says, "The mother provides oxygen, while the baby responds to external stimuli." An event so rare most only read of it in textbooks.

The baby shifts her tiny hands to cover her eyes.

Dr. Greene finds the best angle to apply the amnihook and breaks open the sac. The fluids are suctioned as he gently peels away the protective membranes.

The baby is shocked by the sensation of air touching her skin. As a reflex, she gasps her first breath. The hole in her heart closes, directing oxygen to enter the bloodstream from her tiny lungs for the first time.

The cry of her firstborn yanks Claire's consciousness back into her sweat-drenched body. The sounds in the room fade in and out as she struggles to regain awareness.

"There she is," says Dr. Greene. He hands the baby to the older nurse as he dictates to the other, "En caul birth at thirty-seven weeks. Female. Active response, pink, with a vigorous cry. Please add a side note, if anything falls through with the agency, they are to contact my personal attorney, concerning the placement of this child."

The older nurse tends to the baby, cleaning, measuring, and wrapping it with methodical procedure. The baby attempts to suck its own tiny fist and calmly accepts this treatment.

Dr. Greene turns his attention back to Claire and dictates, "Female neurosis likely contributed to a rare type onset of preeclampsia."

"Doctor," interrupts the nurse, "what is the protocol for this?" The nurse lifts up the amniotic membrane. "Does it go with the baby, or the girl?"

"Superstitions have no place in this hospital," says Dr. Greene. The nurses all look at him like they are not about to simply dispose of it with the rest of the afterbirth. "Have the membrane prepared for the archives."

The young nurse is unclear what exactly that means, so she simply sets the caul aside in a kidney tray.

Claire continues struggling to orient herself, while Dr. Greene rolls his chair into position to stitch her up. Claire manages to form words and asks, "Is she born?"

The older nurse looks to the younger one with a sardonic expression and says, "I bet you'd like to hold it, wouldn't you?"

Claire finds enough energy to nod and attempts to find her arms in order to hold her daughter, but they are still strapped to the table.

The nurse ensures the baby is handled out of Claire's line of vision and lays the child into the bassinet. "This baby doesn't belong to you."

Claire's mouth drops. "But . . ." She searches, looking side to side, "Nurse Ader said . . ."

"Well now, Nurse Ader isn't here, is she?"

Now the baby is born, what little value Claire had before, has dwindled to the nuisance of ensuring she is sufficiently stable for discharge. Claire pulls halfheartedly against the straps, but has no strength left to struggle and flops flat on the bed in complete exhaustion. Hot tears stream down into her ears. "Let me see my baby."

Dr. Greene finishes the stitches and looks up at Claire, the girl who just gave him one of the most thrilling delivery tales of his career. He'll feast on the events of this day for a lifetime. He never offers advice or solace to these girls. There's no point, really, in comforting the feeble-minded. And yet he grabs the nurse's chart and scribbles on it. "Let's add acetaminophen to her meds." He looks at the older nurse, "Remove the restraints, Dorothy." He turns and leaves the room.

"Well, someone thinks you're special," says Dorothy as she unbuckles the restraints.

The young nurse wheels the bassinet out of the room and she asks, "Should we put this one in the Baby Showcase?"

"Yes, until the agency foster nanny comes for pickup. It's the perfect one for display hour."

For the first time, Claire is afraid for her baby. The joyful flutters of her baby have been replaced with chills and muscle spasms. She is oddly grateful she's not conscious enough to fully realize the depth of the emptiness that is overtaking her. She'd vomit again if she had the strength. Fading back to sleep, Claire realizes her only motivation for ever waking up again is the belief that maybe Nurse Ader will live up to her bargain and soon she'll see her daughter.

"What about the name card?" asks the young nurse.

"Just write Baby Girl."

PART 1

CHAPTER 1

Nine months ago

Claire smooths her hands over her new wool skirt and turns from side to side. Is it possible that new clothes are all it takes to transform a high school girl into a college woman? That, and a University of Nebraska School of Humanities and Social Sciences acceptance letter. Shopping bags are strewn about her bedroom as she experiments mixing and matching outfits in front of the mirror. While singing "Sugar Pie Honey Bunch" along with the radio, Claire gives each look its own dance move. The Swim seems to coordinate well with wool. She received enough graduation gift money to update her wardrobe and was thrilled to accept Aunt Georgia's offer to take her shopping. Aunt Georgia is her only relative with the slightest eye for fashion. She is also fun enough to know how to navigate the balance between college dress code guidelines and Claire's secret inner go-go dancer. Aunt Georgia kept the "University of Nebraska Student Guidebook for Women" in her purse to browse through while Claire was in the store dressing room. She earmarked the page with the heading "Nebraska's Ideal Coed" and circled the words "refrain from the unladylike habit of complaining."

"Claire," she says with a quirky smile and an approving nod for the dress that went best with the must-have bright-orange go-go boots. "I can help you look like a coed, but sweetie, there's nothing I can do about your unladylike habits."

The doorbell awakens Claire from her shopping daydream, "I

got it, Mom!" Claire runs down the stairs and, a little out of breath and giddy, she swings open the front door. "I'm glad you got my message," she says, giving Zach a sneaky peck on the lips. "Mom, is it OK if Zach comes up to my room? I want to show him my new clothes."

"Can't you show him down here in the front room, honey? That's where we entertain guests."

"Come on, Mom."

"Fine," says Mom, now at the door with a dishtowel in her hands. "But leave the bedroom door open."

Claire looks at her mom, *seriously*? But she says nothing because, yes, her mother is serious.

Mom and Zach exchange awkward nods of agreement and polite smiles.

They go up to her room and Zach takes his camera case strap off his shoulder. It's a Kodak Brownie 8mm video camera in the custom brown field case. "I want you to have this."

Claire is hesitant to accept. "Your camera?"

"As a graduation present. So you can show me what college is like."

"Wow."

The whole graduation event has slowly driven a wedge between them for months now. It's becoming more and more real that in a matter of weeks, Claire will be at college, while Zach is going back to the same high school football camp he's attended for the last three years. They'll be in completely different worlds, not to mention completely different states.

"Take it. Besides, Mom said she'd get me the latest model for my eighteenth birthday."

Claire accepts the camera and flips up the viewfinder, pretending to film Zach. He smiles and begins doing the hitchhiker dance. He is so darned corny. Claire knows this is like taking a piece of Zach with her, because this boy loves his gadgets. He has two other cameras besides this, also a telescope, a radio, and of course a CB—which is how they originally met. Claire's dad and Zach's dad are in the same CB radio club. It's funny when life goes circular. They met through gadgets, and if Claire does this conversation right, they will separate with gadgets.

"You're sure decked out," says Zach, taking notice of Claire's new outfit and the evidence of the shopping spree that has exploded in her room.

"Do you think I look like a college coed?" Claire makes a little spin.

"Sure. Do you feel like one?"

"Yes." She grabs both of Zach's hands and pulls him over to sit down on the bed next to her, so they can still touch each other but she doesn't have to look directly at him. "That's what I wanted to talk about . . ." She isn't entirely sure how to go about this. She hasn't had much experience with separations. She's lived in the same house her whole life. Never transitioned schools other than entering high school with all her friends. The only thing she ever really had to say good-bye to was the feral cat she fed for two years and that was easy, it just never came back. "You know Dad's dropping me off at the women's dorm soon."

"Soon?" Zach's tone somehow blends his personal sadness with encouragement all at the same time. "Seems kind of early." He reaches his hand around Claire's back and runs his fingers along the seam of the skirt's waist band.

"For summer school. I want to know the place, how it works. So I'm ready to compete with the men come fall term."

"Compete?"

"I'm not going to college to be anyone's secretary."

"Right." Zach patiently listens to Claire's lofty ideas about working outside of the household and effecting change in the world. But he doesn't seem to really believe it.

"I won't have my dad watching over my every move anymore, so I'm looking forward to being . . . independent."

Zach starts to unconsciously bounce his leg. He grabs the camera and folds down the viewfinder.

"I want to . . . explore." Claire tucks a bit of hair back behind her ear. "I think that's important before I consider being a wife and mother." Claire pauses and lets Zach's leg soak up the awkward silence. Of course, someday she wants to get married and have children, that's not even a question. But not just yet. First, she needs to satisfy some curiosity she has about the world. Claire continues to inch toward her point, "We're going to be in separate worlds, and the truth is . . ."

"Look, I get it," interrupts Zach. Annoyed with where this is going, he stands up and looks out the bedroom window with his arms crossed.

"I just don't see where we can go from here." Claire rolls her head up and looks at the ceiling. "I don't know . . . pen pals?"

"Pen pals?" Zach swings around, completely aghast. "Jesus, Claire. Are you serious? After everything we've had together?"

"Well, realistically, what can it be? It's not like we're getting engaged." Claire stops to think. She realizes that Zach may consider the camera an equivalent to an engagement ring, he's kind of like that in a sweet, well-meaning, nerdy way. She takes a deep breath. She must say the words. "I think we should break up."

Zach scratches his head vigorously with both hands and then stretches, arching his back. He walks around the bed to Claire, holds both of her hands, then bends down to look directly into her eyes, "Let's have one more date."

"What?"

"Let's . . . celebrate." Zach pushes the same strand of hair back behind Claire's ear.

Claire looks down and bites the inside of her cheek. This isn't the clean break she planned on.

"You know. Not leave each other with just an anxious goodbye in your bedroom while your mom's trying to listen."

Just then they hear Claire's mom close the bathroom door across the hall. They look at each other and grin. Embarrassed, Claire adjusts the scarf on her ponytail.

"Seriously, let's celebrate our last time together as a couple."

Claire nods. She likes the idea of ending things on an up note. "OK."

"Next week, the CB club plans to rendezvous off County Highway G6R. That means they'll have a bon fire, hay bales circled up, hotdogs, you know—like they did last summer. Think your dad will take you?"

"I'm sure he will. We've already talked about it. My last ever CB club ride along."

"Done." He walks out the bedroom door to see himself out. "I'll see you then . . . Miss Coed Hullabaloo dancer." He starts doing the Freddie.

Claire shakes her head, wondering how such a cornball managed to turn her breakup into their next date.

Chapter 2

Nine years ago

Jo stops in front of the girls' restroom holding the hand of the dirtiest child she's ever seen. She's thankful this school has showers in the restrooms. So many of the country schools don't even have running water. Despite the limited material resources available in the rural schoolhouse, the students are provided an education as good as any they could have gotten in a city.

"Well, Francie, are you ready?" she asks the child who is literally head-to-toe dirt. And not just dust that can be brushed off, but grime that's engrained in every fiber of her clothes, every hair and every crease of her sweet little six-year-old body. She's the only child in the town who lives in a home with dirt floors. Dirt floors!

"Yes, Mrs. Tischler."

Jo loves being called by her teacher name. The children in her class sing her name with a sweet tone, endearment in their tiny voices, extending her the same trust they would give their own mothers. Jo is determined to ensure that all her students have equal opportunity for learning and success in her classroom. The girls the same as the boys. Those quick to learn and those who are slow. They all receive the same treatment. Francie however is a challenge. Her clothes are always filthy, and she doesn't look, or smell, like the other students. She always sticks out, openly ostracized by the other students. Even the two other teachers treat her differently, not only because of her appearance and stench, but because Francie's mother, Jill, was never married—as though holding the child responsible for her circumstances makes any kind of sense.

This morning, Jo arranged something special for Francie. The kindergarten graduation program is this afternoon and Jo took it upon herself to ensure Francie will have the same chance as all the other students to have pride in accomplishment. Jo recruited the two most mature and responsible girls from the seventh grade to bathe and dress Francie. Hygiene was after all an essential part of the home economics curriculum; this would give the older girls practical experience in caregiving as well as give Francie a chance to celebrate with her graduating class.

"Francie, the girls are going to clean you up for the program." Jo passes Francie's dirty little hand to one of the girls, and a bag of clean clothes to the other. In the bag are new underclothes Jo bought from the store, a dress Mrs. Becket the church piano lady donated, and shoes that Jo's best friend Ruth contributed, as her daughter had outgrown them. "Thank you, girls. Just put her dirty clothes in the bag and bring her back to the classroom when you're done."

Jo looks out onto the auditorium that on any other day is the lunchroom. Her face is flushed with excitement as the whole community has come to see the school's spring program. There are limited chairs, and folks are standing in rows along the back walls. Jo looks for her husband, Will, hoping he was able to make it on time to see her kids graduate. The schoolhouse is two counties away from where Will attends trade school and works. He said he'd meet her there and try his best to be there on time, though he might be a bit late. Even though he doesn't have to, Will always goes the extra mile to be part of the school events. He understands the children are always first in Jo's heart. He said he admired that about her. This was the greatest compliment she'd ever received, and the reason she married him.

Jo has certificates prepared to hand to each child once they have walked across the stage. She loves watching the children's eyes light up when their names are announced. Everyone briefly applauds for each child as they walk across the stage. Francie holds the sides of her dress out like an adorable little princess when she walks. It's unfortunate, but not surprising, that Jill is not there to see her beautiful daughter's big moment. Jo does her best as a stand-in and gives Francie a wink as she hands her the certificate. Not a single student is shy; they all beam with pride as they receive their first academic achievement. "Congratulations to the kindergarten class of 1957," says Jo, filled with happiness for each and every one of her kids. She steps down from the front stage to go stand with the crowd and watch the second part of the program. The rest of the children from grades one through eight line up on risers and prepare to sing a few songs as accompanied by Mrs. Becket.

"Is that Jill Laney's girl? In a clean dress?" says the woman with a tightly pinned bun sitting just in front of where Jo is standing.

"Well, I'll be. I couldn't tell at first," says the lady in the black hat sitting next to the woman. "Sure enough, she blends right in with the others."

Jo smiles and mentally pats herself on the back. Why yes, she does. Because she *is* just like the others, beautiful and filled with potential.

"You know," offers the woman on the other side, "Jill's seeing a decent man now." The women glance at each other. "*The trucker*," she mouths, her voice not audible, but her raised eyebrow making it clear she has the skinny on Jill. They nod at each other and look back at the program. The woman continues, out the side of her mouth. "He proposed. Said he'd adopt the girl."

The first song is over and the children bow as the audience applauds.

"No amount of scrubbing will wash away the fact that she's illegitimate," says the lady in the black hat.

The children shift positions to highlight four dancers with the second tune.

Jo is aghast, digesting the last comment she overheard. It's no fault of the child that an irresponsible man took advantage of her mother. Once adopted they'll be a family. End of story.

"If you ask me, it's not fair to the proper children, treating her the same as them."

Jo's face is now flushed with anger, her chest hot, the tip of her nose bright red. Not fair? To the *other* children?

Just then Will shows up. He scoots all the way down the wall behind the other spectators and puts his arm around Jo's waist as a silent hello. Jo looks at Will, her body stiff, eyebrows furrowed as she attempts to contain her rage. Will recognizes the look. *What?* he mouths silently.

At an angle that only Will can see, Jo crosses her arms, nods, and, raising an eyebrow, points a finger toward the women sitting in front of them.

"Regardless, clearly Mrs. Tischler is a talented teacher. A gift to the community really." The women around her nod in agreement.

Will raises his eyebrows to Jo, telepathically communicating, *That's a good thing, right?* He squeezes her and smiles with pride.

Jo bites her cheek and shifts her eyes in suspicion.

"She'd be a fabulous mother," says the lady with the bun. "I'm surprised they don't have children of their own by now."

"Apparently she can't get pregnant," says the lady in the black hat.

"Oh. That's too bad."

"Poor dear," says the other.

The crowd applauds loudly now as the children take their final bow. Everyone begins standing up and clearing the chairs.

Jo looks down at her shoes and turns toward Will, hiding behind him, hoping the women don't see she's been standing there.

"Hey." Will raises Jo's gaze, his reassuring eyes telling her not to give the thoughtless chatter a second thought. "Grab your things." Will squeezes her hand adorned with the modest wedding band he slipped on her finger three years ago. "I'll take you home."

CHAPTER 3

Claire fidgets with the Woolworths wedding band on her finger that is a half-size too big. She'd have taken the ridiculous thing off if she didn't think she'd lose it otherwise. From Claire's view the ring is a symbol of shame, but the Matron of the maternity home requires all the girls to wear rings when they go out in public to protect them from social persecution. That's a laugh.

Claire shifts her weight awkwardly to look into the rearview mirror and adjust her favorite orange head scarf. Her huge belly barely fits behind the driver's wheel of the sedan that Lilli loaned her for one final girls' night out before the girls are due to deliver.

Claire squints out the passenger window to the front door of the converted mansion. The entrance plaque reads, "The Franklin Maternity Home — Dedicated to the reform of fallen women to whom we offer salvation and hope." Her reformed friends should be coming out at any moment. What's taking so long?

The last of the afternoon light dances off the thin layer of snow on the ground. Shimmering stars zigzag Claire's vision as she rubs her eyes. She rummages through her tote bag sitting on the seat next to her and digs out a bottle of aspirin. She throws one down dry hoping to hedge off the inevitable migraine.

From inside the house, Riley pulls back the curtain and waves. Once she's gotten Claire's attention, she holds up a finger and mouths, *One more minute.*

Claire smiles and nods. That goof. Sweet Jesus, it doesn't seem possible that fourteen-year-old bundle of innocence is going to have her baby any day now. In truth, there's no telling who will go first: Claire, Riley, or Stella. All three were admitted to Franklin on the same day, that's how they became friends. An assumed name is assigned to each girl when she is admitted as a resident. The list of fake names is in alphabetical order so Riley became Betty, Stella became Cathy, and Claire's name became Debby.

"To protect your identity, use your assumed name at all times." That's what it says at the top of the house chore list that hangs just next to the community phone. Yet another thing that is supposedly protecting them. Besides not being able to use your own name, or your own marital status, there are many other things they can't do while residents of Franklin—like not eat sugar and no taking or sharing photos. Everyone knew this was complete malarkey and breaking those rules is the theme of tonight's grand finale girls' night out.

Just the thought of eating sugar set off an uncontrollable wave of candy craving. Claire reaches in her bag for the box of Sugar Babies she picked up to share as treats for tonight's show. She shakes a few into her palm. No one will notice.

After what seems like so much more than one minute, the two pregnant teens open the front door cautiously and look side to side, anticipating the inevitable ambush. Claire looks from her angle, and waves them in. Stella and Riley slide quickly out the door and move forward as a pair, each girl gripping her side of the stair railing, heads ducked down. Once safely down the cement stairs, they begin the dash toward the sedan.

Midway to the car, a couple of neighborhood boys jump out from the hedges and throw rotten fruit at the dashing pregnant women. Easy targets, they both take a hit in the middle of their backs. They grit their teeth and continue as fast as they can to the car, yank open the doors, throw in their bags, and roll their bodies into the backseat.

Claire rolls down her window just enough to shout at the little shits. "Take a day off already!"

The girls slam the back seat doors and Claire hands them towels to clean off the back of each other's coats and the car seat. The car wheels spin a bit in the icy slush alongside the curb as they pull away.

"Everyone OK?" asks Claire over her shoulder.

"All OK," reports Stella, busy wiping up the mess.

"Everyone got their movie snacks?" asks Claire.

"Got 'em," says Riley. Slightly out of breath, she holds up her stained glass–printed Pucci tote bag her Grandma gave her for Christmas. Smiling at Riley's face in the rearview mirror, Claire notices that though Riley is enthusiastic, she's visibly tired and uncomfortable. They all are.

But Claire promised to show them the fruits of her daily labors at the library and this was pretty much their last chance. She's been working under the direction of Lilli setting up the new technology equipment, and sharing the home movies she made with Zach's camera seemed like a fun way to try out the new projector. At any rate they will all eat snacks and talk in private one last time before the babies came. "It'll be like our own personal hideout."

"Only Claire Jordan can make going to the library sound like a legit night out," says Stella.

Claire smiles and adjusts the radio. "The library is one place where the assholes aren't."

"Hey, did you notice?" announces Riley with a hint of pride in her voice. "Today Betty is at the top of the chore list. Any day now it's goodbye Betty and nice to see you again Riley."

It's adorable that Riley openly announces she misses her old self. This dream weighs heavy on all the girls at Franklin.

"I'll be back, just like nothing ever happened." Riley repeats the phrase she's been trained to believe. A thickness hangs in the car as the girls digest that idea. Sweet Riley, she's too naive to realize that her old self will never exist again.

"Wouldn't that be wonderful?" says Claire. The caseworkers know just what to exploit to gain compliance. They insist that after the relinquishment, they are free to continue their lives unencumbered by the responsibilities of motherhood. Claire often wonders, how do you leave your firstborn, like nothing ever happened, when clearly *everything* happened?

"It is true, once a name leaves the top of that chore list, that girl is never seen or heard of again." True and unsettling. Claire is hopeful that the chance to share their stories will somehow help them come to terms with it all. This is their last night together before they start dropping off the chore list. Soon everything they've been through will be nothing but a dark secret.

Riley reaches over and grabs Stella's hand, holding it tight. It's almost dark now and Claire flicks on the headlights. They ride the rest of the way to the University holding hands and listening to the Beatles on the radio singing "Help," the girls' unofficial anthem.

As they enter the library, Claire inhales deeply and smiles, feeling at home in a place filled with college students who are refreshingly preoccupied with their own business. The girls stomp snow from their shoes and then simply stand there, excited but confused. "This way," says Claire. Though she typically walks with the confident prance of a runway model, her stride has been entirely appropriated by the size and weight of her baby, leaving her with the characteristic late-pregnancy waddle. Claire leads the waddling friends single file through the library—around the card catalog, past the study rooms, to the very back, where they come up to the door of the brand-new audio-visual room. Claire digs through her bag for the key Lilli entrusted her with. Once opened, the dark room releases the familiar smell of new carpet. She flips on the lights and rushes to the back of the room to turn on the record player, placing the needle at the groove of her favorite song.

Claire prepared the room today before the end of her usual work shift. The screen and projector are set up. The table to the side of the room has napkins, cups, and three small bags of popcorn she picked up from the cafeteria. Claire reaches into her bag and pulls out the box of Sugar Babies, shaking them to tempt her friends.

Winter coats and scarves fall to the floor and the girls reveal the truth of full-term pregnancy. Riley is petite in every way except for her low-riding baby bulge. She tries to remain small in presence and tucks a whisp of her short wavy brown hair behind her ear. "This is perfect, Claire," she says. "A secret cave for us three sisters."

Sisters in a cave. Claire wonders if Riley also sees in her mind's eye three beauties magically turned into monsters as a punishment for something they had no control over.

Riley pulls a pink bag of Dunkin Donuts from her bag and adds it to the table. "Dad came to yesterday's visitor night and brought these, and I saved them for you two," she says, proud of her discipline and loyalty. "Next time he sees me it will be . . . after . . . to pick me up." Riley looks down at her belly, her shoulders raised in a brief shrug, too ashamed and afraid to even have words for what's going to happen to her.

Stella puts her arm around Riley and gives her an empathetic squeeze. Though she's only seventeen herself, Stella looks out for Riley. Stella pulls out three cans of Sprite from her leather tote and hands one to Riley. Stella's not shy about being excited for the treats and grabs her favorite jelly donut. She sits down with her legs wide and uses her belly as a table. Easily balancing the donut on her belly, she stretches her arms out and shows off, "Look Mom, no hands!" The sisters giggle. They pop open the cans of soda, savor the sugar, and enjoy the music. Stella looks around the room and comments, "So this is where you work every day while we're scrubbing toilets and doing laundry?" she says with a hint of jealously.

"Yes," says Claire. "Who knew signing up for summer-term typing would end up with all this as a perk." The idea that any part of the experience of being unmarried and pregnant was a perk, puts a wry smile on her face. The benefits of this educational experience just keep on coming. She tilts the box of candies so a few more Sugar Babies roll into her hand. "We won't really have a chance to tell our stories after the babies come, so I thought we could . . ."

"Tell our secrets?" interjects Riley.

Of course, Riley thinks it's a game, but what does keeping a secret for a lifetime really do to a person? Take for example the home movie that Claire made with every intention of sharing it with Zach. What was she going to do with it? Carry it around as a secret from her future husband? Store it in a box in the attic where her future children might discover it once she's dead? What about the movie she's created in her mind with Sarah? Is there a storage unit deep enough or remote enough to hold that?

"Which secrets?" says Stella, waggling her eyebrows with impressive dexterity.

"Our hopes and dreams?" says Claire. "Those seem to qualify as secrets nowadays"

Riley puts down her soda, digs through her bag, and pulls out her wallet. She flips through the photo holder and presents a picture of her and her boyfriend all dressed up for prom.

"He's the father," she says just like that.

Stella and Claire slide together and hold the photo between them. There was a staged background with painted palm trees and they stood on a stage of sand decorated with shells. Riley had a wrist corsage, and a pearl necklace.

Claire allows herself to feel the nervous energy of a first prom as shared through Riley's photogenic smile. The excitement seems to flow into her baby, as it kicks and stretches into her bladder, causing immediate discomfort. She passes Stella a bag of popcorn,

"Ray and Riley, Southwest High's cutest couple," states Riley, very matter-of-factly.

Stella makes a sarcastic eyeroll, apparently too cute for her. She shoves a handful of popcorn in her mouth.

Riley flips through her wallet again and emerges with another photo of Ray. Here he's leaning against a Ford Mustang with his arms crossed. "His folks got him a brand-new car for his sixteenth birthday. We'd go to lots of places. A&W, the drive-in."

Claire imagines Riley swinging on the swing set, entertaining herself and others as they wait for the darkness to set in.

"I dreamed about being his wife, making his lunch, decorating the house with flowers." Riley stops her train of thought, embarrassed she may have revealed childish ideas of married life. "The only thing Mom ever told me about sex is 'never go behind the bushes with boys.' That's it. There are no bushes at the drive-in, so I figured it was OK."

Stella stops chewing, knowing there's more to this secret.

"To be honest, I wasn't sure if it really happened," Riley admitted. "It was all so . . . fast . . . and wet."

Riley maybe wasn't sure, but the picture was clear to Claire.

"He said, 'You belong to me now.' "

"Oh Riley . . ." Claire murmured, feeling sadness for the innocence taken like it could be owned.

Riley convinced herself otherwise, "I liked the idea of belonging to someone."

Riley pokes through her wallet again and presents a family portrait, like the kind you would take in a department store. They look amazingly similar to the *Father Knows Best* cast, Riley being the youngest of three. "I destroyed my mother," she admits, her soft voice filled with guilt. "My folks said I couldn't marry Ray because he wasn't Catholic." The next shot is of her parents standing at the front door of their home holding hands in an obviously posed fashion. "I overheard my father on the phone with the doctor. He said to send me to a home for feeble-minded girls." Riley turns to Claire, "Is that what we are?"

Claire frowns as she formulates a response. Feeble-minded? The record reaches the end of the album, making a dull, scratchy hum. Claire presses herself up out of the chair with a small groan, "We're the definition of strength." She puts her hand on Riley's shoulder as she walks by, "I don't see anything feeble about us." Claire flips the album over.

Riley nods and seems satisfied with the notion of seeing herself as strong. "After that, Mom made me hide in the house. Insisted I keep the drapes closed. I wasn't allowed to answer the door." She flips to another photo, this one of her in the yard with her black poodle Coco. She shared many Coco stories as polite conversation at Franklin. Here she was holding his front paws and they were dancing. "After a while, Ray stopped coming by . . . I guess I didn't belong to him anymore." Riley bites her lower lip and looks off, drifting away with her eyes fixated on the wall clock. "Any moment now, I won't belong to his baby either."

"What are you going to do, when you're back home?" asks Stella, shifting the conversation from the forbidden topic of who the babies will belong to.

"I don't know. Be a retail salesclerk? Something like that, until I'm a respectable wife, who can cook and clean for my husband. Then we can have a baby I can take care of."

Stella looks down at her fake wedding ring and shakes her head.

Riley notices her reaction. "What are you thinking, Stella? You don't think I'll be respectable again?"

"Of course you will," Stella is quick to respond and set Riley's heart at ease. "The thing is, I dreamed of my boyfriend too," she says, looking empathetically at Riley. She grabs her bag and pulls out the photo collection in her wallet. It's not as neat as Riley's, Stella just laid in several photographs on the other side of the cash pocket. She holds the small stack in her hands and shuffles to one. "This is Johnny."

The image is of a confident teen couple, laughing together. Johnny was leaning over her shoulder as Stella was thumbing through a stack of records. Claire imagines he was teasing her about her taste in music.

"We were in love, me and Johnny. He had a part-time job. When he finished for the day, we'd listen to records and play Frisbee." She shuffles to another photo of Johnny holding up a condom he just took from his wallet. He has that proud "see, I got it" look on his face. "He always told me he'd take care of everything. He managed to get condoms off the black market."

"How's that possible?" asked Riley.

Riley and Claire look at each other as though to say, *That's a good question*. It's no easy thing to get condoms or any kind of birth control. "I'm not entirely sure," admits Stella. "He and a friend road tripped to Chicago; they came back with condoms."

"Is that your secret?" says Riley.

"Well, after the first time we . . . used one . . . I thought it was, you know, romantic, beautiful. When he leaned close to me, I smiled, waiting to hear him say how much he loved me. But when he whispered in my ear he said, 'We were dirty.' "

"Jesus . . ." huffed Claire, shaking her head.

"Ya, you'd think I would have known better after that, but I thought he'd . . . mature." The next photo she offers is an adorable shot of Stella wearing an oversized man's jacket, one would assume Johnny's. She's smiling bright, her blunt-cut bangs perfectly framing her glowing face, like she's feeling oh so cozy in love. "We were pinned. You know, engaged to be engaged. I thought what we were doing was perfectly normal." Stella pauses to take a sip of her soda. "Until my period was late."

Riley and Claire raise their eyebrows. *So true.*

"I used Humphreys #11; you know, to . . . bring on the period. But still nothing."

Claire's friend Laura used this pill to ease extra painful periods. She had a cousin who suggested it for that same purpose . . . and to deworm the kittens. She'd heard other girls mention it could be used to bring on a late period if you were worried about being pregnant. Stella just confirmed that's a rumor, which Claire always assumed was the case because anyone could pick up a bottle at the Walgreens.

The next picture is of Johnny and another boy roughhousing like they were imitating professional wrestlers at the final pin count.

"This is the day I told Johnny I was pregnant." The kids in the background sitting at a picnic table were laughing. "Then out of nowhere, he slapped me . . . hard . . . and called me a scuz." Just the thought of it made Stella's face red, as though the betrayal was happening now. "I wasn't a scuz all those times we had sex before I was pregnant. It's like getting caught was somehow different, and now Johnny wanted to be sure everyone knew I was a bad person."

Claire pictured Johnny in that same jacket Stella was wearing in the previous slide, now backhanding her with such force it brought her to her knees. Somehow the boys always find a way to deny responsibility. She's feeble-minded, she's a slut . . . and the boys are held accountable by absolutely no one, not even themselves.

That last photo is of Stella and another girl alongside a road.

Stella was wearing a long skirt and holding a suitcase in one hand and her other hand has a thumb up, looking to hitch a ride. "There was one thing everyone could agree on—I wasn't enough. Not responsible enough, not old enough, not enough money . . . according to everyone, my own family even, I could never be enough to be a mother. So, I just . . . moved on." Stella inhales loudly, slowly runs clawed fingers up both sides of her scalp. She crosses her arms, exhales, and cracks her neck. "My cousin told me about Child Horizons, and come to find out, I'm not even enough to love what I feel growing inside."

Claire puts her hand on her belly, the baby is really pressing hard now. It's true, they seem to think we're not capable of loving these babies and expect us to believe that bunk. Claire looks over at Riley, who is jamming the last huge bite of a sprinkled donut in her mouth, literally swallowing any emotions she may have on that topic. "Where are you going . . . after?" she asks, wiping up a few crumbs that didn't go down.

"I'm heading to California, changing everything. Designing my own life. One thing for sure, I *won't* ever get married or have kids. Nope. I learned *my* lesson." She holds her back with both hands and tries to lift her chest up for a little more space to breathe. "Your turn, Claire."

Claire, suddenly feeling nauseous, takes a moment to finish her soda. She pushes herself to standing and rolls a reel-to-reel film projector cart into position. Riley is instantly re-energized. "Now we're talking. Home movies."

"Courtesy of Zach, who gifted me the camera, and Lilli, who gave me this job with access to all the new media technology." Claire channels Zach's corny nature and attempts a princess-style curtsy to prompt a bit of forced applause.

"Flip that thing on and get straight to the secrets, Claire. We're going to have to get moving to make curfew," says Stella.

"And leave some time so we can watch the movie in reverse. My cousin did that last Thanksgiving, it's a gas," adds Riley.

Claire switches on the projector and it whirls up to speed. The first clip is of her dad driving his truck, talking on the CB radio, the last time they laughed together. He's expertly using CB lingo; it's a shame the only sound of the movie was the hum of the film going through the projector. They were both smoking Pall Mall cigarettes and drinking Pabst beer. Her dad kept trying to pass her the CB mic. Clearly, Claire got her charismatic smile and expressions of persuasion from him. The cameraman changed and now everyone can see Claire, feeling embarrassed in front of the mic as she gives it a try. "It was the last time I went out with my dad," narrates Claire. "That's how Zach and I met; our dads were both in the CB club."

The next clip goes slowly around the bonfire, showing everyone sitting on the bails of straw, roasting hotdogs, drinking beer, and passing around and inspecting radio parts. It stops on Zach, who waves. You can read his lips saying, "Hi, Claire." Riley giggles. "He's a cornball like that," says Claire. "While our dads talked about the latest equipment, we would go off and explore. "Be back in twenty minutes," my dad would say, like he was setting boundaries. But really it was just public permission for Zach and me to run off and be alone together. Which was fine by me."

The movie cuts to looking down an old dirt road with an abandoned house in the distance. There are several cuts, each time getting closer and closer to the old house. "They call this 'the old Craig's Place.' The high school stomping ground, where kids would go when ditching class." There was a firepit with old bottles and cans in the dirt. The rickety front steps had pillars that looked oddly similar to crumbling ruins you might see in history books.

"We pretended it was our house, and we were newlyweds," says Claire, thinking her image of marriage wasn't really much more sophisticated than Riley's.

The movie becomes a tour of the old house now with Zach behind the camera and Claire pretending to be a spokesmodel for the home, pointing out the various features of the living room and the kitchen, where remnants of ancient furniture and appliances remained.

"That's a dream and a secret all in one," says Riley.

"Very true," agrees Claire. "We both knew this was the last time we'd see each other. I was heading to college the next day. He was going back to high school for his senior year."

The movie continues the house tour and shows the bedroom with an old wrought-iron bedframe in the corner. Claire remembers their hungry embrace and deep kissing that took her breath away. Zach held her so close, so tight. She could feel his erection pressing against her. He unbuttoned his jeans and put her hand on it, guiding her to his rhythm.

"Did you . . . you know . . . act like newlyweds in *that* place?" asks Riley as though she is reading Claire's mind but having a hard time believing a dirty dump could be romantic.

"He said to me, 'You're not going to college a square, are you?' "

Claire runs the dilapidated house tour in reverse to entertain Riley. "Maybe I was a square. Everyone knows all college girls have sex."

"So the answer is yes," Stella answers Riley's original question.

Claire fills in the blanks, "He said, 'Don't worry, I'll pull out.' "

"We all know that isn't going to happen," says Stella as she tips up her soda and slurps the last drops.

"I actually believed he had my best interest in mind," said Claire, mostly to herself.

Claire fast forwards to a view of walking through campus and the camera hones in on a sign at the front of the building that reads *College of Political Science*. "I felt . . . grateful, like Zach gave me something I needed to be successful in college." The next clip is of a typing class. A row of women enthusiastically typing away, throwing the carriage return, and continuing typing without missing a beat. "Typing came easy to me." A classmate took over as cameraman briefly and there was Claire in front of a typewriter, waving and putting on a big smile.

"Hey, you have glasses . . . you look nerdy, Claire." Riley points and jokes.

Claire nods and explains, "I started feeling off. Had headaches. I vomited *a lot*. I figured I was working too hard and picked up some glasses and aspirin at the Walgreens." The next clip is a tour of the woman's dorm—her roommate, the registration desk, the mail slots, and whatnot. "I couldn't believe it when the nurse said I was pregnant. Zach didn't return my calls, so I sent him a letter to tell him I was pregnant. He sent me a letter back, I still have it." Claire keeps Zach's letter stashed to the side of her dresser drawer along with her underwear and socks. She isn't sure why she kept it, as it only makes her feel more alone. "He said, 'Do everything you can so the baby never knows who I am.' Then he said he 'didn't want this to ruin his life.' "

Stella belches loudly. Riley looks at her in disgust.

"I agree," Claire acknowledges Stella's completely appropriate response. "He didn't mention a thing about *my* life." Claire looks down at her belly as she touches it gently, thinking about how much she wants the baby to know who *she* is. "Or the baby's." Claire remembers that day in her bedroom she told Zach she was looking forward to being independent. In truth, that desire hasn't changed. Oma would warn, "Be careful of what you wish for, you may just get it." Claire wonders, *Am I getting what I asked for?* "The university expelled me. Revoked my access to the woman's dormitory. I had nowhere to go, so I called my folks thinking they would provide some support. My mom just cried and put Dad on the phone. He said, 'Don't bother coming home.' Just like that . . ."

The film comes to an end and flips off the now empty reel and flaps around the full side. Claire flips the projector off and removes the spools. "It was the RA who gave me the Franklin House pamphlet with Lilli's card stapled to it."

Claire begins unplugging equipment and winding up cords, to put things away so they can get back to their destiny of going through labor alone to relinquish their babies to families they'll never know. "You want to know my real secret, Riley?"

Riley sits back and crosses one arm over her belly and holds her face with the other hand, while she taps her lips, waiting see where Claire is going with this.

"Every day when I come here to index microforms, type instructions on how to use this technology, or whatever it is that Lilli kindly invented for me to do so I can pay the Child Horizons fees . . ." Claire shifts her agitated energy to collecting the napkins and popcorn bags and tosses them in the trashcan. "I talk with my baby. We have full-on conversations, Sarah and me." The room is suddenly so still, the hum of the wall clock becomes the dominating sound. "At some level," continues Claire, "she's learned everything I have," says Claire, raising an eyebrow and gently holding her belly. "We've had every day of her life together and to be honest, I'm having a hard time imagining what my days will look like without her."

Riley looks over at Stella and then back at Claire. "Claire. Sister. We're not supposed to do that."

"Not supposed to do what?" Claire's chin quivers. "Acknowledge we love the person growing inside our own bodies?" A sickening headache sweeps over Claire as she winces and rubs her forehead.

"Hey, are you OK?" asks Stella as she grabs her elbow to steady her.

Claire nods and looks up at Stella, "How do I go on without her?"

"When you have no choice, you just keep moving."

Chapter 4

Jo kicks a cardboard box up against the cement steps at the front of the Union Bank. The sidewalk is busy with people walking by, so many people she doesn't know or trust. A gust of wind catches the dismissal letter she set on top of the other items that typically sit on her desk. Jo quickly snatches it and secures it back under her name plate that reads "Johanka Tischler" in white block letters. A name that only strangers or distant relatives might use. She would have preferred it said "Mrs. Wilfried Tischler," which is the name she signs on checks and other official documents.

Jo awkwardly tries to sit "ladylike" on the stair next to the box. She brushes her skirt and clasps her hands around her bouncing knees. Looking down into the box, she sees the word "Congratulations" written in calligraphy on the Hallmark card slotted in an opened bright-yellow envelope that has an image of a stork on it. A lump forms in her throat as Jo sits up straight to remind herself of what dignity she has left.

Jo expects Will to pick her up any minute now. Traffic noises echo off the buildings, hitting her nerves. She bites at her already ragged nails, realizes her habit, and clenches her hands in her lap. After what seems like ages, Will's LA Contractors Guild truck pulls up. "I left as soon as you called," he says. Jo grabs her box. As soon as she's seated, she reaches over and flicks off the blaring radio.

"Will . . ." A car honks from behind, and Jo looks annoyed. "Could you?" she asks as she makes motions for Will to roll up his window. Will flicks his cigarette out onto the street. As he rolls up the tar-stained window, the American flag tattooed on his arm waves across his well-developed muscles formed from years of swinging a hammer. He puts the truck into gear, yanks the wheel, and pulls into traffic.

"OK now, what's this about?"

Jo, feeling sheepish, admits she has kept this from him. "I . . . resigned."

"Today?"

"No, of course not. I gave my notice last month, per policy."

Jo grabs the rolling thermos from the seat and places it in the box on her lap. "Everyone thought . . . I *received* notice . . . because . . . I'm expecting."

Will looks at Jo with confusion. His eyes shift back to the road, his brow softening with sadness.

Jo continues, rattling away, explaining herself, "They knew I was going to the obstetric appointments. After all the testing . . . all the planning . . . It's easy to believe . . . I'd have a baby."

"Jo . . ." Cut off by a honk, Will looks over his shoulder and changes lanes.

Out the passenger window a mother stands on the sidewalk, boggling a shopping bag, and helping her child button his sweater. If only she could be buttoning up her child's sweater.

"Will, I don't think you fully understand, but, when people realize we've been married without children for *ten years* . . . the looks . . . the words . . . condolences, pity."

Jo jumps as an aggressive honk sounds from behind. Will waits for a drunk to stumble across the intersection against the light. Jo wrinkles up her face in disgust. Will doesn't seem to care in the least about the whole scene.

"Jo . . ."

This time Jo cuts him off. She's going to say what she's going to say. "Two people don't make a family, we've always said that . . ."

She stops and looks at Will for confirmation. He gives a down-ward slanting nod, glancing at her over his prescription glasses. Jo goes on, "A home isn't a home without children. That's a big part of why we married." She sighs and sucks in a breath as emotion works its way up her throat. "Now . . . it's been made clear, we can't have a family. Not here, for Christ's sake." She waves an agitated hand at the drunk on the street.

"Not with this . . ." she touches her trembling lips, then slides her hand down to her heart and rests the blaming hand on her empty womb surrounded by rogue endometrium.

Will flips on the blinker to take the next turn. The blinker clicks rhythmically, filling the cab with a mechanical heartbeat.

"Will . . . I can't stay here anymore," Jo speaks to the window, her head cooling on the glass. "I want to go home. I want to teach. I miss my kids."

Will glances over at her, "Jo, we've talked about this."

Jo remembers how proud she was of him that day when Will graduated from trade school. She knew it would be hard on him to shift from farming. They were both emotionally exhausted from the struggles of infertility, and this change was filled with possibility. The promise of the LA construction boom and access to world-class doctors re-energized both of them. It was like they were newlyweds again, until it wasn't.

"Yesterday . . . after hearing the test results . . ." Jo, now actively trying to hold back tears, bites her lip. "Even the doctors in LA can't help us . . ." At this point she totally breaks down into shoulder-heaving sobs.

Will pulls into Ralph's Market and parks the truck in the back of the lot. He takes off his glasses, exposing white streaks on his sun-tanned face. He massages his brow briefly, then wipes a tear from his eye with his thumb before putting his glasses back on.

Jo pulls out a hanky and blow-honks her nose surprisingly loudly for what a small person she is. Her voice still trembling, she says, "Ever since the first day we were married, we wanted a family . . ."

"Jo," he says, cutting her off. "I agree with the doctor. It's time we stop waiting and hoping . . . pretending." He rolls down the window and lights another cigarette. "We *can* still be a family. The construction work here is . . . unlimited. The teaching's in Nebraska."

Jo looks at him, ready for wherever he's going with this train of thought.

"Hell, there's enough work in Saline County to keep us going. I just told the foreman last week I was thinking of starting up my own business." Will reaches for Jo's hand and twists the plain and simple wedding band he gave her a decade earlier. It was all he could afford at the time, a symbol of their commitment. She'd never trade for anything fancier.

"Jo," Will says, "let's move back home . . . and adopt."

CHAPTER 5

Though the kitchen is hot with the morning baking, Babička is already dressed for the festival in full traditional folk costume. A white eyelet cap pinned atop her neatly braided white hair. Her white blouse sleeves are cinched with red ribbons. Shiny rickrack edges her vest, and her bright red skirt is accented with a white apron ornately embroidered with roses. Every piece of clothing is meticulously starched.

All the women and girls in the community will be dressed similarly today, but for now Jo is fortunate to feel cool in her one-piece lifeguard swimsuit. Typically, she'd be scolded for being in the kitchen barefoot in a swimsuit, but her mom's preoccupied with baking and the men are out putting together the parade floats, so why not be comfortable?

"What a fine hand you have, Babička." Jo bends over and kisses her grandma on the cheek.

Babička sits on an old dining room chair positioned at the doorway to an enclosed porch, long ago converted to a sewing room. Behind her, within arm's reach, are stacks of remnants and countless spools and bobbins of thread. Her elderly hands move with precision as she expertly applies a silver applique in the shape of a crossed hammer and saw to a men's black festival vest.

Jo runs her hand over the stitching and the embroidered flowers, "Will's going to love this." The admiration for her grandma's handwork is heartfelt. For some reason she never could embroider, or crochet, or even sew on a button. "Always too much pulling," her mother would say when attempting to teach the basic craft every woman was expected to master. The men completely took this skillset for granted. Not once had she heard a man comment on his appreciation for a darned sock that doesn't irritate the skin, a knee patch that can withstand a roofing project, or the miles and miles of beautiful embroidery that adorns their traditional festival costumes. It's of course the women's duty to compliment each other's handwork. "It matches the signs on his truck perfectly," says Jo as she gives her grandma a big hug. "Soon the whole county will know about Tischler and Zajíček Carpentry."

"Expect 20,000 visitors, they said. Such a crowd." Jo's mother, Marta, speaks with the familiar accent of her Czechoslovakian heritage, though the family was always encouraged to speak only in English. Her words sing in the low tone of slight disapproval, that somehow comforts and threatens the listener all at the same time. "Every one of them will have koláče."

Jo nods her head in shared amazement as she refills her cup of coffee and takes a big bite of thickly buttered toast. Today is the opening day of the annual Czech Days festival the town is famous for. A sign that reads "Vítáme Vás" is permanently posted at the highway entrance and today it will welcome the thousands of visitors who come primarily for the food. One might argue they come for the parade, but that's really just the kickoff for entry to the beer gardens. Every woman in the community has been busy all week baking pastries and grinding sausage. It's common knowledge that Marta's cherry koláče are the best in the county, as they are often put at the front of displays.

"Do you need any help, Mom?"

Marta ignores this offer, which is typically the case when she's deep in her baking groove. She moves with efficient precision as she prepares the last two trays of koláče. She applies egg wash with a goose feather pastry brush, then spoons in canned cherries and finally tops each pastry with a sugary butter and flour sprinkle.

The screen door slams behind Will and Emi, both in black pants and short-sleeved white button-up shirts. Emi also has his embroidered black festival vest on. Will smiles at Jo while Emi wobbles on arthritic knees. "Smells good, Marta," he says.

Everyone glistens with sweat from the humid summer day, the heat of the kitchen, and the extra festival clothing. Emi reaches to take a warm koláče from the cooling rack, and Marta slaps his hand away. "Get yourself rye bread, old man." She waves the men over to the breakfast table. "Fresh from Žitnik's."

"Alright, alright." Emi groans but is easily redirected to the breakfast table snugged up against the back wall.

"Lifeguard duty, Jo?" says Will.

Marta now takes notice for the first time of Jo's skimpy attire, "You'll cover up on the way there."

"Yes," says Jo as she pours coffee for the men. "I'm filling in for an hour so Don can dance in the polka contest." Jo sets the cups down on the small white and grey Formica-topped table. The men take this service without notice or acknowledgement. They are busily slathering goose grease on slices of rye bread.

"You know we need you on our float, Jo," says Will as he wipes a drip of grease off his chin with the back of his hand.

Jo watches her dad and her husband sitting across from each other doing the exact same things. Chewing on crusty bread, dripping with grease, slurping on coffee, sweating in their costumes. Adorable, the both of them. She was always impressed with how Will embraced her family's ways and traditions. Now that Jo's brother is in the Navy and stationed overseas, and her sister recently divorced, there's a dry family joke that Will is their number one son.

"I wouldn't miss the chance to be on the float that introduces your new carpentry business to whole world." Jo puts her hand on Will's shoulder. "Ruth offered to come help me close the pool." She catches his eye to see if he makes the connection. "We'll talk about the adoption agency."

There have been several controversies in the family when it comes to the topic of adoption. Initially they thought it wouldn't be a good idea, especially if Will and Jo ended up having a child of their own. Old Doc Trav said the endometriosis doesn't always prevent miracles from happening. The notion that the Černý family inheritance would only go to the bloodline child didn't set right with Will and Jo. Will's side of the family didn't feel the same way, but that didn't change anyone's mind. When it came to "whose fault" it was that they couldn't have a baby, everyone seemed to universally assume it was Jo's fault. It wasn't until the very final tests in LA that they discovered the infertility was due to issues from both Will and Jo. With that, everyone knew for sure they would never have children of their own. The family conversation immediately shifted to what's the best way to adopt a child, and Emi was sure there was only one right way.

"Joey, gawd dammit already." Emi slurps grease from his thumb and grunts as he talks. "Call Ike. Having an ass of a lawyer for a brother-in-law should come in handy for something."

Babička mumbles under her breath, "Má máslo na hlavě."

Jo and Will share hidden smirks, agreeing with Babička.

Uncle Ike's business is built on the fact that he's the only lawyer in the area. People turn to him as a last resort usually because they can't afford the fees of the attorneys in the nearby cities. He is arrogant and has a reputation for chasing women during his "business trips" to Lincoln. His wife Judy pretends not to know even though every other woman in town does. Yet Emi and Marta will always stand by family loyalty.

"He's over at Judy's now getting his damn fancy black shoes," says Emi.

Marta slams the oven door and walks with heavy feet toward the men. She reaches between them to pick up the wall phone receiver and lays it on her shoulder while she wipes her hands on her apron and dials the rotary.

"Judy? Marta. Yes, the boys are on their way with the koláče. Can you put Ike on? Joey and Will want to adopt. Ya, they finally came to their senses." With a raised eyebrow, Marta calls Jo to come to her then firmly puts the phone receiver into Jo's hand.

Jo glares at Marta and jerks the receiver, making the cord flop into Will's face. She puts a smile on her face before she begins to speak. "Hi, Uncle Ike. Yes, it's been a long time." Jo looks out the kitchen window and can see the shadow of Ike through his own kitchen curtain. They've always lived just fifteen steps away from each other and yet he's the one relative she keeps in touch with the least. "What? You can get us a baby just like that? Dr. Greene? Should you be sharing your clients' names?" Jo is actually impressed that he could convey his lack of ethics in less than sixty seconds. "That sounds . . . sudden. Yes, we have money." Jo looks at Will and rolls her eyes. "Meet Will in the beer garden today? Uncle Ike, we're in the parade. OK, he'll see you after. OK. Bu-bye."

Everyone looks at Jo expecting a rundown of the conversation they all just heard. Jo looks back at everyone and hangs up the receiver. She gives Will the 'thank you for dealing with that' look.

"Welp . . ." starts Emi.

"No," interjects Jo. "Not that way."

Marta shrugs her shoulders and goes back to the baking.

Jo grabs her whistle off the key hook and heads for the door. "See you downtown."

*　　*　　*

Jo wraps a towel around the last kid getting out of the pool and gives him a big hug.

"I'm glad you're back, Mrs. Tischler."

"Me too, sweetie. See you at school in a couple weeks. If I don't see your mom at the parade, say hi for me."

Jo pats the child's back, sending him on his way, then plops down in a pool chair next to Ruth. They watch the boy pedal off on his bike. Finally, a chance for a private conversation. Jo has been anticipating this moment ever since Will suggested they come back home to adopt. Jo wrings her hands, not knowing where to begin.

"Thanks for meeting me here . . . and for lending us the doll. It's perfect for Will's float theme."

Ruth waves her hand, indicating it's nothing.

"You are great with kids, Jo. You've taught my Jamie everything from how to backstroke to how to read and write."

"I had her Sunday school too," adds Jo.

"I don't know how you do it," says Ruth. "Did you miss the kids?"

"Well, I couldn't be a bank teller, that's for sure." Jo isn't shy about saying how she felt about working in LA. "But teaching, that's always been easy for me. Just watching them grow is enough to make me fall in love with each and every one of them."

Jo decides to bring Ruth up to speed with the fertility doctor's findings, "We are positive now. The doctor confirmed Will and I can't have children of our own."

"I'm sorry, Jo. But just knowing. That's a good thing, isn't it?" Ruth shades her eyes with her hand and looks for Jo's reaction.

"That's how Will and I see it," she says.

"Does that mean you will have the surgery to finally take care of the fibroids?"

"Not yet. One thing at a time," says Jo, intending to keep her parts and what hormones they provide her as long as she can. "We came home to . . . start a family. Adopt, like you and Hal."

Ruth puts her hands together as in prayer in front of her mouth, inhales audibly, and holds her breath in excitement. She swings her legs around toward Jo and leans in.

"The bond . . . as soon as you see your baby . . ." Ruth's eyes tear up. "The love. Is fast. Once they're in your arms, you know you'd stand in front of a truck for them."

Jo sees such joy and devotion on Ruth's face and knows in her heart *that's* the very kind of joy she's going to have when she becomes a mother. Her eyes tear up too just thinking about it. "How do I get started?"

"The process is simple." Ruth sits up straight in her chair, ready to list out the logistics, "It starts with a call, then filling out all the forms. I'll give you our caseworker's number."

Jo nods with gratitude, her wide eyes encouraging more detail. "Then . . ."

"You give them everything they ask for. Medical records, bank statements, letters of recommendation, church participation. They inspect every part of your life." Ruth stops to check in with Jo, to see if there's any reaction to this.

Jo adjusts the strap on her suit. That doesn't bother her or Will. What could get more intrusive than what they've already been through?

Ruth continues, "They match your family traits with the natural mother and father's family. You pay the fees. That's about it."

"What about using a lawyer? Do we need one? Mom had me call Uncle Ike this morning."

Ruth raises her eyebrow at the mention of Uncle Ike.

"I know. But he *is* family. He said it was easy to get a baby."

"We didn't know how to do it either," says Ruth. "Pastor Grant told us about Child Horizons. He said since they are also an orphanage of sorts for children who are wards of the state, they have the long-term welfare of the child in mind."

Jo nods, absorbing every word. Of course, the whole point of adoption is to serve the child.

"Pastor Grant gave us a referral and explicitly told us to steer clear of anyone making it sound like a quick and easy transaction."

"There's nothing easy about creating a family," says Jo.

"I suppose lawyers can hand babies over to couples for a handsome fee," says Ruth. "But at what risk?"

The sun shifts just enough to be right in Ruth's eyes. She and Jo drag their chairs across the white concrete toward the shade by the office. "The privilege of being an adoptive mother, is . . . an incredible gift, but it's not easy," says Ruth, more comfortable now in the shade. "The agency is very clear on all the ways they can take back the baby, even after placement."

Take back? Jo hadn't thought of that. Sure, they have to know the baby is safe, but after all the screening, how often do they really have to do that?

"You must keep in continuous contact with them," continues Ruth. "Including a continuous stream of donations."

Jo and Will hadn't considered an *ongoing* financial relationship with the agency. They had a good idea of the finances around raising children, keeping them safe and healthy, but she always thought the agency costs were a one-time kind of thing.

"What the agency has done for us . . . we'll always be grateful. Our kids are everything to us." Ruth, now enthusiastic to help Jo get the process rolling, says, "Jo, call them right away." She nods her head in the direction of the pool office phone. "The number's in my little blue address book under Child Horizons." Ruth jumps up and snaps Jo's leg with her towel. "I'll sweep up out here, you go ahead. Call them now. Before the parade."

Jo jumps and rubs her leg, smiling, "That smarts."

In the office, she pulls the little blue address book out of Ruth's bag. She hesitates for a minute, wondering if she should talk this through with Will first. "There's a child waiting for you, Jo," she reminds herself out loud. There's also about a hundred ways this process can be ended, so no reason to invent another one. Jo dials the number, then bites her thumb nail as she waits for it to be picked up.

"Child Horizons, how may I help you?"

Jo feels oddly surprised that someone just up and answered her call to become a mother. Her mind goes temporarily blank, then thankfully she remembers her name. "I'm Mrs. Wilfried Tischler," says Jo. "We'd like to adopt a child."

A frazzled woman in a white sash bearing the words *Vítáme Vás* waves at Jo, who is now dressed in full festival attire, "Hey, it's time to line up. Will and Teddy are looking for you." She smiles at the dressed-up doll, "And they're looking for you too, you little cutie," she says as she playfully shakes the little plastic hand.

"Thanks, Betty. Where's our spot?"

"Between Jelinek's dance school and Žitnik's bakery wagon."

Jo looks down the block and sees Will dutifully manning his float just behind the group of children practicing their step-hop-steps.

"The dance school is always my favorite entry!" says Jo, already excited about following children skipping all the way down Main Street. She imagines her own child as part of that entry someday.

"Actually, once the kids heard you'd be on the new entry float, they begged to have Mrs. Tischler next to them. Žitnik's was kind enough to swap places with Will."

Jo breathes in the festival, feeling more deeply connected and at home than ever. She skips past the huge grills lined with home-made jitrnice and jelita. The smell of flame-kissed sausage makes her mouth water. Jo smiles at the women serving them up on plates with huge helpings of fried potatoes and sauerkraut seasoned with caraway seed. The polka band on center stage is going strong. Accordion players' fingers are flying as their arms bring breath to the familiar tunes that will echo through the streets the entire day. Polka dancing contestants with numbers on their backs are seated in the shade now, finished with their competition, drinking lemonade and cooling off. *Did Don win another trophy this year?* Jo wonders. Finally breaking away from the dense crowd, Will sees Jo and welcomes her with a wave and a smile.

The high school marching band plays their school fight song as the traditional "the parade's going to start now" indicator. The polka band stops and the crowd shifts to line Main Street.

"Right on time," says Will. He pats the head of the doll. "Nice touch. Better jump into our spots now."

"Will, there's something we should talk about."

"It's going to have to wait." He slaps the truck twice, indicating to Emi to go ahead and start the truck. "Here's your candy bowl, the polka kids already ate half of it." He grins as he hands it to Jo.

On a platform build on the bed of his work truck, Will made a little framed house and painted it red. There is a rocking chair in the center where Jo is to sit with her dressed up doll on her lap. Her job is to make the little house feel like home, wave, smile, and toss candy. Meanwhile, Will and his partner Teddy pretend to hammer and saw, demonstrating how they provide housing for the women and children. The signs affixed to the side panels of the truck read "Tischler and Zajíček Carpentry—Welcome Home." The truck is of course ornately decorated in flowers and ribbons from front bumper to hitch ball.

The Master of Ceremony is jabbering away, creating a continuous flow of chatter and advertising over the loudspeaker, to entertain the crowd and encourage them to support the small-town businesses.

After the dance school finishes their polka demonstration the MC blasts, "Let's give the Jelinek School of dance a big round of applause." The enthusiastic crowd cheers as the kids take a bow and march off together.

Jo feels a spark of excitement run up her spine as Will's big introduction is up next.

"We have a new entry this year, folks. Tischler and Zajíček Carpentry, custom building and cabinetry for the comfort of your family. Weeelllcome home."

The crowd cheers. The kids poise themselves for candy collection. Jo waves and throws candy out the little home's faux windows. She can hear their adorable little voices call out, "Mrs. Tischler's back!" "She's back!" "Hi, Mrs. Tischler!"

The float is right up to the MC's stand now and he begins to start up a conversation with Will right over the loudspeaker. "Welcome home indeed. It's great to have you back, Will, and your lovely wife Jo. Two fine citizens of Wilber, always serving our community."

Will nods and acknowledges the personal touch, and indicates he's done with it by giving one of those saluting goodbyes to the MC.

The MC moves on to put the spotlight on Jo. "Jo, you're teaching the kindergarten class this fall, is that right?"

Honestly, Jim, what in the world, just keep the focus on Will's business, will you? Jo simply nods and smiles at the children who are busily chomping away at the candies.

"Yes," confirms the MC. "That's a big bright yes," he announces. The crowd cheers again. "Wait a minute, is that a baby on your lap?"

Jo looks at Will with the *when will this ever end* look.

Will just returns a smug glance that says, *Well, you get what you ask for.*

Jo smiles and holds up the festive doll.

"Well, a little bird from the attorney's office tells me the Tischlers will soon be holding their own *real* baby." The crowd collectively gasps and takes this public announcement as permission to set off an immediate murmur of small-town gossip.

Jo's mouth drops open and her face turns red. She looks at Will, who has now completely checked out of his pretend hammering and steps into the little frame house and stands next to Jo.

Will waves his arm and nods his head indicating a yes.

"It's been a long wait, everyone, let's start the congratulations early!" The entire town applauds and hoots in celebration.

Teddy jumps in the cab of the truck prompting Emi to drive forward, and follow the procession to the next block, where they round off of Main Street.

"Well, we won't need to spend any more on company advertising," says Will. "We can just keep Ike up to speed on the business and the word will make it around town in mere hours."

Jo bites the side of her cheek; this too is part of small-town life. "When you have that beer with Uncle Ike at Růžička's Tavern, you can tell him we don't need his services because . . . we already contacted Child Horizons adoption agency."

"We did?"

She nods with hopeful excitement, "We have an appointment, week after next."

CHAPTER 6

Their appointment was set two weeks in advance and Jo used every moment of that preparing. She arranged for written recommendations, gathered financial statements, had copies of medical records made, memorized names and positions of the Child Horizons staff she had phone conversations and written correspondence with, prepared her outfit, ironed Will's shirt with extra starch, and put gas in the car. It was exhausting and exhilarating all at the same time. And now they are finally here, at the in-person applicant interview.

Will and Jo sit on straight-back chairs next to a closed door that simply says, "Adoption Unit." Jo drank two cups of coffee before they drove up to Omaha and she glances at her watch to see if there is time for her to go the ladies' room before their interview time. Nope. She bounces her knees, causing the heels of her modest pumps to tap softly on the tiles.

Will puts his hand on her knee to stop the tapping and gives her a reassuring squeeze.

Jo opens her handbag, pulls out a hanky, and blow-honks her nose. As much as she planned, she could not prevent her hay fever acting up today. Hopefully the caseworker won't assume anything negative about her red and watering eyes.

The door opens and a young couple comes out, looking somewhat exhausted and relieved.

"Thank you again, Mr. and Mrs. Martin. We'll be in touch."

Will and Jo stand as the couples size each other up, briefly assessing the competition. She's younger than Jo, slimmer, and . . . are those real pearls? Who would waste money on such a thing?

"Mr. and Mrs. Tischler, please come in and have a seat."

The men nod at each other in polite acknowledgement as they pass each other. Will steadies Jo with a firm grip on her elbow, guiding her into the office and toward the next uncomfortable chair.

"Thank you so much for coming into the city today. We like to have an in-person interview before anything proceeds."

Verna Prescot, their caseworker, sits down behind her small and practical desk. The whole office is small and practical, without a single effort put toward warmth in décor. The walls are white with only a single framed certificate hung. A certificate of what, Jo can't tell from where she sits. The bookshelf is filled with what looks like textbooks and state law reference volumes. Even though there is a large grey filing cabinet, the bookshelf is lined with manila folders, as is the side of her desk. The amount of paperwork required certainly is impressive. In front of her, Verna has a spiral bound Harvard Square notebook and two sharpened pencils.

Will and Jo smile nervously and sit in their designated chairs.

Verna, clearly not into small talk, goes straight to her questioning. "Please tell me, why do you want children?"

Jo looks over at Will. He nods, indicating she should go ahead and respond. "I simply love children. That's the primary reason why I became a teacher. I believe it's our duty to see that *every* child has the opportunity to reach their full potential." She looks at Will. He nods back, encouraging her. "Will and I always talked about having a family. We don't think a home is really a home without children. We've often dreamed of having two children." She looks down at her hands and, realizing she's clutching, purposefully releases into a more lady-like posture. "We've been considering adopting for some time now."

Verna briefly smiles and takes a few notes. "You've been married for . . ." She flips quickly through the file to check exactly the form to which she's referring, "Ten years." She looks directly at Jo and asks, "What are your feelings about not being able to have a child of your own?"

Jo clenches her hands. "It's been quite a disappointment." She pauses, thinking about all the people she's let down, her mom and dad, her husband. Is it right to talk about feeling guilt? She swallows and exhales loudly through her mouth because her nose is plugged.

"We were hopeful for years," offers Will, "then we began seeking medical advice. The tests showed we both contribute to the problem."

Jo chokes up a little. They cried many times together. She smiles at him sweetly with gratitude that he just said the difficult thing straight out like that, so it was over and out there. "I sent the doctor's report," added Jo.

Verna flits through their file and makes a brief nod of satisfaction when she finds the report. Her manner is all business, maybe even too much business considering her job is about forming families. She's wearing a modest but professional houndstooth suit. She is well prepared and speaks calmly. Yet it seems odd to Jo that Verna had no emotional reaction, no empathetic gaze to offer after they just revealed the details of such a deep wound that has been causing her and Will pain for a decade. She must be callused from hearing similar stories from hundreds of couples, that would be the only way Jo could imagine that anyone could move on with such insensitivity.

"Tell me, how do you feel about the natural mother. Do you think you would be more comfortable with the situation if she was married or not married?" Verna looks directly at Jo for a response. "If the child asks you about his natural mother, how would you explain?"

Jo thinks back to the only unmarried mother she's ever known, Jill Laney, Francie's mother—who lived in a house with dirt floors.

Jo would have loved to be the mother of a child like Francie if Jill had asked for help. But Jill never did and was determined to keep her child. In ways that were never spoken out loud, the community considered Jill to be the town slut. But Jo would never tell Francie anything negative about her mother. Of course not. She would be sure Francie understood how brave and loving her mother was to seek out a better circumstance.

"We would be honest about the adoption from day one," says Will to set the foundation of the importance of truth, as he does in all matters. Jo reaches for Will's hand. His honesty is one of the many reasons she fell in love with him.

Adoption is about the child, and Jo knows the key to a successful adoption is in her ability to fill the role, as much as possible, of the natural mother. To give the love, affection, and security a child needs. From a teacher's perspective, she would do all she could for her child to understand how to thrive in the world. From a mother's perspective, she'd ensure her child would understand love. In this moment, Verna must hear everything she needs to feel confident in making Jo a child's mother.

"I'd describe the love the natural mother must feel for the child. So much love that she would give him to an agency, knowing he would go into a home with people who would take good care of him and love him like their own."

Verna shows no emotion or judgement around this answer.

"I give the natural mother a lot of credit for choosing to do something she can do to take care of the child."

Verna is diligent and continues to take notes. But her eyes have a sadness that Jo can't quite put her finger on. Where does that come from? Maybe something Verna knows about the natural mother?

Moving on to the next question. "What age child are you interested in? Is there a preference for boy or girl?"

"We'd like to adopt an infant if we could, a boy or girl doesn't matter. Just as long as they are healthy," says Jo.

"So, you wouldn't be able to take a child with medical conditions?" presses Verna.

Jo is suddenly anxious she may have said the wrong thing. She bites her lip and her knees start to bounce gain.

Will steps in, "Taking care of our family health is a top priority, Ms. Prescot. We take care of Jo's allergies. We treat any injuries. As part of our family, we would ensure the baby always receives proper medical care. We carry insurance and are prepared to address whatever life hands us."

Verna checks some boxes and Jo stops holding her breath.

"Preferences on the background of the child?"

"Irish, Italian, or whatever their extraction or eye color doesn't matter. Except," Jo looks over at Will, "we couldn't take a colored child."

"There aren't enough people to take care of our perfectly healthy fostered colored children," encourages Verna. "They are often kept in the facility for over a year and have never learned to walk or experience the outdoors. They could use a teacher."

"I don't think the world is ready for it," says Will with a sad tone. "We don't think it would be fair to the child."

Verna looks at them both over her glasses to validate they are both in agreement and checks the box. "How would your family feel about adoption?"

"They're all for it. I don't think there would be any issue there," says Jo. Finally feeling complete confidence about one of the questions, she inhales deeply and shifts in her seat, realizing how frozen in place she's been.

Verna makes the final check on her list, sets her pencil down, and exhales, ready to deliver a prepared message to close the interview.

"As you can imagine, it's very important that an adoption occur through the right channels."

Is there some way Verna may have knowledge of their relationship with Uncle Ike and his dealings with facilitating private adoptions? Jo looks at Will with her brows furled. Will gives her the "calm down" look.

"It is our task here at Child Horizons," continues Verna, "to match the children, who are wards of the county, with couples who want to adopt a child for the child himself. I am required to disclose that the natural mother may exercise her right to reclaim the child all the way up to the legal relinquishment."

Jo and Will share a look of surprised interest as this is a new piece of information they were never previously aware of.

"Child Horizons mitigates that risk by partnering with the University of Nebraska Medical Center and the Franklin Home for girls. These kinds of partnerships are not available to private attorneys and are a way for us to spend time with the natural mother while at the same time we are getting to know our adoptive parent applicants. Allowing us to make the best possible match for the child."

Jo is a bit confused with the complexity in the matching process, but at this point she doesn't need more detail, she will do anything it takes to have this agency qualify her and Will as suitable adoptive parents. They're simply not going back to Uncle Ike.

"Additionally, we have a probationary period. We require no-notice inquiries and home visits, which can result in taking the child back and placing them in foster care until a subsequent, more suitable placement is arranged for." She looks over her glasses at Will and Jo to see if they have a response or questions.

Both Will and Jo are silent, focused and determined to submit to any condition presented.

"Here at Child Horizons, we know our children very well. We

perform a very thorough investigation of qualified applicants, until we are convinced the children are getting the superior adoptive parents." Verna stands up. "Thank you so much for sharing your thoughts today."

Jo and Will awkwardly rise, off guard with the seemingly sudden ending of the conversation.

With one final glance at the paperwork, Verna picks up their folder from the desk, "There are a couple of reports outstanding you must complete as soon as reasonable."

Jo feels embarrassment that anything could be missing. The tip of her nose turns redder than it already was; she was sure she followed all of the instructions perfectly.

"Jo, you will need you to submit to a female medical exam and send us a current negative syphilis report. We will also need your work resignation on file. We require all our mothers to be at home, full-time."

Jo flashes a look of confusion and slight panic to Will. She must resign teaching? Ruth didn't mention that.

Will stands up and grabs Jo's elbow, helping her to her feet.

"The home visit is not offered to all applicants and is the final step of the investigation. If you are found to be suitable, you can expect a caseworker to arrive at your home with short notice, who will inspect your home to ensure the environment is nurturing."

Everything seems to be coming at her so fast now, Jo can hardly keep up. Weren't they just about to leave?

"I have your current address, but I don't see evidence of home ownership," says Verna.

Jo explains, "Oh, no, we don't own our home. We just moved back from California and are living in my Aunt Gwen's rental property."

"Well," sighs Verna, "I strongly recommend you attain ownership of a home. This would put you in a more favorable position, showing long-term stability and financial capability."

Jo is now completely in a daze.

"Thank you again, Mr. and Mrs. Tischler. We will be in touch." Verna extends her hand. Will accepts Verna's handshake and puts his arm around Jo.

Verna opens the door to the office and there is another doe-eyed couple standing just outside, waiting to enter.

The couples awkwardly shuffle out, then in, the office door. This time Jo notices absolutely nothing about them as she's still trying to digest what just happened in the last two minutes.

They burst out of the agency's front door as though they were thrown out. Will has Jo by the elbow and ensures her safety crossing the street to their car. She is all the way inside her head, completely flabbergasted.

"It doesn't even make sense to have one person stop working *and* buy a home." Jo grabs both of Will's arms to address him squarely in the eye, "What will I do if I'm not teaching my kids?"

Opening the car door for Jo, Will says, "We've come this far, we'll figure it out." Jo plops herself in and crosses her arms. Then Will leans in and says, "Maybe you can take up baking?" Then he firmly swings the car door closed and walks around to the driver's side. "Bring it on, Verna."

<h1 style="text-align:center">CHAPTER 7</h1>

Claire sits on one of the two straight-back chairs next to a closed door that simply says "Adoption Unit." She's sat in this chair three times including today. Once to sign a consent to adoption and be placed in a maternity home. Once to pay the bills associated with the maternity care, room, and board. And now to sign the relinquishment of her baby, Sarah, who she's not been allowed to see. The previous two times, her baby was her companion. This time she sits alone. Her uncombed hair hangs around her face as she contemplates the brown button on her wool coat, which she hasn't bothered to take off. The uncomfortable chair makes the stitches pull. She shifts her legs a bit and wonders if she has time to get to the ladies' room and change out the sanitary pad.

The door opens and a young woman comes out of the office. Her head is hung low, so Claire bends forward to see how she's doing, hoping for any indicator of what's to come. The woman's lips remain closed, but her eyes speak plainly. *I was duped . . . and so are you.*

"Goodbye, Miss Wayne," says Verna. She turns to Claire, "Miss Jordan, come in and have a seat."

Verna Prescot, Claire's caseworker, is one of those people that's constantly surrounded by grey. She works in a tiny grey office off a grey hallway. She wears grey suits with gawdy fake pearls. She shuffles papers in and out of a grey filing cabinet all day. The women who emerge from her presence are surrounded by grey emotion. Her voice is monotone, her mannerisms mechanical. Does that really sound like someone who's dedicated her life to doing work that's "best for everyone"?

Verna pulls out a pre-filled form from a manila folder and pulls a pen from her lap drawer. "This is the last step in the process, Claire, when you legally sign your consent." Verna squares the one-page document in front of Claire. "We find it helps to read aloud." Verna points to the body of the form and taps her finger about a third of the way down on the document. "Start here."

"I do hereby relinquish, and surrender said child," says Claire. She stops. That's it? It's done in one sentence? Sarah is already reduced to the "said child"? Not even two weeks in this world and she's just another child in a stack of nameless children to be assigned to a line-up of rich married women. There must be something else. Claire brushes Verna's cold grey hand aside and picks up the paper to read the whole thing from the top.

I, Margaret Claire Jordan, the mother of said child, in consideration of the expense and care already given and hereafter to be given to my said child.

I do hereby relinquish and surrender said child and the absolute custody and control thereof to the Child Horizons Institute.

I do hereby further authorize said Institute to place said child in a family home for adoption or under special contracts and do hereby consent such adoption and relinquish all right and claim to her and her services forever.

I hereby agree that I will not interfere with or attempt to have any part in the management of said child. That I will not ask to discover the whereabouts of said child or the parties who may have her or to molest or deprive them of said child and that I will never visit or attempt to visit said child or make my identity known to her.

*　　　*　　　*

Verna grabs Claire's wrist. Her touch sends an electric spark up Claire's neck. The faint odor of cleaning fluids brings on a wave of nausea as the grey cloud that makes up Verna expands, threatening to engulf Claire. She looks up for a way out of the storm and sees darkness beyond the ceiling of the Adoption Unit. She looks down at the room and sees a young woman sitting at the desk with restraints on her wrists and a gag pulling on the corners of her mouth. A woman with no voice, and no choice.

"You've had sufficient time for review," says Verna. She squeezes Claire's wrist to release the paper and slaps it on the table with a pen. "Now sign."

This demand snaps Claire back into her empty body and she wipes beads of sweat from her upper lip. Placing her hand on her swollen belly where Sarah used to be, Claire looks to Verna for accountability. "This is what you call consent?"

Claire knows she can't possibly sign, she hasn't even seen her baby yet. Isn't there something in this damn document that says the mother has to see the baby? "I don't understand this part." Claire says in desperation, pointing to the bit about how Child Horizons is her attorney-infact.

"I'm sure you've been over this many times with the Franklin counseling staff. That simply means *we* do all the work to find *proper* parents." Verna clucks her tongue with impatience.

Claire isn't surprised Verna is in a rush, the next girl she plans to dupe must already be sitting in the hard chair outside the door.

"We make sure you give that baby to good, decent people. People who will take care of it and love it, in spite of your obvious flaws."

Claire looks up at Verna as she begins to believe what she's saying is true.

"That's right. A person with your mental, social, and financial problems?" Verna stands up and walks around the desk and hovers behind Claire, bending over to speak directly into her ear, "You couldn't possibly provide for a child."

Claire feels Verna's breath on her neck and shrinks in shame to admit that Verna's words are true.

"If you're ever going to redeem yourself in God's eyes, you'll give this baby to a good Christian family. Now sign here and move on with your life."

Claire hears her heart pounding in her head as she observes her disembodied hand sign on the line.

Verna grabs the document, puts it in the manila folder and secures it in the grey cabinet. "The services provided to you by Child Horizons are now complete. You will not return to our office concerning this case. You're expected to pack your things and leave Franklin tomorrow."

"Where do I even leave to?" Claire looks down in her lap for answers.

Verna flips through her grey spiral-bound notebook. "The last contact with your family indicates you can go back to Clarkson and live in your parents' household. I recommend you start there."

Verna opens the door and dismisses Claire, "Goodbye, Miss Jordan." She turns to the next woman sitting on the chair in the hallway, "Miss Winters, come in and have a seat."

Claire walks out the door quickly, as to avoid eye contact with Miss Winters. She doesn't have the strength to see another woman broken by this process and has no hope to offer.

CHILD HORIZONS

OMAHA, NEBRASKA

RELINQUISHMENT AND CONSENT TO ADOPTION

I, _______Margaret Claire Jordan_______________________________, desiring that

my child, ____, born MXX (out of) wedlock at

_______Omaha____________Nebraska_______________________ on the 3ʳᵈ day of

_______January__________, 19 66 , receive the benefits of Child Horizons , a Nebraska corporation, and said Institute being willing to receive......her...... upon the conditions hereinafter set forth;

Now, I, ________Margaret Claire Jordan_________________, the _____Mother_______ of said child, in consideration of the expense and care already given and hereafter to be given to my said child, _______I_______, do hereby relinquish and surrender said child and the absolute custody and control thereof to the Child Horizons , and I do hereby further authorize said Institute to place said child in a family home for adoption or under special contract and do hereby consent to such adoption without further notice to me and relinquish all right and claim to .....her...... and .....her..... services forever.

I hereby agree that I will not interfere with or attempt to have any part in the management of said child, that I will not seek to discover the whereabouts of said child or the parties who may have.....her..... or to molest or deprive them of said child, and that I will never visit or attempt to visit said child or make my identity known to.....her..........

I do hereby make, constitute and appoint the Child Horizons my attorney-in-fact for me and in my name, place and stead, to enter my appearance for me in any proceeding to adopt said child; and for me and in my name to waive the service of any and all notices or processes in all such proceedings for adoption and to release all errors and waive all right to appeal in my behalf; and I hereby waive the issuance and service of any and all process in any such proceedings.

Witness my hand at......Omaha.........,.....Nebraska........., this .....7..... day of......Jan......, 19 66

Witness:

Verna M Pierpont   _Margaret Claire Jordan_

STATE OF NEBRASKA }
COUNTY OF DOUGLAS } SS.

Vera Anderson
Notary Public

My commission expires:
October 22, 1970

Chapter 8

Will drives Jo and Aunt Gwen in the work truck, the three of them shoulder to shoulder across the bench seat. Jo wiggles her hand under her aunt's elbow and shifts her weight to lay her head on her. Jo is ear to ear smiles as she watches the road from a diagonal perspective. The truck bumps roughly as they transition from pavement to gravel. "Oh!" says Aunt Gwen as she tightens her grip around the purse on her lap. Someday Elm Street will surely be extended, Jo is confident of it. When that happens their little plot of ground will have a regular residential address, but for now it's simply Lot#11.

"Aunt Gwen, you can truly work miracles! We wanted to move back from California; you had a rental. We need to own our own home; you help us find a way."

"Where there's a Gwen, there's a way," says Will with a wink, flipping the saying that people so often direct toward him thinking they're extraordinarily clever.

It's sweet of Aunt Gwen to want to be part of their little groundbreaking ceremony. Today's the day construction begins, and Gwen insisted she visit the worksite with them. Will gives Aunt Gwen a hand out of the truck and gives her the cane he stowed behind the seat. She sways for a couple steps on her bowlegs and steadies herself. He lights a cigarette and unrolls the blueprint on the hood. Jo scoots out and stands next to Aunt Gwen.

"You are officially the proud owners of all this." Gwen opens her arms wide with a sparkling smile.

The three look out at the empty lot, the tall grass bending in the autumn breeze.

"The location couldn't be better," says Gwen. "Pospisil's across the street, three blocks from the school, six blocks from Zimmerman's grocery, and, importantly, eight full blocks from your in-laws." Gwen looks over her shoulder at Will and winks with a palatal click, "That should be far enough to detour Emi from wandering into your house unannounced."

Jo snickers. Will hates it when her dad just walks in. Apparently, one morning Emi decided to stop by their place to use the toilet and walked right in on Will sitting on the stool. With a baby in the house, it's very likely her mother will also be walking in on them.

Teddy drives up in the company truck, "Tischler and Zajíček Carpentry" with the crossed hammer and saw logo adhered to the side box. Will looks up from the blueprint, cocks his head up, and exhales a cloud of smoke as a greeting.

"Got the labor locked down with Glenn's guys?" says Will.

"You betcha boy." Teddy has a chewed cigar out the side of his mouth. "Laura double checked the permits and is coordinating materials deliveries. I picked up salvageable cabinetry from the Travnicek fire job, and our tight electrician even gave the family discount."

"It's so nice to see the town come together in support of you two," says Gwen, grabbing Jo's hand and giving it a see-I-told-you-this-would-work squeeze.

Teddy looks around and then at his watch. "Now we wait for the excavator. Those the plans?"

Will rolls up the drawing and hands it to Teddy.

"My first design, soon to be our premier model home: Three bedroom, one bath, one thousand square foot. Cozy, to code, no messing around. Thirty days from now the women can start the interior work." Will stands with his chest high knowing his design is solid. Practical and on point, as always.

"There's already inquiries about replicating your plan in lot#28." Gwen waves her cane, "Just west of here." Then with a little song in her voice, "Expansion is in the air!" As if on cue a warbler joins in, *deweet—dewoo.*

Jo breathes in the gentle breeze and ponders what expansion means in her world. It used to mean more grades of curriculum to prepare, but now it means taking care of a house and a family. Sure, there would be more visitors and more family celebrations, but also more beds and more plates. More laundry. More work!

The excavator drives up now filling the air with the sound of machinery. Will waves them in.

Jo pulls out her new camera, a gift her brother sent when he got news of their plans to adopt. He instructed her to take plenty of pictures so he could share all the precious moments with them, when he got back home from his time in Japan with the Navy. Jo takes on family photographer as a welcome new role. A complete set of photos of the home construction will not only be useful for Gwen's real-estate business and Tischler and Zajíček marketing, but will serve as information to share with Child Horizons, as evidence of their stability and financial capability. Jo feels secure with an inner quiet knowledge that once this home is built, a baby will come and they will be a family.

Jo captures every stage of the home-building process: excavation, footings, foundation, framing, mechanicals, and drywall. The whole community committed to worked together in order to have the home baby-ready in just one month. A full crew of men kept at it from dawn to dusk, Will right there with them. Marta and the Pythian Sisters brought in lunch for the men each day. Meanwhile, Jo planned the interior and coordinated the efforts of the church ladies to help with painting and sewing curtains. There was absolutely no need for the expensive trendy wall-to-wall carpeting Ruth attempted to talk Jo into. Marta's hand-me-down rugs are filled with childhood memories and will look lovely on the simple, yet durable wooden floor. Jo spruced up the rehabbed kitchen cabinets Teddy procured with varnish and paper shelf liner. The patterned vinyl tiles in the kitchen made it feel more modern than it was. Secondhand furniture from her and Will's families filled the little house with warmth. Jo especially loved the family heirloom walnut high headboard bedframe that was hauled in from Will's mother's basement.

When it came time to pour the cement for the sidewalk, Jo was tempted to put in her handprint, but Will was against it, so she refrained. He made her a little mold for a cement garden steppingstone instead, for them both to put their handprints in and keep as memento. The final touch was the exterior paint, light pink with white trim.

"Terracotta," says Will, correcting Jo. He's standing on the sidewalk watching Jo as she's bent over, planting a bush at the front of the house. She stands up realizing he's watching her. She dusts her hands off and walks up next to him with a slight wiggle in her hips. They stand arm-in-arm and admire their creation.

"Fine. Once the bushes and trees grow in, they'll look great with the *terracotta* paint," says Jo. They kiss each other in mutual gratitude for all the effort put into their family home, built with their very own hands and hearts. "Maybe some lilac next year."

Will nods in that-sounds-nice-honey fashion. "OK, Verna," he says as the sun sets behind the house, "your move."

Jo looks anxiously out the front window and sees a car pull up. "Will, she's here." Jo checks herself in the entryway mirror and pulls her blue sweater down over the waist of her wool skirt. Will says the dress perfectly matches her eyes. Ever since then it's been her favorite sweater because she can't help but feel special in it. "It's Mrs. Hoffman, she does the home studies, not Verna."

Will emerges from the hallway, looking fresh shaven. The scent of Avon's latest aftershave fills the room. He's in the pressed shirt Jo laid out for him and is tucking it in as he walks. Jo sets down a plate of chocolate chip cookies and rose leaf mints on the coffee table. Will buttons and buckles his pants.

They both look out the window and watch the caseworker get out of the car and step cautiously on the thin layer of snow that came with the grey clouds this afternoon. Even with her winter coat on, the woman is clearly very pregnant. "Verna said this visit is to ensure the needs of the child are met in the household," says Jo.

"They're checking that the living and sleeping areas have cross ventilation," says Will as a matter of fact.

"Will, what this is," says Jo as she picks a piece of toilet paper off his neck, "is our make-or-break moment."

"Jo," says Will, taking the toilet paper out of her hand and putting it in his pocket. "We've already passed. You heard Verna, not everyone gets a home visit. We've already made it. Relax and enjoy showing off your new home."

They both see her almost lose her footing and Will jumps out the door to give her a hand up the front step. For crying out loud, what in the world is she doing in those heels, in the snow, while pregnant?

Jo greets her at the door. "Hello, I'm Jo, won't you come in?"

"Who knew a dusting of snow could be so slippery." She extends her hand, "I'm Jean Hoffman. I'll be performing your home study today." Everyone wears polite smiles as Will helps her with her coat, then hangs it on the hall tree Emi made from the huge walnut tree cleared from the lot.

"A charming rural neighborhood," notes Jean out loud, as if dictating to someone.

Jo can't quite tell if Jean finds rural life backwards or if she's giving a genuine compliment. Just like Verna, Jean offers very limited personal expression. Jo wonders if they take training on how to conceal what they're really thinking.

"I understand you recently moved in."

"Will designed and built this home himself." Jo glows with pride. "We're still working on a few finishing touches."

"Impressive." Jean bows in Will's direction with acknowledgement.

Will modestly nods, silently accepting the compliment. Jo fidgets with her necklace.

"Would you like to see the rest of our home?" offers Jo.

Jean politely nods.

Will steps over into the front room and out of the way of the women, indicating he will wait here while they do the home tour. He immediately grabs a cookie and lights a cigarette.

Jo can't help but want to scold Will for going straight to the cookies like a child. Will senses Jo's dismay and assumes it's the smoking that got to her, so he shrugs and stamps out the cigarette.

"This," Jo waves her hand, offering Jean to go on in, "is the master bedroom." The walnut bed is beautifully dressed in a quilt handmade by Will's mother, Dolly.

"I love your wedding picture," says Jean. "Such a unique frame."

"The frame is from my mother's side, brought here from Czechoslovakia."

"You got married in a suit," Jean notes with a tone that assumes every woman's dream is to be given away in an off-the-shoulder dress with a ball-gown silhouette. Jo and Will's wedding attire was modest. Will is in the suit he wore to trade school graduation. Jo wore a skirt and jacket with a matching netted pillbox hat.

"Our parents gave us wedding money to do with however we decided. We chose to buy a work truck over a big wedding;"

"Umm, stylish *and* practical."

Jo continues on to the next room. "This is our spare bedroom for guests, and where I do crafts and sewing projects." She actually hates sewing, and only learned to as a necessity to repair Will's work clothes. In this room Jo is thankful for what *couldn't* be seen, the many boxes of teaching materials stacked in the closet. Jo decided to keep everything. She wasn't sure why. There was a piece of her that thought she should donate it all to the school. But still, she hoped maybe someday, she would find the opportunity to use them again. It took almost ten years to acquire all the things that support lesson plans that span several age groups. She just couldn't bring herself to part with it all.

Finally, Jo shares her favorite room in the house, the one where she often stands at night, imagining a child sleeping peacefully. "This will be our child's room." Jo has a small bookshelf already lined with various children's books, a stack of wooden puzzles depicting shapes of nursery rhyme characters, and a toy clock with hands that can move to various times. The small nightlight-style lamp on top the tall-boy dresser radiates a calming golden glow in the room. Ruth offered the use of the crib her children outgrown. Jo thought it best to wait until they knew for sure about a baby before she accepted it.

Jean lightly turns a hand on the toy clock. "The teacher in you is showing, Jo," says Jean and then she adds with a bit of a wink, "We like that."

"I do miss my class. I look forward to seeing the children at Sunday school."

Jo's seen plenty of teacher staff meetings where discussion around the children's family situation can shift from professional planning to town gossip. The adoption review process can't be all that different.

Jo would love to be a fly on the wall during the agency's matching conversations, hearing how they judge and compare every aspect of the applicants' lives in the attempt to match parents for the children. Matching in physical traits seems straightforward enough, but matching religious background seems like over management. Would a loving God even care?

Besides, there's so much that can't be seen on the paperwork. Even the home study is limited. Jean can tell if they are clean, and apparently if the home ventilation is acceptable, but how would they know if the couple argues or fights nonstop? If anyone in the family drinks? If they spend time and money wisely or waste it on things that don't benefit the children? They couldn't tell that Jo is still reliant upon borrowing her dad's car. All that said, when it comes right down to it, she's *glad* they consider every aspect of the applicants' character and lifestyle they can. They should, after all; children deserve it.

"The bathroom." Jo shifts focus to the other side of the hall. Jean just leans her head in the doorway as Jo leads them back toward the front of the house to conclude the tour, "And this is my kitchen."

"That's Jo's domain," Will waves his cookie and smiles. "She's quite a cook."

"Well, baking really," says Jo, feeling the compliment is much too broad. "That's what I enjoy." Jo opens her hand to the living room couch, offering the most comfortable place to sit, "Can I get you something to drink?"

Jean looks grateful for the chance to get off her feet, "Yes, thank you." She sits with a slightly awkward plop and sets her notebook on the coffee table. "It's just under a month until the baby comes."

Finally, the elephant in the room is released! Jo is curious how her own experience waiting for the coming of a baby compares to Jean's experience. How is Jean dealing with the idea of giving up her career? Is it easier if you have the reminder of the baby growing within you?

Will passes her the cookie plate, which Jean accepts and grabs a little rose-molded mint and pops it in her mouth. Jean rests her hand on her protruding tummy, "One of my favorites."

"I bet your office has planned a beautiful combination shower and going away party," suggests Jo as she brings in a coffee. Jo knows the church ladies are just dying to organize a shower for their child. They don't even try to hide their nosiness anymore and expect an adoption progress update each Sunday.

"Oh, I won't be gone that long. I hope to keep working right up to delivery day," says Jean. "Assuming all goes smoothly, I'll be out the recommended six weeks recovery." She reaches into her briefcase and pulls out a small packet of paperclipped papers. "We are so fortunate my husband's sister lives near us, she'll be watching the baby when I go back to work."

Jo and Will exchange shocked expressions.

Jean doesn't notice Jo and Will's reactions as she is waving a mint about while she talks about how to prepare their home for a baby. All of which Jo isn't really hearing.

At first Jo thought sending a pregnant woman to an infertile couple's home study was just a careless result of poor staff planning, but this kind of double standard is just . . . rude. Did she just say she's planning on her sister-in-law raising their baby while she works? The full-time mother rule isn't an agency rule? It's just an *applicant* rule?

Jean pauses as the sight of her watch reminds her to look at that time. "Oh my, where did the time go?" She pulls a few more papers from her briefcase and hands them to Jo.

Jo feels her face grow hot and she hides the blush by burying herself in the documents.

Jean presses herself up off the couch. "Please read these carefully.

They're for your reference as we move closer to bringing a child into your lovely home. You'll need all the supplies listed as soon as reasonable." She drips out the rest of her sentence as she notices the confusion on Jo and Will's faces. "Don't hesitate to call . . . if you have any questions . . . What is it, dear?"

Jo puts the papers down and bites her lip as she figures out how to say what she is thinking in an acceptable tone, "I thought . . . the agency might require . . . *your* resignation."

Jean answers without hesitation, unable to see any similarity in their situations. "Oh heavens no. I don't know what I'd do without my career, I just love what I do."

Is this a test? A training moment? Like something you do to a dog that's dirtied on the rug? Is she rubbing my nose in it? Well, thank you, Jean Hoffman. Thank you very much for reminding me of your superiority.

Will helps Jean with her coat and opens the door. Noticing that Jo has completely lost the ability to speak, he adds, "Thank you for your visit. It's been nice meeting you, Jean."

Jean raises her eyebrows and smiles with the satisfaction of another successful home study under her belt. "We'll contact you when the review is complete."

Jo's mouth hangs slightly open as she stands in the open doorway watching Jean walk down the sidewalk in her city shoes, back to her car, her family, and her career.

Will pulls Jo out of the doorway and closes the door.

"They sent a pregnant career woman," says Jo like a child tattling on a bully.

"Yes," says Will as he puts his arms around Jo and kisses her in an attempt to make it all better. "They did."

CHAPTER 9

Claire stands in silence at the open door of the Microform reading room. She sees Lilli is completely absorbed in her work. She looks just like any other forty-year-old working woman. Average height, average size. Modest in every way. She wouldn't stand out in a crowd and yet Lilli manages to provide housing, money, and friendship for unwed pregnant students when no one else will. Why? Claire still hasn't figured that out. Lilli never shared anything personal about herself—just that she was married to an attorney and had no children. There must be a story deep inside her that drives her compassion. There's nothing Claire could ever say or do to repay her. Lilli's been nothing short of an angel in Claire's life and there's no rush to interrupt her now. No need to knock, call her name, or even clear her throat to get attention because this . . . is goodbye.

When Lilli senses a presence, she breaks away from the viewer. "Claire." She stands up to give Claire a hug. "Are you OK?" She pulls out a chair, inviting Claire to sit. "How'd it go?"

Claire realizes how much she needed Lilli's warm, comforting voice. As her defenses weaken, she fights the urge to cry, "Well . . . I signed the paper."

"Do you want to talk about it?"

Claire wants to open up, but she has no idea how. She doesn't even feel sad. They told her she'd feel relieved, but that was just another lie. All she feels is numb. Claire just shakes her head.

"I see." Lilli takes off her glasses and exhales audibly. "So you believed them."

Claire doesn't look up. She doesn't know what to believe anymore. Lilli begins, "Claire . . ."

"Verna said I should go back home." Claire rolls her head and stretches her neck. "I called Dad, to see if that was true." It was the first time Claire and her dad talked since he told her to not bother ever coming back home. "He didn't ask how I was doing, how the baby was, nothing."

Lilli turns off the viewer's power switch with a smack.

"He said I could come home . . . but only until I found a job. And 'it better be a good job' because he 'doubts any decent man would ever want me.' " Claire mocks her father's words, then lowers her gaze and distracts herself with her coat button again. "They're right, you know," says Claire.

"What?" Lilli shakes her head, showing her disagreement with Claire's thinking.

"Verna said I can't provide for a baby. It's true. I can't even provide for myself."

"Claire," says Lilli, "no one who's put in your position could."

"I'm pretty sure I put me in this position."

"Really?" says Lilli, spooling up for a rant. "And Zach? Your dad's choice to turn his back on his daughter? Your mom? She went along with him. How about whoever decided to make birth control only available to married women? Or the lack of education for women about their own bodies. Don't get me started on how the University policies play into it. Don't you see?"

What Claire sees is Lilli's soft brown eyes light up with fire.

"You were *put* in this position."

Of course, Lilli's right. All of those choices stripped Claire of everything she had until there was nowhere for her to go, no one to count on, and absolutely no chance at becoming the successful mother she wanted to be.

"As for the Vernas of the world," Lilli continues, but then just shakes her head. She pauses to collect herself. "Don't believe them," she says almost in a whisper. "Leave their words of indoctrination behind, along with any shame they conveniently pushed off of themselves and onto you."

Claire's mind and body are laden with enough shame and guilt to last a lifetime. At this very moment her breasts are engorged, still leaking milk, a constant reminder that she will never nourish her own baby. How does she even begin to leave this behind?

As if Lilli read Claire's mind she says, "It's time to be kind to yourself. Especially while you grieve."

"Grieve? My baby's alive. Doesn't seem right to grieve the living."

"The grief is for all you need to let go of," says Lilli. She opens a drawer and pulls out a large manila envelope. "I know it seems impossible, but it's time to put yourself first." She gives the envelop to Claire, "My grandma used to tell us, 'Only when we know the joy of being beyond suffering, will we walk in stride.' "

Claire figures there remains only two things she trusts in the world: Grandmas and Lilli.

"Open it."

Claire bends the metal clasps and pulls out her last paycheck. She notices she was paid for the weeks she was in the hospital. She smiles in gratitude and wonderment at how Lilli never fails to look out for her in any way she can. Next Claire pulls out a bottle of prescription medication—diazepam. She shakes it and raises her brow.

"Dr. Hastings from the Medical Center asked me to give you these. Atypical depression is real, Claire, even for women in the best situations. These can help you through this rough patch."

Claire nods and wonders what comes when the numbness wears away.

The last thing she pulls from the envelope is a magazine. On the cover is a large, colorful photo of two chic and sexy women in fashionable air hostess uniforms. Claire's inner go-go girl is naturally curious but mostly confused.

"This also came from Dr. Hastings's office. It's an airline recruitment pamphlet. An option for you to consider."

Claire can't remember the last time she was offered an option. Is this something she could honestly say yes or no to?

"It's not anything like the degree you came here for, but travel might be the expansion you need." Lilli flips the pamphlet open. "Give yourself permission to simply explore, shed anything that's holding you back, and discover your next chapter."

Claire envisions herself literally flying away. Away from Sarah. Away from the family she once knew. Away from the feelings she doesn't recognize.

"They want women with some college, good with people, tall, beautiful. Their uniforms are made by French designers." Lilli taps at the photo, "If those boots don't say Claire Jordan, I don't know what does." Lilli's voice shifts to make clear the bare essence of this offer, "Once your application is approved, there's a five-week training that includes room and board."

Claire snaps with the realization that this could actually work. "How?"

"Dr. Hastings golfs with the airline training coordinator." Lilli raises her eyebrows, "And he's a decent man who actually cares about women." Lilli continues with instructions like it's already a done deal. "The world being what it is, you'll need an internal exam to complete the application—they make sure you're . . . *single*."

As absurd as that sounds, after all she's been through, Claire's not surprised.

Lilli grabs a pen and writes on the pamphlet Dr. Hastings's phone number. "Be sure your appointment is with him. He's familiar with the airline policies and will ensure your paperwork has everything needed for you to enter the next cohort."

And just like that, the emotions come flooding in and there is no holding them back. She grimaces, her shoulders heave.

Lilli hands her a tissue.

"I thought I could do this on my own," Claire blubbers, "but that's . . . impossible." She quiets herself a bit and swallows to clear her throat. "Thank you."

"You're welcome." The two women continue to sit together in the moment, appreciating each other's strength.

"I'll never forget you, Lilli," says Claire.

"Promise me two things?"

Claire nods. Nothing will prevent her from keeping this promise.

"Stay in touch? Send me a postcard every now and then."

Claire nods. "I will . . ." She waits for the second part.

Lilli runs her hand around the side of her head, smoothing the hair up in the bun that sits atop her head. She takes a deep breath in and exhales fully, "I saw you in the media room one day," reveals Lilli. "You were talking to your baby the way you did most days."

"You could hear that?" says Claire, who had been thinking all along that no one knew.

Lilli nodded. "That day, I heard you name her . . . Sarah."

Claire nods and tears begin to flow again, "They said she wasn't mine to name. I prayed that some part of her would know the name I gave her. The name her first mother gave her."

Lilli brushes a strand of hair behind Claire's ear, "I have no doubt Sarah heard her name and felt your love." She puts her hand on Claire's and looks into her eyes for a commitment, "Promise me you'll keep breaking the rules."

"Break the rules?"

Lilli nods as she speaks, "There's a lot of women counting on you to do that."

"I promise."

Claire wipes her face with the soaked tissue and puts her things back into the envelope. She thinks about how she can start living up to her agreement. "Can I ask just one more favor?"

Lilli adjusts her earring and looks sideways at Claire with a smile, "Just name it."

"Can you drop me off at the agency?"

Claire plunges into the adoption agency, stuffing down the urge to retreat. She just promised Lilli she'd break some rules, and she's not going to back down the first day in. She glances around to see if anyone notices she is in the very place to which she was told not to return. Even though she was here just yesterday, it looks oddly unrecognizable. She may have been a wreck then, but now she's a wreck with determination.

A young receptionist at the front desk talks on a phone that she's balanced on her shoulder. The receptionist multi-tasks, filling out a form on a manual return typewriter, striking the keys every so often in between phrases of her phone conversation, not noticing Claire.

"Well, every day. Every day I see dazed teens in front of me, her baby's not even real to her yet. They're taught nothing, have no resources . . ." She pauses to listen while she types. "I guess I end up agreeing with them. The best-case scenario seems to be placement with one of the many couples waiting to adopt. And yet . . ."

Claire steps up to the desk and looks around for a bell to ring to interrupt the phone conversation she can hear. Who knew that being referred to as a "dazed teen" would somehow be better? The receptionist finally notices her and signals "one more minute" with her finger, but then at second glance recognizes Claire and quickly ends her phone conversation. She pops the phone receiver off her shoulder and onto its cradle. "Is there anything I can do for you, honey?"

Claire is surprised to find her tone indicates genuine concern. Claire notices the name tag pinned neatly on her jacket and makes her demands as clear and as simple as she can, "Bonnie, I need to know if my baby is OK, and exactly how you find a family that will truly love her."

Bonnie bites her lower lip and raises an eyebrow, as if that's a request she's never before heard. Claire can't imagine why every single girl who's been through this atrocity of a process wouldn't ask for the very same information. Bonnie remains silent, processing. She appears young, couldn't be much older than Claire. Surely, she's been trained in what to do if a girl shows up after her baby's been . . . kidnapped. How much of a fight is this going to be? Claire steadies her stance and purses her lips, "I'm not leaving until I know."

Claire assumes Bonnie's been given some sort of script, just like everyone else involved in the adoption process. They all willingly learn words designed to get possession of the baby, collect payment for services, and then simply get rid of her. Not today, Bonnie.

Bonnie looks around her to see if any supervisor is nearby. There's a large potted peace lily next to the reception desk and a sea of cubicles, but no one in line of sight. It's just the two of them. She waves Claire in to walk around the reception desk to sit down at the chair right next to her. Just maybe Bonnie is ready to break the pattern.

"Honey, there are so many lovely, established young couples coming to us. Just as soon as we place a baby, there are ten more qualified applicants in line for the next."

"Please, tell me . . . anything about my baby," pleads Claire. "Is she well? I was sick when she was born." Claire clenches her hands into fists inside of her coat pockets to remind herself to stay present so she can absorb whatever Bonnie is willing to offer.

Bonnie inhales, about to speak, but then stops herself. She taps her pen and bites her lip.

Oh my God, it's going to happen. Come on, Bonnie, you can do it. You can do better.

"Hold on, let me take a look. Your name again, honey?

"Margaret. Claire. Jordan." Now Claire is also looking around to see if anyone is coming.

Bonnie flips through the files right there in the tray on her desk. "You go by Claire, right? You just recently met with Mrs. Prescot?"

Claire nods.

"Honey, the moment the baby is placed in our foster care center, it has its own file, separate from yours. The baby's file is protected by our county and state laws. There's simply no way for me to answer any question about the baby."

Tears begin to stream down Claire's face. "I just want to tell her I love her." *This place is filled with social workers, for god's sake. Can't they understand? How will Sarah know how special she is to me?*

Bonnie hands Claire a couple tissues from the box on the side of her station.

"Thank you." *Be kind to yourself, that's what Lilli said. Bonnie, please have a way to help me do that.*

Bonnie gives Claire a brief smile and continues to search her desk for some kind of solution. "Here's what you're going to do," says Bonnie, now with the confidence of a woman with a plan. "You're going to take this card." She pulls out from under the corner of her desk pad a Hallmark card that's folded in a bright-yellow envelope and places it in front of Claire. "I picked it up today for my niece's birthday, but I want you to have it." The front of the card says, "To a DEAR GIRL On Her Birthday."

"Wa . . . what?" says Claire in between sobs.

"It's for you to write in, honey. You sit right here as long as you need and write everything you feel the baby should know about how she's loved. Can you do that?"

Claire wipes her nose with the tissue and looks at the card, deciding if this will do.

"Here's a pen. When you're done, I'll put it in this envelope." Bonnie pulls out a big, smelly, squeaky permanent black marker and writes on the large manila envelope 'FILLED WITH LOVE' in big bold all capital letters. "Then I'll see that this envelope gets in the baby's file."

"You would do that for me?" asks Claire, rapidly blinking, surprised at her genuine concern and generosity.

"Oh my God honey, yes. As a matter of fact, after today, you can write a card as often as you like. Just send it in to us, and I'll file it right here along with this one." Bonnie looks at the birthday card, "Maybe you could write to her on her birthdays."

"I will . . ." decides Claire. "Thank you." Claire's own commitment to an ongoing relationship with her daughter, even if it is just through writing cards, feels like the first right choice she's made in a long while. Her and Sarah's relationship is not over. The tightness in her chest releases ever so slightly.

"Don't even worry about it. Listen, honey, it's very normal to be sad. If you write about love every time you feel down, that might help you know everything's going to be all right."

Claire licks her lips, cautious hope seeping into her heart.

Bonnie pulls out a bag of candy from her drawer, "I just got this bag of caramels; you want some while you write?"

Claire looks up at Bonnie with gratitude, takes two caramels, and picks up the pen.

Dear Sarah,

What a beautiful girl you are. You've been growing so strong. I am proud of you.

Having a daughter, knowing you, means more to me than anything ever has or ever will. I love you.

Your first mother,
Claire

The whole house smells of caramel. This morning, Jo busies herself learning a new recipe. Betty Crocker's *New Picture Cook Book* is laid open on the counter. Jo reads, "Work quickly to avoid the candy hardening at an uneven consistency." She tips the heavy stainless-steel skillet with one hand, spreading the bubbling hot syrupy mixture across the greased baking pan with the other. The kitchen wall phone rings. Jo looks up at the phone and frowns at the unfortunate timing. She picks up the receiver and places it on her shoulder, freeing her hands to deal with the sticky skillet.

"Tischler's . . . yes, speaking." Jo freezes. "Do I want to pick up . . . our *baby girl*?" Her heart stops as she tries to process the words she just heard. She clears the lump out of her throat in order to respond. "Today?" She steps back a little to catch herself, her eyes welling up with tears. "Yes. I . . . yes . . ." She can hardly breath now. Jo swallows hard to gain composure and, grabbing the pencil, writes on the roll of paper always kept by the phone. She scribbles down notes as she repeats every instruction. "Yes, both of us will be there." She glances at the old schoolhouse clock that was a housewarming gift from her co-worders. Quarter to ten. Will should still be near the bank about this time. "Yes, I have all the items on the list." She writes, *diaper, set of clothes, blanket*. "Yes, I'll be writing a check." Perfect timing sending Will in to make a deposit today. "Two p.m. Thank you so much."

Jo hangs up the phone with a surprisingly rough nervous slam. She sits down and exhales into folded hands. It's happening. Then she runs her hands up the sides of her head and slips off the bandana she was wearing and uses it to wipe her eyes. Realizing now that she set the skillet down on the counter, Jo springs to her feet and picks it up in a panic. No burn marks. She laughs with relief. But then she stiffens again, she's going to be a mother in a matter of hours. She looks at her trembling hand holding the skillet and laughs out loud as she turns it upside down with spoon and candy thermometer completely stuck.

Jo and Will are sitting at a round table dressed in their Sunday best. They borrowed Emi's car so they didn't have to drive the baby home in the work truck. Drive *their* baby home. They sit stiff and wide eyed, which is something Jo hasn't seen on Will in a long time, he's usually so relaxed. She counts on him to be the one that has it all together. The emotional mixture of fear, impatience, and excitement has Jo biting the inside of her cheek. It's hard to believe this is the end of the longing. The end of the unworthiness. The journey to this moment has been so, so long. Jo wonders how long a person can be expected to physically sit and wait in this room. The adoption room has two doors, the one they came in is behind them. Jo considers the side door, door number 2. That's the door that will reveal their child. She's been negotiating for a decade for that door to open. Negotiating with God, Will, doctors, pharmacists. And now the adoption agency will open the door to motherhood.

After a brief mental image of *Let's Make a Deal*, Jo is reminded of her students waiting for Valentine's cookies. No one may begin eating until everyone has a treat on their desk. Jo always started with the more mature children because there was no way the youngest could restrain themselves that long. The children would stare at the heart-shaped cookie sitting in front of them, waiting to devour it like they hadn't eaten in years. Jo stares at the adoption room side door. Her senses are on high alert. The faint odor of cleaning fluids makes her nose itch. She twitches her nose and then becomes aware of a ticking. It's Will's wristwatch. At first, she was mildly entertained by her ability to hear it at this distance, but now finds it annoying and consciously reminds herself that's not something she can scold him for. Then she hears the scratch of the latch on the strike plate and sees the knob twist. Will and Jo lean forward as the door creaks open in slow motion.

Verna enters holding the door just wide enough to slip herself in and close it behind. "Our investigations determined you to be superior adoptive parents." Verna seats herself at the round table. "Congratulations."

Jo and Will look at each other, then at Verna, smiling bravely with chins high. "Thank you."

Verna continues, "Up until now, the baby's received excellent care in our foster center. Today you'll make the decision to take responsibility for the care received to date and for all the child's care going forward . . . for a lifetime."

Jo and Will nod as they listen to Verna describe what they have already committed to many times over in their hearts. There is no need for further preamble. *For the love of God, Verna, bring in the child.*

"During this time, you have a chance to meet the baby and ask any additional questions before making that decision. Are you ready?"

"Yes, ma'am," answers Will as he grabs Jo's hand.

Verna walks over to the door at the side of the room and knocks twice. Will squeezes Jo's hand. She can feel the sweat in his palm. Their eyes are fixed on the door. Verna looks back over her shoulder to Jo and Will, "She's six weeks old."

A foster nanny emerges holding their baby, swaddled in a blanket. Jo and Will stand up as the nanny brings the baby to them. Jo holds her heart with one hand and her face with the other as she leans in to see her daughter's face for the first time. "She's awake," says the nanny as she loosens the blanket, uncovering the baby's entire face.

Jo covers her quivering chin, feeling a joy larger than she thought possible. Will puts his arm around Jo in comfort and support. "Would you like to hold your daughter?" says the nanny.

"I have a daughter," says Jo looking at Will, reminding herself this is not a dream.

Will nods as the nanny carefully transfers the baby into Jo's arms.

Jo smiles as she looks at the baby. The baby considers Jo, with fearless eyes trying to focus. "Hi," Jo adjusts the blanket and rubs her thumb across the baby's check.

"She's so tiny," says Will, which is more than an observation, it's an immediate commitment to her protection. "Her eyes are blue like yours, Jo." He laughs softly as he wipes a tear from behind his glasses with his thumb.

The baby engages with Jo, and in that moment, there is the bonding. A feeling of oneness. The sensation of absolute trust extends from the baby, creating a warmth deep in Jo's chest. She stops breathing and surrenders, permitting her heart to break wide open to allow the child in. Too overcome to make words, she lovingly mouths her daughter's name, "Julia."

Julia coos with acceptance.

Jo doesn't hide her tears; she wants Julia to know that what's happening to her right now is important. An unexpected rush of gratitude flows over Jo. There's so much she's never understood about the obstacles she's faced in becoming a mother, but now she's grateful. Grateful that God planned for her to become a mother in this way.

Verna gently interrupts with the legally required inquiry, "Do you accept this child?"

Verna's voice prompts Jo and Will to return to the physical world of the adoption room. They look at each other with great affection and exchange an acknowledgement that this is an incredible accomplishment. They now share what was previously impossible, the love of a child. "Yes," they say in unison.

"Did you bring the clothes and wraps requested?" asks Verna.

"In my bag." Jo nods at Will, indicating he should retrieve them. Will hands the meticulously folded stack of cloth to Verna. The nanny moves to take the baby back from Jo.

Jo and Will both look up at the nanny, reluctant to let anyone take their baby from their possession. "I'm happy to change her," offers Jo.

"It is our policy," insists Verna. "Jenny will dress the baby while we finish the paperwork."

Verna indicates Jo and Will should sit back down at the table, then opens the side door and places the stack of clothes on the counter just inside the next room.

Will shifts in his chair unable to sit still, his eyes fixed on the baby as they leave the room. They can hear Julia coo "ah-ha" as the door closes. Will nudges Jo with his elbow and speaks without shifting his gaze from the door, "Jo, go ahead and take out the checkbook."

Jo, reaches into her bag, grabs a hanky, blows her nose with a honk, then pulls out the checkbook.

Verna places several forms and an invoice on the table. Then she presents paperwork for Will to sign while Jo writes the check the Child Horizons: *four hundred and no/100 dollars*. That leaves only $10 in their account. No problem, she'll just transfer some from savings tomorrow. The paperwork shuffling and signature pointing is guided by Verna with well-practiced rhythm.

"Do you have a name picked out?" she asks.

"Julia Fae Tischler." The child's full name unfolds into the air like a song from Jo's heart.

"We'll call her Jules," says Will as he smiles at Jo.

"Jo and Jules," says Verna, "very nice."

Verna points to where Jo is to fill the name in on the paperwork. "The birth certificate is modified to show you as Julia's father and mother. Please look this over and verify all the information is correct. Going forward this is the only birth certificate released by the state and county courts."

Jo and Will glance at the documents, barely interested in paperwork, willing to sign and agree to anything at this point, while continuously scanning for any activity from the side door.

Satisfied with the signatures, Verna announces, "Your probation period begins today."

Will and Jo look at each other, readily accepting any condition to their parenthood.

"We require a year of written progress reports, and you may expect a no-notice home visit."

Jo replies with her most practiced hostess voice, "I'll make sure you have everything, exactly as requested, Mrs. Prescot. You are always welcome to our home. Please come by any time."

Verna nods and goes back to her paperwork shuffling. Jo can hear Will's wristwatch again and can't stop herself from chewing her nails. Will rubs a patch of dry skin along the side of his index finger against the edge of the table. They glance at each other with a bright-eyed support and encouragement when they're not staring at the side door.

As the door opens, both Jo and Will stand up. Jo floats across the room to the nanny and takes Jules in her arms. For the first time in her life, Jules wears her very own clothes. Kicking her feet and throwing out her arms, she seems to be proud of herself for being dressed in the mint-green going-home outfit that Babička adorned with colorful embroidered flowers on the collar and matching bonnet.

"May we take a photo?" asks Jo.

"We can permit a photograph with just the three of you," says Verna.

Will pulls the camera out of Jo's bag and hands it to the nanny. Will puts his arms around his girls, and the new family poses for the shot.

"We're a family now," announces Jo.

"Let's go home," says Will.

PART 2

Claire spins the rack of birthday cards, browsing for the most colorful. Sarah turns three this year. Already. The holidays were exhausting, and though delays due to de-icing are inconvenient, Claire is relieved to have a bit of extra time to catch up on sleep in one of her favorite Hiltons. They recently updated the gift shop with a nice selection of paperbacks and greeting cards. If they had the latest Agatha Christie that would be okay, but she was specifically looking for something a little more John le Carré if they had it. At registration, the rest of her crew and the pilots are still receiving their keys.

Celebrities from the moment they enter training, stewardesses by regulation are young, slim, attractive, and single. Every man, woman, and child in the lobby has halted to look up to them with either admiration or desire. That *is* the point, after all. Airlines can't compete for customers with airfare since that's regulated by the feds, but they certainly do compete by who has the most attractive stewardesses. When the crew gathers, whether it's in flight, in the airport terminal, or in the hotel lobby, they are on full display.

The stewardesses radiate glamour, wearing custom-fitted uniforms with skirts only a couple inches longer than their stylish pink and orange bicolor jackets. The matching cap hats are a nice touch, but Claire's favorite part of the uniform is the knee-high boots. Even their luggage is the latest modern material and shapes. Fully booked flights and packed hotel bars are evidence those uniforms are worth every bit of the marketing money. Claire does feel like a million dollars in her uniform, but she's not really proud of her job. For the most part she's a glorified waitress. Taking meal orders and mixing cocktails. Paid to be charming, stylish, and happy to have drunk men eyeball her every move. She *is* at the center of the man's world, but not in the way she'd once imagined. All the stewardesses knew it wouldn't be long until someone younger, prettier, or thinner would take over their position. One of her crew members did not make weight this morning and was disqualified from flying. Weigh-in is never a concern for Claire since she is always well underweight. Termination is always looming, and according to their contract it would transpire when they got married, pregnant, or turned thirty-two years old.

Though the stewardesses may be the glamour, it's the pilots who are the crew's power. Their uniforms are inspired by the military rather than runway fashion, with wings of gold on their chest and bold stripes of authority on their sleeves. To do their job, pilots have to be confident, competent, and in more cases than not, Claire has found the pilots to be conceited. Generally, she chooses to stay away from them, all except one that is, who she's found to be kind and more aware of the stewardesses concerns and wellbeing than the other pilots.

It's at that very moment, as though he could read her mind, Claire realizes Tony, the most junior pilot of today's crew, is watching her. He smiles like he caught her at something.

Claire briefly smiles, then spins the greeting card rack. She knows exactly what she is and isn't looking for. She grabs the bright pink and orange birthday card and a small bag of caramels, then hands her cash to the checkout clerk.

Tony is still watching, and she ignores him as she rejoins her co-workers at the front of the line accepting the final key in their group block. Across the lobby, the lounge hostess hands each member of the crew an invitation card to a Tiki-themed happy hour. Claire accepts the card with a smile assuring the hostess she will be there and overhears Tony briefly coordinating with the two older pilots.

"Yes, Sir. Dinner at 19:30." As the senior pilots head directly to the lounge, Tony remains and lights a cigarette. He follows Claire and the stewardesses toward the elevators.

A bellman holds open the door. The women enter the elevator and Tony goes to step in, but the bellman puts out his hand, obstructing Tony's path. "I'm sorry, sir, please take the next lift, this is going to our ladies-only floor."

The whole crew including Claire face Tony, who is left in the lobby.

"Yes, of course." Tony inhales his cigarette, looking at the women with a sheepish smile.

The girls wave bye-bye and laugh as the doors close.

The flaming volcano is a party drink they can't replicate onboard flights. For a good reason, 151-proof spirits are not allowed on the aircraft. If the bottle were to light, it would explode. The ceramic is painted with Polynesian dancers, and a raised volcano shape in the middle of the bowl has a puddle of rum waiting to be lit. Claire asked the server to hold off on the flaming presentation until her flight crew members joined. Meanwhile, sitting alone at the table with this giant cocktail feels ridiculous.

The hotel bar is transformed with driftwood, coconuts, and bamboo. The golden glow of the Tiki lanterns combines with the house band playing hapa-haole music, creating an exotic mood. Claire realizes her co-workers have been snatched up by hungry men as they plated snacks on toothpicks from the hors d'oeuvre table. The girls wink and wave at Claire as they accept a change in plans more attractive than the originally discussed girls' night out.

She reaches for her bag and pulls out a pen and the birthday card.

This just became a private party, between her and Sarah. Claire pokes at the maraschino cherries floating in the iced rum punch and sips through the long blue straw. The warmth of the rum immediately soothes the ever-present ache in her heart that seems to grow less dull with each passing year. "Happy Birthday Sweetie," Claire writes in her best handwriting. She pauses and puts down the pen to brush away the tear that slipped from her eye. Drinking from the depths of the volcano, feeling exposed, Claire looks around and decides she's sufficiently hidden from the crowd nestled in a little nook next to the huge fireplace. On her last trip to the agency, Bonnie's promise gave her a lifeline. This year she decided to share a little bit about her current circumstance with Sarah. It's become a recent nagging concern that Sarah will soon be old enough to form an opinion about her. The truth isn't perfect, but it's filled with love and hope. Claire dreams that Sarah will be proud of her somehow, so it would make sense to share some accomplishments. Maybe someday that would develop into them having common interests.

Happy Birthday Sweetie,

I can't believe how big you've gotten. Don't forget to make a wish before you blow out all three birthday candles. You can do it! Someday I'll tell you stories of my adventures as an air hostess. Always know how much I love you.

Your first mother,
Claire

Claire takes another sip and lifts her brimming eyes in the direction of the hors d'oeuvre table, where Tony pretends he wasn't really watching her as he puts a few skewered snacks on his plate and swipes the cheese ball with a cracker. He's dressed in a conservative dark suit with a collar over lapel, a pocket square in his breast pocket.

Claire enjoys seeing the pilots dressed in anything other than the pilot uniform. It's a chance to assess their inner sense of style, and Tony is decidedly . . . foxy. Claire puts her pen back in her bag and is beginning to put the card in the envelope when Tony appears right in front of the table, "That's quite a drink for a table of one."

Claire greets him, then swirls the straw in the volcano. "I've always wanted to drink from a bowl of fire."

He pulls out his golden Zippo lighter and shakes it. "May I?" Tony tilts his head at an empty seat at the table. Claire nods and feels an anticipatory tingle of excitement. It's silly to think she would not agree to his joining, but she's appreciative he was polite enough to ask. Good manners are an incredibly attractive quality in men.

They've socialized many times before when their schedules coincided during a layover, and the last time they had a night with just the two of them, their connection was undeniable. But Claire remains guarded, afraid of scaring him away with the truth of who she really is. Claire picks up the long red straw the server left on the table and puts it in the volcano bowl in the direction of Tony.

They both ooh and aah when the drink ignites, then sip from their straws.

"That's the smile I'm used to seeing," says Tony, putting no effort into hiding his pleasure.

Claire acknowledges she does feel better. She takes another sip, and catches the glance of two women across the room. They're making comments to each other with trenchant expressions. The focus of their conversation is so obviously centered on Claire, they might as well just be pointing fingers at her. "Check them out." Claire tilts her head in their direction. "But not so they notice."

Tony nonchalantly glances in the direction Claire suggests. "You think they're talking about us?"

"Sure, they are." Claire recognizes them from the lobby when the crew checked in.

"Does it matter?" asks Tony.

Claire shrugs as she sips from the bowl of fire. "What they don't know is a lot."

"Meaning . . ."

"Well, they act like they're envious. A stewardess with a pilot, drinking from a flaming volcano. Just another day of glamourous, carefree adventure. Blah, blah, blah."

"Isn't that the case?"

"It might be for you," offers Claire, "but what I have isn't something they want." Claire takes another long drink and considers if it's safe to reveal her true feelings. "No one wants it."

"What's that?" Tony asks as if he truly wants to know.

Claire turns red, and she wipes her face with defiance. She wants to share with him her ever-present feelings of guilt, shame, rage . . . downright anger. But . . . he doesn't want to hear that. No one does. "You don't want to know."

"Everyone has regrets, Claire" Tony swirls his cocktail weenie in sauce, but decides not to eat it.

Claire freezes and stares at Tony.

"You aren't the only one to screw up," he says, attempting to read her stare.

Could Tony possibly know what's behind her feelings? Technically, the pilots are in charge of the entire flight crew including the stewardesses and have access to their employment files. But the only way the airline would have any of *that* background would be if they did some kind of independent investigation of her medical records at the University Medical Center. Could the airline know about Child Horizons?

Tony attempts to somehow clear up the unspoken confusion in

Claire's silent stare. "I mean the Captain Bob thing," he says without complete confidence. That's what the crew calls the senior pilot Captain Robert Tyler, notorious for fooling around with the naïve girls, usually the not so bright stewardesses. He thinks nothing of extramarital affairs. Claire feels genuinely sorry for his wife. Just last week Bob was apparently bragging that Claire was the most recent notch in his belt. Not only did Tony call Bob out for spreading such an outrageous lie, he also took the time to make sure Claire knew the bullshit Bob was spreading, so she didn't hear it from someone else.

Claire is relieved that Tony's comment had nothing to do with Child Horizons. But just the thought of Captain Bob, makes her blood boil. Again. "I'm no one's notch," says Claire.

"Really?" Tony pokes.

"Really." Claire plucks a maraschino cherry from the punch and pulls the stem from between her teeth.

"As soon as I heard it, I knew something didn't add up," says Tony. "It just didn't sound like you. You keep to yourself. Stay in your room."

"You're damn right I do," says Claire, now worked up thinking about just how low Bob was willing to go. Claire takes another long sip trying to cool off. "Thank you, by the way, for setting him straight, so I didn't have to." The incident made working with Bob ridiculously awkward, but thanks to Tony, it quickly became a non-issue.

"You're welcome." Tony looks into Claire's eyes. He seemed genuinely happy to be in position where he could assist her.

Claire is tempted to lose herself in Tony's gaze, but instead she shifts her eyes to the volcano and takes another sip. "You notice I stay in?"

"Well, Claire," says Tony leaning in, "I notice a lot of things about you." He says this very matter-of-factly, like noticing everything about Claire is obviously a very natural thing for him to do.

Claire challenges him to stand behind such a statement. "Like what?"

Tony pauses to light a cigarette. "You're not like the others. They compete so they can travel, shop, find husbands." He exhales the smoke out the side of his mouth and looks at Claire to see if he's on track.

She remains quiet and allows him to continue.

"You look out for the others. Cover up their mistakes, step in when old fat businessmen are assuming and rude. You're usually assigned the pre-flight safety briefing. Because you're one of the few with a presence of authority. And yes, you stay in, so I assume you spend only your own money. Your free time is for writing cards." He nods down at the envelope Claire has yet to stash back in her bag. "And reading spy novels." He sets the cigarette down, "I see . . ." Tony waits for Claire's eye contact, "a woman with a secret purpose."

A secret purpose. Claire feels like Tony does see her. She hears a narration of her life as a spy in her mind. *Double Agent Jordan. Jet-setting stewardess by day, secretly seeking the location of her kidnapped daughter by night. She's no stranger to coercion and will break every rule to be part of her child's life. Agent Jordan's mission: to break the chains of guilt and shame and put the evil Verna Prescot behind bars.* Claire takes another long sip from the volcano and promises herself that it's the last one because when your inner dialogue sounds like a spy novel narrator, you've decidedly progressed beyond tipsy.

Claire speaks in a low tone to the one man who may actually get her, "During night flights, when passengers are dozing," Claire's mind drifts now to the many times she's sat by herself staring out the window of an aircraft, "I look out into the black sky. I think, someday I'll have to face all that darkness." She looks to the dance floor where her gorgeous crew members are flirting with every man in the room.

"So far, I've protected myself from the darkness simply by staying out of its way."

"So, you're afraid of the dark?" asks Tony.

Claire considers what Tony knows well, that anyone can navigate the darkness with the proper equipment.

"I was told I could leave the pain behind, but no matter where I fly, there's no moving on from her."

Tony's brows draw together. "From *her*?"

Claire holds her finger up to her lips, shooshing herself.

Tony pulls her hand from her face and holds it in his, smiling warmly into her eyes. "Let me ask you this. Are the secrets you're keeping yours to tell?"

There's a world of difference between having the power of a secret and being silenced. Everyone held up their end of the secret, but the only one affected long term is Claire. Being pregnant, giving birth, her baby. All are part of Claire's identity now. Attempting to forget who she is, isn't moving on, it's agreeing to remain still. If she wants to feel alive again, Claire knows she has to face the dark. Maybe telling Tony can be a start.

"My daughter." Claire is surprised by the sound of her own words. She looks down at the card. "There's no moving on from . . . my daughter." Claire holds her breath. She looks at Tony, waiting for his reaction.

He leans back, reaches in his pocket and offers Claire a cigarette.

Claire releases her breath slowly and leans forward for a light. He's still here. No polite excuses to leave. He decided to stay. Claire holds the birthday card with a trembling hand and manages to blubber an explanation, "I write her a birthday card every year. It's been three years. Since I . . . signed for adoption." Claire faces the ceiling and exhales, "I doubt you can understand . . ."

"Adoption." Tony repeats the word. He looks at the card, "You still want to know her?"

"I do," says Claire. "It's a need really. I need . . . the impossible." She sips again from the straw in front of her, knowing she's already had enough. Being an air hostess has had many benefits, travel is interesting, and the work keeps her mind and body busy, but this so-called glamourous life isn't nearly enough.

Claire taps the birthday card, remembering when she accepted Bonnie's suggestion to tell Sarah how much she is loved. "The very next day after signing those papers, I decided to keep her in my life, even if it seems impossible. Even if she's far away, living with another family."

Tony looks deep into Claire's eyes. "Proximity doesn't make a family."

"What *does* make a family?" This is a genuine question. Family seems so complicated now. Seeing herself as a mother but not a parent is so confusing. If only she could be reminded what family is, that would be something.

"I don't know," says Tony. "Love?"

CHAPTER 12

"Thanks for bringing the food color," says Jo. There's a naked Barbie doll standing in the center of a three-layer white cake waiting to be clothed in frosting. Jo's kitchen, which on any other day is immaculately organized, is a controlled whirlwind of birthday party preparations.

"No problem," says Ruth. "Don't forget to take pictures. We should submit your doll cake to this year's Pythian Sisters cookbook."

"Good idea," says Jo as she stirs a few drops of color into the frosting and puts her focus on decorating. Jo has built quite a reputation for her developing skill in baking even though it's a genuine challenge to find time to bake. Time for anything "extra" is a rare commodity. Looking back on the last three years, she seriously underestimated the amount of time and energy required for mothering. Jo was aware of the unspoken expectations for mothers. Dress the children in beautiful clothes, keep a beautiful home, cook beautiful food, entertain with cleverly themed parties, see to all the polite correspondence, the list goes on. That's all part of the privilege of being a mother. Planning, shopping, preparations, making sure everyone is served, cleaning up, all while tending to the children's wellbeing and development. She's watched the women in the community do all of this, and manage to make it appear deceptively effortless.

And that's not accounting for all the not-so-beautiful moments. The things no one talks about. Like the fact that Jules howled the entire way home that first day they picked her up from Child Horizons. *Owh owh owh*. The. Entire. Way. Once they finally got home, Jo had to call her sister to come over and show her how to give a baby a bath. Jo traversed every human emotion that day, from anxiety, pure joy, and pride to feeling like she failed motherhood in the first few tender hours. Her perfect dream of the homecoming never happened. Reality happened. The reality is, it's a lot of work. And there's no breaks. And the men are, frankly, little help. Will means well, a wonderful provider, but the fact is he's never changed a diaper, made a bottle, given a bath, or even read a bedtime story. He's not once gotten up in the middle of the night, he just snores right through it. Will pretty much goes to work and comes home hungry like he always has. He says women are made for nurturing children. Jo guesses he's right, and Will requires plenty of nurturing too.

Jo has considered the comparisons between being a mother and being a teacher. Of course, the love of her own daughter and son is the most incredible feeling imaginable, but in teaching she could call in the principal for tangible backup. She had regular staff meetings where she could ask for advice and blow off steam. She had substitutes available for when she was sick. Jo is a little surprised at how slim the support structure for motherhood really is.

"How are you feeling?" asks Ruth, pulling Jo out of her thoughts. Jo continues to subconsciously crank out frosting flowers in a spiraling row around the cake.

"About the party?" says Jo. "It'll be fine. Mom took the kids so I can finish up the cake as a surprise for Jules." Marta's duty is easy since it's dance lesson day. The instructor is teaching the kids the cutest cowboy dance, prompting Karl to wear his cowboy hat and little toy holster all day every day. That will work out fine tonight, he can wear his special cowboy outfit, while Jules wears her special birthday party dress. That alone should help with the inevitable jealousy issues that will arise. Karl loves being the big brother when he's in charge and the center of attention. This has been his little attitude since the day they brought him home.

"No," Ruth huffs with a laugh, "not the party. I mean you. How'd the last doctor visit go?"

Ruth is the only person who still asks about her condition. Everyone else, even Will, pretty much gave up. Jo purposefully downplays it because managing chronic pain, especially when it's particularly bad during that time of the month, isn't part of polite conversation, certainly not to be mentioned in mixed company. Jo is concerned that if Child Horizons got word of her pain management, recommendations for surgery, and subsequent time in recovery, they may construe that to mean she's an "unfit mother." Ruth tried to talk her down from that fear, but no amount of discussion can convince Jo otherwise. She would never do anything that might risk losing Jules and Karl. If that means putting aside her own needs, so be it.

"He confirmed what I already knew," says Jo as she refills the piping bag. "The growths are large now, including the ones on my ovaries. He recommends surgery. That and Tylenol."

"Jesus, Jo. How long can you keep putting this off?" Ruth swipes up the little glass bottle of food color and returns it to the box, annoyed and concerned at the same time. "You know that's a huge strain on your body."

Jo nods, knowing Ruth is right, but she's doing it anyway. "Just until we're a safe distance from the agency's line of sight and small-town gossip," says Jo.

"Still considering moving?" asks Ruth. The move to LA didn't pan out. So now Jo and Will are considering Colorado. When Jo's Uncle Arno died, Karla decided not to return to the small town in Nebraska and now lives alone in the mountain cabin. As it turns out, Karla's cabin is a favorite vacation destination for the entire extended family.

Jo nods again, biting her lip as she puts down the frosting to check on the soup and give it a stir. Emi requested Jo's dill gravy as the meal for the party. Jo initially laughed at the idea, but the traditional hearty soup is always welcome in January. It's easy enough to make a large batch, and simple to serve, which is a blessing because their table isn't quite big enough for six adults and two children.

"Will's decided. We are moving," says Jo. Moving seems too small of an idea for what they're planning. Selling the business, the house, everything. They're planning to start a new life. To raise a family free from the obligations to family and a small town.

"Soon?" says Ruth.

"We start packing as soon as the snow melts."

Will's been looking for a way to expand his business for some time now. The trip to visit Aunt Karla's cabin last summer was primarily a location check and an opportunity for Will to make connections with a construction company that just opened a location near Horsetooth Reservoir.

"When are you telling your folks?"

"Tonight."

"Blow out the candles, Jules," encourages Will.

Karl attempts to blow them out from across the coffee table, but only manages to spray a bit of spit on Jules's face. Will scoops him up. "Hold on there, cowboy."

"I do it!" says Jules, frowning at her brother and wiping her face.

"Go ahead, Jules," says Jo. She's all lined up ready to snap the picture. It took some convincing, but everyone singing the birthday song persuaded Jules to stop playing with the new tricycle Grandma and Grandpa Cerny bought her long enough to make the traditional birthday wish. Jules has her hands in her mouth as she assesses the three glowing candles. Through the camera viewer, Jo sees that the blue of Jules's velvet party dress and the blue of the doll's cake dress is a surprisingly close match. Nice.

Jules takes a deep breath and manages to blow out two of the three candles. Frustrated with the results, she reaches out to the last remaining flame and pinches it between her index finger and thumb. The roomful of grandparents collectively suck in a breath of concern. Jo is surprised at how quickly that managed to happen and guesses maybe she's seen her dad put out a match out like that. Jules looks wide-eyed at her scorched fingers and bursts into tears. She runs over to Will's mother, Dolly, and buries her little face in Grandma's huge bosomy lap. Dolly gives Jules's hand a quick assessment, smothers it in kisses, and throws her head back and cackles a jolly laugh, magically transforming the lesson about fire into just another fun moment of surprise and excitement.

Jo swoops in and grabs the cake to take it to the kitchen for cutting and serving. Even though it's snowing outside, the tiny room is hot. Jo feels sweat dripping on the back of her neck and notices Karl is now fingering shapes in the condensation on the front window. Jo chooses to ignore that usually forbidden activity and makes a quick note on the paper pad by the phone to remember to create an article for the *Wilber Republican* about the visitors that came to town to help celebrate Jules's third birthday. The newspaper is always asking for things to publish in the Community Events section, and this way she can send clippings of the family events to Child Horizons as a way of keeping their records current. This is easier than writing the monthly letters, which are thankfully no longer required.

Per usual protocol at family gatherings, the men separate from the women and begin smoking or chewing tobacco and talking about their latest discoveries in fishing, farming, or construction equipment. Marta pats the cushion next to her, inviting Dolly to join her on the couch so they can entertain themselves by flipping through the baby book Jo set out on the end table. Jo created the album binder from two pieces of paneling wood left over from the home construction, to serve as a memento of their first family home. She dutifully maintains the album not just with photos, but with all the communications with Child Horizons: every application letter, receipt, and probationary progress report. She wants to be sure the kids grow up knowing the whole and honest truth about how their family came together. She wants her entire family to understand, the whole community for that matter. Because truth is where love begins; no one could convince her otherwise. There is no place for secrets in this family.

"So many beautiful letters." sings Marta as she brags to Dolly, "Jo's my best writer."

Marta holds the typed letter with the Child Horizons pink letterhead that includes an illustration of a smiling, blue-eyed, chubby-cheeked baby in a blue bonnet. It reads:

> Here is the letter bringing you the news for which you have so long waited!

> We have a little girl who would very much like to have you for her Mommy and Daddy.

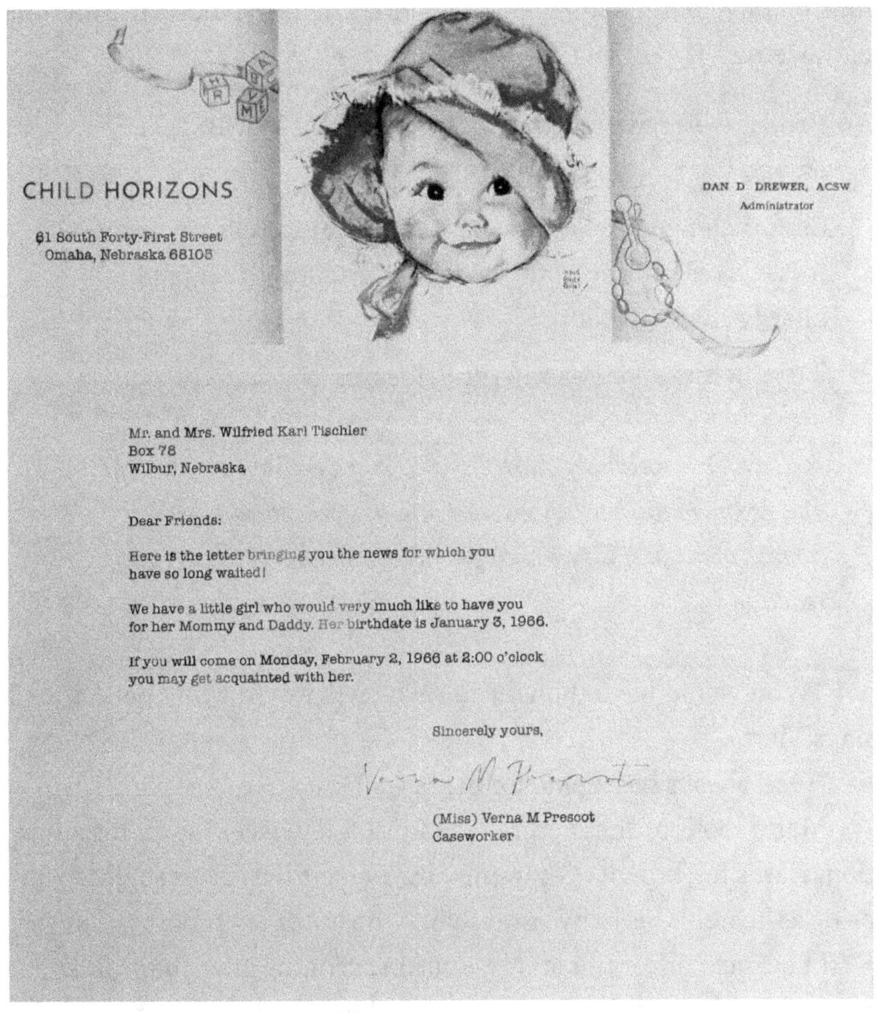

The two grandmothers sigh out loud thinking back to that joyful moment. "I had to kick Emi to get the fishing equipment out of the car so the kids could go pick up their baby. They could have gotten a hook."

Emi grunts from across the room, acknowledging he heard his name and was somehow being chastised.

Marta and Dolly smile at each other and turn the page. The next letter has the same adorable illustration of a baby in a bonnet, but this time on blue letterhead. There is an index card stapled to the bottom of the letter. Typed on the card it says:

Brown eyes, curly brown hair, complexion of Italian extraction.

Child has spent considerable time (20 months) in our foster care nursery due to hepatitis testing and food allergy management.

Then in red-inked handwriting it says:

Jo Tischler is uniquely qualified as a rural community educator and a person with allergies that understands the daily commitment in lifestyle changes needed to navigate allergic reactions.

"Who would have thought Jo's allergies would bring her a son?" sings Marta.

"God always has a plan for us," says Dolly.

Marta looks at the picture taken just a few weeks after his adoption. Karl's big brown eyes framed by long curled lashes sparkle with pride as he holds his baby sister Jules, who is just ten months younger. Karl became part of the family just nine months after Jules. Jo knew of women who had children close together like that, but she was the only person she knew who had the oldest arrive last. It took a little explaining at first, but it didn't take long for people to consider Karl their "first child."

Who would give up such a beautiful child?" says Marta, still trying to understand how adoption of healthy infants is even a possibility.

Jo follows the conversation from across the counter between the kitchen and the living room. "We tell the kids that their natural mothers loved them so much, they wanted them to grow up in a loving family." This assumes the natural mothers didn't have loving families, which is all that Jo could come up with when she asked herself the same question.

Marta hears Jo's words, but they don't seem to really sink in. On the next page they see the receipts of their fees paid stapled to the back of the availability letters: $400 for Jules, $2100 for Karl. "A small fortune," says Marta. Dolly nods. They continue to flip pages.

N⁰. 790

FORM R

CODE 041-000 200.00
002-010 200.00

Wilber — Nebr
CITY — STATE — CHURCH

2-2-66 — Adoption Fee — $ 400.00
DATE — CREDITED TO — AMOUNT

$ 400.00 — $
OPER. — OTHER — DESCRIPTION

Sent by Mr. and Mrs. Wilfried Karl Tischler
Address Wilber, Nebr 68465

CHILD HORIZONS
61 S. 41ˢᵗ STREET
OMAHA, NEBRASKA

BY va

Next is a series of family progress newsletters, neatly typed with the month and year clearly at the top of each page, and a donation receipt stapled to the back of each one. Marta clucks her tongue and sings with a laborsome cadence, "Ev-er-y month."

"It's a privilege, Mom," says Jo, almost done with plating the cake and ice cream. "Just another labor of love." All three women nod. If there's one thing the women can all agree on, it's all the labor behind the love for children. "Besides," continues Jo, "it was the perfect way to document their first years. It's all there for them to read whenever they're ready."

The kitchen counter is lined with plates of cake, each with a scoop of ice cream. Jo prepared three special plates, cowboy treats that exclude milk and wheat products. It's a cookie she decorated with the blue frosting and popsicle. These are for Karl, but she always makes more than one so he doesn't have to feel left out. "If anyone else would like the cowboy cookies, go right on ahead and help yourself."

Grandpa Fats, Will's step-father, takes two helpings of Karl's special treats and snuggles right up next to Karl at the table eating up the cookie like Cookie Monster, mimicking the latest character the kids watch on TV. The kids explode with giggles and then proceed to eat everything as though they were Cookie Monster with crumbs flying in every direction.

"We'll need a dog, Jo, to help with the crumbs," teases Will.

Jo smiles a not-so-smiley smile. They've been discussing the idea of getting a dog for the kids, but my God, another thing to take care of?! "OK, OK. Enough with the Cookie Monster," says Jo. "Everyone, Will and I have an announcement."

Marta looks at Dolly and sings a wish so softly it's almost a whisper, "Another grandchild?"

"No. I heard that, Mom," says Jo. She looks at Will, who takes a drag from his cigarette and nods, waving his hand a bit to encourage her to go ahead.

"We're moving to the mountains."

The room goes silent as everyone freezes, except Will of course. Cool as a cucumber he stamps out his cigarette in the ash tray and prepares to address the battery of questions that will come once everyone catches their breath.

CHAPTER 13

Three years later

Standing arms crossed on the porch of her Aunt Karla's log cabin, Jo assesses the clouds of the summer storm. She remembers the times when as a lifeguard, she shut down the pool because of clouds like these. The children would moan and give her sad faces as they got out of the pool. They had no idea the danger she thwarted. Funny how disappointing them can be just another part of loving them. "Kids. Time to come in," Jo yells from the cabin porch. The pine trees bend with the gusts of wind, spreading loose cones and small branches.

"Ollie Ollie Oxin Free!" yells Karl. He has his T-shirt off his torso, but still on his arms above his head to catch the wind like a sail. He learns the wind isn't strong enough for a liftoff, so he purposefully kicks up rocks behind him to create swirling clouds of dirt with every step.

Jo holds the cabin door open and stops him by the elbow as he breaches the doorway, "Shoes off. Wash your hands. Where's your sister?"

"I don't know. Hiding." He kicks off his shoes and scoots in.

"Jules!" Jo rolls her eyes and grabs the metal beater hanging by a length of fishing line and circles round the triangle dinner bell.

"I'm here."

Jo hears a muffled voice from the doghouse just a few feet away under the porch steps. She bends over and looks inside. "How'd you get in there?"

"Easy. Me and Tipper are hiding from the thunder." The senior dog wags her tail. "Can I stay here with her?"

"No."

Jules crawls out and brushes dog dirt off her face and chest. Her clothes are covered not only in dog fur but also black soot.

"Jules, in under fifteen minutes you've ruined your clothes?" Jo tries to hide her smile as she licks her thumb and tries to rub a bit of soot off Jules's face but only smears it.

"Karl and I did an experiment." She points to the outdoor patio fireplace, smiling with pride. Will built Karla an outdoor fireplace from recovered brick the first year they arrived on the mountain. A gift, for all the support she provided while the Tischler family transitioned to life in the Rocky Mountains.

"An experiment, was it?"

"We wanted to see if Santa could really get down a chimney," says Jules. "I don't know, Mom," she says, now with evidence supporting the possibility of disbelief, "I barely fit."

Karla's now on the porch to assess why the dinner bell was ringing.

Jo nods to indicate all is well.

Karla's hosted a lot of kids on her property and takes the use of the bell seriously. It's one of the few things the children are not allowed to play with. Almost every one of Jo's cousins have brought their kids here for a summer adventure, and the first aid kit hangs on the porch by the bell for a good reason. Fishing hooks, cactus needles, rock climbing, wasps, pocketknives . . . the mountains provide plenty of lessons. Karla thrives on hosting her family's mountain adventures. Though she rarely interacts with the kids, she keeps the equipment, lodging, food, and drink ready and available. She's the only person Jo knows who considers graham cracker sandwiches a staple.

"I see," says Jo. "How did Karl keep out of the soot?" Jo grabs the bottom of the soiled shirt, "Arms up." She pulls it off in one swift yank and then uses the shirt to wipe Jules's face.

"He said he'd keep a look out for Big Foot while I did the experiment."

"Well, young lady, get a shirt from the bag in the back bedroom and wash your hands."

Jules juts out her lower lip and marches past her mother into the cabin.

"Still looking for Big Foot?" asks Karla with a grin.

"He's always on the lookout. Last week it was black bears. Before that rattle snakes."

"The joy of children," says Karla as she secures the first aid kit and anything else hanging on the porch in the built-in deck box.

"Meanwhile, Jules gets into everything. She fell into a cactus bed on Horsetooth Trail last week. Took an hour to tweeze out the needles."

Jo puts her arm around her aunt and gives her a big squeeze. "Thank you for letting us invite ourselves over, filthy kids and all.

"You know I love having you," says Karla, "and thankful for Will's help at the dock."

"We've managed through other storms in the trailer," says Jo, feeling the need to attest to the safety of their mobile home, which has served them well. They got it at a good price and it allowed them to live right on the mountain, just a few miles from the lake and Karla's cabin. It was the perfect environment for curious kids. Exploration was a daily event. All that said, severe weather events hit differently when you're living in a mobile home. You can't help but feel more exposed when the sounds of rain and hail are amplified and the entire thing sways ever so slightly with the gusts of wind. The storm coming now was expected to involve high winds and funnel clouds. Public warnings sounded, and everyone is preparing. "Karl had a complete meltdown when his father was heading out to help secure the boats. He insisted the storm would sweep Jules away, and we would only be safe here at your cabin."

"The mobile home park does get its share of hail damage."

"Too much Wizard of Oz, if you ask me."

"Well, if it makes you feel any better, Alice, our neighbor? She feels the same as Karl. Baby coming soon, her husband away on business, she didn't want to be alone."

Lightning cracks, and the rumble of thunder echoes through the hills. Karla and Jo look up at the darkening sky. The kids scream and then giggle at each other's screams. Jo smiles at Karla, "Storms aren't scary when you're with people who make you feel safe."

The women head to the kitchen to put together some iced tea for the adults and Kool-Aid for the kids.

"You know, Jo, you don't have to wait for a storm to bring the kids over," says Karla. "Or a week in the hospital."

Jo acknowledges she could do better at making consistent social visits with Aunt Karla and not just reach out to her when there is some kind of logistical need. Karla didn't hesitate to help out when Jo finally went in to take care of the endometriosis. Since then, she's been so busy just trying to get back into the swing of things.

"How are you feeling?" presses Karla, looking over her glasses.

"Better." The pain left along with the cysts. And that was the end of that. There just wasn't a lot more information to share. The doctor preferred to talk with Will about the details. Jo always did what the doctor prescribed, trusting he knew what he was doing. A full hysterectomy wasn't easy, but life seems back to normal.

Karla pats Jo on the hand. "Good. It's about time."

"Good enough to go swimming last week." Jo was tempted to wear her red lifeguard suit since she still had it and was pleasantly surprised it still fit. Instead, she stopped by Sears and got a modest blue suit with white piping that was on sale. "Took the kids to the Ft. Collins public pool for the first time."

"Remind you of your lifeguard days?" says Aunt Karla. Karla is openly afraid of water and refuses to walk on the dock where she keeps Arlo's old fishing boat. She never did and never will go out in it, but she keeps the modest boat maintained and ready for her visitors to enjoy—at their own risk. "Bring your own lifeguard," she always says. Jo and Will love going out in the boat, so they often accompany family visitors while Karla watches the kids. Jo insists Jules and Karl can't go out on the boat until they've had proper swimming lessons and passed a swimming test.

"Funny you say that," says Jo, "I had to rescue Jules."

"Rescue?" Aunt Karla's whole being stiffens. She is immediately triggered by any report of water-related incidents.

Jo relives the events in her mind, careful not to articulate too many scary details. Like all emergencies, it came on fast and when least expected. "One moment, she was in the shallow end and the next she stepped right off into the deep end."

"That child tests everything."

Jo nods. That is an accurate description of Jules's nature. When Jules feels safe, she will try anything. A blessing—most the time.

"The lifeguard didn't see it, but I saw her sink like a rock."

"Good thing *you* were watching," says Karla, shaking her head at the incompetence of the lifeguard.

Jo nods and is thankful she knew exactly what to do. She dove right in and pulled Jules up to the surface. "She coughed up a bit of water and had a little cry."

Karla sips her tea and looks at Jo with wide eyes.

Maybe mentioning she coughed up water was a little too much detail for Karla. "Then Jules said the strangest thing."

Karla pulls back the lever on the tray of ice and shakes the mold free.

Jo catches a cube that sprung loose, then continues her story. "She reached up and touched my face and said, 'I wasn't scared, Mommy, they said you'd protect me.'"

"Who's they?" says Karla.

"That's what *I* asked," says Jo. "She said the angels told her."

"Huh," says Karla with a wink. "How lucky to have a mother angel lifeguard." Karla wipes up some melted ice from the counter, "Having you nearby is like having immunity from death by drowning."

Jo shakes her head and tries not to laugh openly at Karla's sweet and extreme perspective, bless her heart. "I went straight over and signed them both them up for swim lessons. They won't need me to protect them from water much longer."

Karla gives a shiver, shaking off the heebie jeebies brought on by all the swimming talk. "Good for them."

Jules agrees. It is good. Lots of things are good right now. Will's new business is growing. The kids are healthy and active. They are a state away from possible unexpected intrusions on their family, and Jo is beginning to remember what it feels like to be free of pain. "The kids were happy when I could cook again," says Jo. "They refused to eat one more of Will's milk-toast dinners."

Heavy rain starts pouring down, and the sound of it on the metal roof is loud enough to conceal some of the thunder and lightning, creating a cozy calm in the cabin. Everyone assembles around the grand stone fireplace in the living room. Alice prepared a tray of fixings for a casual indoor cookout with hotdogs and marshmallows. Karla untwists wire coat hangers so the kids can use them as roasting sticks.

"Oh, my baby's kicking," says Alice with delight in her eyes. "Would you like to feel it?" she offers the kids.

"Not me!" says Karl as he scoots two feet further away from Alice.

Jules steps up and puts her hand on Alice's tummy, making a face at Karl while demonstrating her bravery. "There's a baby inside of you?" asks Jules, more skeptical than confused. "Why?"

This is the first time the kids have been up close with a pregnant woman. Jo never really spent time discussing pregnancy. It's not something she has any experience with or much exposure to. The emphasis with the kids has always been around how adoption is what makes a family.

"Well," Alice glances at Jo to see if she should continue with an answer to Jules's inquiry. Jo nods and gives her the "why not?" shrug. Alice clears her throat, "Because, this is how children are made." Alice guides Jules's hands, circling them around her tummy, "The baby grows inside their mother."

Jules narrows her eyes and bites her lip, trying to put ideas together. "Before they're adopted?"

"Well, yes and no," says Alice, not wanting to provide inaccurate information. "When my baby is done growing, she, or *he*," says Alice, glancing at Karl, who is paying close attention even though he's still at a distance, "will be in my arms and part of our family, no adoption needed."

Jules scratches behind her ear, then looks at her mom, "Then whose tummy did I grow in?"

The room goes oddly silent as all eyes shift to Jo.

Jules looks around at the avoidant faces, then up at her mother. "Did I say something wrong?"

"No, you didn't say anything wrong," says Jo to both Jules and Alice, who is shifting in her seat showing some discomfort that her condition has set off such a sensitive learning moment.

"You grew in your *birthmother*'s tummy," says Jo.

"Birthmother?" Jules looks over at Karl and they both look back at Jo.

"Me too?" asks Karl.

"Yes," says Jo, leaning forward and rotating her hotdog over the flames, "both of you have birthmothers."

Karl smiles proudly at Jules and sits up tall.

"Why doesn't our book say anything about birthmothers?" asks Jules.

Now that's an interesting question Jo has even asked herself. The only time the agency mentioned the birthmother was at their very first interview. Nowhere in the documentation were any details about her. No personal characteristics, no history, no circumstances of the pregnancy or delivery, nothing. Jo assumed all this was protected by law and included in the "closed records" that as far as she could tell were accessible to absolutely no one. The agency certainly didn't share the relinquishment papers. Jo had no idea at all about the legal agreements the birthmother made, which is probably why there is always a nagging worry in Jo's busy mind that somehow the birthmothers could find them and demand to have their beautiful child back. Verna did mention original birth records existed; but Jo never saw them. There was nothing. It's as though the birthmother was erased from existence. The idea that the legal system could do that to someone, to a mother, gives her the willies.

In the absence of any response or information, Jules is quick to invent her own story, "I bet my birthmother looks like a princess," says Jules to Karl, attempting to one-up him giving her the sibling advantage with this new discovery. This doesn't generate an interesting response from Karl, who clearly is not into princesses, so Jules digs deeper with her mom, "Why didn't my birthmother want to keep me, like Alice is keeping her baby?"

"That's easy," says Karl without missing a beat, "because you're a girl."

"Shut up," snaps Jules, "Your birthmother didn't want you either."

"Knock it off!" says Jo with such force it's practically yelling. OK, yes, it is yelling. Surprised and embarrassed by her own reaction, Jo looks at Alice and Karla, feeling the compulsion to apologize. Instead, she chooses to close her mouth and sits back with crossed arms. The one thing! The one thing she always wanted to shield them from had somehow already developed in the children's minds. The idea that they weren't wanted. How did that even happen? Jo sits stewing in her fresh failure.

"I don't know about all that," says Aunt Karla. Quick to offer a distraction, she hands the kids chocolate squares to build s'mores. "What I do know is you both look just like Tischlers to me."

Just then the front door bursts open as Will enters the cabin along with a gust of wind requiring a focused effort to close the door. "It's a good thing we're all here," says Will. "A twister is being tracked. Looks like the trailer park is in its path." From Jo's perspective, there's already a twister right here in the cabin. Some tornadoes you cannot avoid.

Chapter 14

An unfriendly cool breeze permeates Claire's nightgown, giving her goosebumps. Grey clouds advance from behind a mountain summit distinguished from the rest of the range by a large stone monument, in the shape of a giant's cleft heart. Lightning flashes across the sky and shocks it to life. The enormous unembodied heart beats with rhythmic pounding, causing falling rocks and clouds of red dirt to stream down the mountainside. Throbbing sound waves emanate in all directions, creating ripples in the clouds above and the lake below.

A young girl in pigtails fearlessly makes her way across the rock scape, walking with calm intent.

"Sarah!" Claire calls out to her. "Sarah!" But the wind swallows Claire's voice.

The girl follows a path that leads to a blue trailer by the lake. A dark rotating column of wind forms in the distance and moves toward the trailer from the opposite direction. The girl calmly pulls on the silver lever, the trailer door opens, and she steps inside. Safe.

Claire is relieved for the safety of the child, but quickly realizes her own exposure to the storm. As she advances toward the trailer, she runs into a baby carriage blocking the path. Inside, Adam lies sound asleep. "Son! Who brought you here?" cries Claire. She picks him up just as the wind grabs the carriage. It tumbles away and is lifted into the hungry tornado that has grown one hundred times in size.

As she clutches Adam tight to her chest, Claire's legs can barely move forward against the strength of the wind. After what seems like an eternity of struggle, she manages to reach the trailer. With her last ounce of strength, she yanks the door handle only to find the door is locked, the roar of the wind so intense it usurps every sensation in Claire's body. The inescapable tornado is directly upon them and sucks up the entire trailer. The silver door handle is torn from Claire's grasp as it rises. She collapses on her knees, clutching her sleeping son as she watches the trailer swirl away into the outer limits of the grey sky.

"Jesus, Claire, wake up!" Tony shakes her arm.

Claire gasps, still sensing the pungent aroma of a lightning storm. Her heart pounds, wondering if she's still dreaming. Claire looks up and sees a dark sky filled with stars above her bedroom ceiling. She looks down and sees a woman in her nightgown on hands and knees in bed next to Tony.

Mother!

Claire hears the voice of her daughter, a child she's never seen.

"Adam," cries the woman below as she springs up and rushes to their son's room. The nursery lamp is on, and the thin woman who appears frail scoops up all thirty pounds of the sleeping toddler and carries him to the bedroom to climb back into bed with Tony. Warmed by her son nestled within her arms, Claire returns to her body and feels whole again.

"That's the third time this week, honey," whispers Tony.

"I know," says Claire. "I know." She rocks herself and Adam, kissing his head. She's tried to explain the stormy dreams to Tony, but she hasn't attempted to share with him the feeling of being out of her body. There's no way to put words to that without sounding like she's one step away from an asylum.

"Thursday, when I'm back from this trip," says Tony, "we'll talk."

"I'm sorry," says Claire.

"No sorrys." Tony rolls over and puts his arm around both Claire and Adam.

"We just need to take care of it." He squeezes them both, "I love you." His breath begins to regulate as he's already starting to drift back to sleep.

"Tony?" Claire has been thinking about this for a while, and asking now seems like a sure way to get agreement.

"What?"

"I need to make a trip to Child Horizons."

Tony remains quiet, his half-asleep brain processing. "You do?"

"I need to find out how Sarah's doing. Is that OK?"

"Ah," he scratches his head. "Sure. You want me to come?"

"I need to do this alone." Claire kisses Adam again on the head. "Can you watch Adam?" This would mark the first time Tony and Adam would experience a full day together, just the two of them. It should be pretty easy now. With any luck, Adam would poop on the potty like a big boy and save Tony from facing his first poopy diaper.

Tony is quiet.

Claire is wondering now if he went back to sleep of if he's trying to figure out how to say no.

"Ya. I can do that."

Wow. That worked. Claire promises herself to ask for things in the middle of the night more often.

"Thursday, when I'm back from this haul," Tony yawns, "we'll plan."

Claire pours herself a cup of coffee and ponders the best way to set things up for Tony to be successful in taking care of Adam. Tony's been flying routes that get him home every four or five days, which is helpful, but in the end, he's absent from family life 70 percent of the time. Being a housewife has plenty of upsides—like being able to always be with Adam—but it hasn't been easy. Claire's been on and off anxiety medications ever since Lilli gave her that first bottle years ago. Unfortunately, no drug she's tried has brought on true calm or a restful sleep. Claire knows that bringing Adam to their bed is creating a literal and emotional wedge between her and Tony, but she can't help it. Holding her son's sweet sleeping body next to hers is the only reprieve she's found to date.

Claire picks at the banana slices she's cutting for Adam. He's usually hungrier than she is in the morning. She puts the plate of scrambled eggs and banana in front of him. He puts the little baby fork in his mouth empty of food, then uses his other hand to pick up a banana slice and manages to smash it around the fork and into his mouth.

"Good start, buddy," says Claire. At least he's doing something with the fork other than tossing it on the floor. Then it comes, like it does every day; the inevitable flood of unanswerable questions begins to bombard Claire's mind. *I wonder if Sarah would have picked the eggs first or the banana? Was Sarah able to get food on a fork when she was twenty-two months old? How is Sarah doing at potty training?* As Adam progressed through each stage of growth, Claire would imagine Sarah at those stages. And for some reason Sarah was always more advanced than Adam, like he had to catch up to her. Claire stares at Adam and looks for Sarah in his face. The two often blend into one and sometimes Adam is both himself and Sarah. He's never allowed to be just himself.

Of course, these thoughts are absolutely ridiculous and can't be healthy. She's never heard other mothers mention anything like this. The enslaving cycle of unanswerable questions followed by guilt is a constant shadow. If she is feeding Adam, she feels guilty about how she never fed Sarah. During bath time Claire obsesses over how she never poked a little toy boat toward Sarah, or ever put her down for a nap, or picked her up and kissed her knees when she fell, or the million other things a mother does for their child.

Claire is positive her racing mind and relentless guilt are somehow causing the dreams, making it impossible to get restful sleep. It's also made it difficult for Claire to eat. Feelings of guilt often arise during meal preparation, ruining her appetite. She stopped getting periods and the doctor suggested she eat more. Every day is an endless loop of anxiety.

Tony's absolutely right. This can't go on. Thankfully, Tony is right most the time and Claire counts on him for guidance. He was right they should date a few years before getting married. That way she could keep her position as an air hostess until he was promoted to the next pay tier. He was right they should elope instead of having a large wedding. And he was right they should start a family right away. It took a while for her body to wake up, but in a couple years she was pregnant with Adam.

Adam bangs his Tommy Tipper cup on the table. "More."

"What a good eater you are," says Claire. She puts more juice in the cup and gives Adam a little bowl of applesauce to practice with the spoon. Adam keeps the spoon in one hand and puts his fingers in the sauce with the other hand. Claire wonders if maybe he's left-handed. Maybe Sarah is. She sighs heavily noticing that even right after she's brought her attention to her thought patterns, they still incessantly gravitate to Sarah.

The more she tries to ignore it, the more prominent the troubling thoughts become. Claire has firmly committed to keeping Sarah in her life, but things have somehow gone sideways. Last January marked the tenth year of writing her birthday cards. She and Tony have already discussed that when the time is right Adam will know he has a sister in the world, even though Sarah may never know of

Adam. So the problem isn't thoughts of Sarah, the problem seems to be that Claire has no memories of her. No information from which to build an image of her own daughter. She's using the son she's raising to create memories of the daughter she's not raising. *Christ! I have no control over how pathetic I can get.*

"All done," announces Adam.

Claire takes his bowl to the sink and picks up a washcloth to clean him and the table up. "All done" is right. All done is Claire putting a phantom child onto the lives of her husband and son. She needs a reconciliation. To somehow connect the Sarah she knew as a tiny soul growing within her and the real-life person she's become. And there's only one place that can help her find resolution: Child Horizons.

Claire steps over to the little craft table she's set up in the breakfast nook to the side of the kitchen and picks up her purse and digs through it, pulling out a small address book. She picks up the avocado-green wall phone and holds her breath while dialing their number.

"Child Horizons, how may I direct your call?"

Claire realizes she has no idea how to direct her call and slams down the receiver.

"Down," says Adam.

Claire pulls out the chair, unstraps Adam from the booster seat, and sets him free.

This is going to take strategy. What would they do if she just straight up asked to see her daughter? Give her an appointment? Ha! No. Hell no. An in-person unannounced visit might have a shot. Who knows, maybe there's someone there who's like Bonnie was all those years ago. Someone willing to break a few rules.

Claire begins to unfold a plan for visiting Child Horizons. Tony can easily help her set up standby travel. With a red-eye on the way down, she could be back in time to fix dinner that night.

*   *   *

After staring into the darkness for what seemed like a lifetime, Claire sees the first signs of sunrise through the window. First the clouds turned purple to pink and then came the hot red spark of a new day. Tony was incredibly supportive of Claire's idea to visit Child Horizons and seek information about her daughter. He even seemed excited about him and Adam having their first full day together. According to Tony, they are going to get in some quality "male bonding."

Claire didn't know what all to pack, but she dug into her old filing folder and decided to bring the relinquishment paperwork. She opens the document, which she folded in quarters to fit in her purse. Maybe there is some way to rework the agreement. This is the section she's interested in changing, hopefully removing entirely.

That I will not ask to discover the whereabouts of said child or the parties who may have her or to molest or deprive them of said child and that I will never visit or attempt to visit said child or make my identity known to her.

Claire considers the glass door as she enters Child Horizons. They've updated their name to add a logo with triangle mountains and three stars emanating from it. She exhales and pulls the door open. A cool wave of air-conditioning blasts her hot face. As soon as her stylish white sandals step into the lobby, a flash of emotional memory makes it seem like just yesterday she was in this place, still bleeding from giving birth to the daughter she's never seen. Her head now swimming, Claire is disoriented and surveys the lobby for signs with directions. She's not sure what she's looking for, but Lost and Found comes to mind. Smoothing out her bright-yellow sundress, Claire realizes her hands are sweaty and shaking. She manages to poke one eye a bit as she grapples with her sunglasses. While putting them into her purse, she debates maybe keeping them on. Would the dark circles under her eyes give away something she doesn't want to reveal? Deciding to just sit down and get her thoughts together, Claire plops onto the first empty chair that isn't behind a desk. She reaches in her purse and pulls a Certs breath mint off the roll, then pulls out the relinquishment document to remind her what she's here for. To find her daughter. The love centers her. She notices the name plate on the desk in front of her says "Bonnie" in bold white lettering.

"Can I help you?" says a woman, approaching her from behind.

Claire turns expecting to see the same Bonnie who encouraged her to fill Sarah's record with love all those years ago. It's not her. This woman has a tired seriousness, with thin brown hair held back in a barrette at the nape of her neck. Her grey pencil skirt is paired with an untucked brown short-sleeve blouse and practical flats. Hoping to find an ally in this place that has so frequently been the location of her nightmares, Claire optimistically asks with a quiver in her voice, "Is Bonnie here?"

"Bonnie's at lunch. Did you have an appointment?"

"No. I just flew in from Idaho. I . . ." Claire unfolds the document with her sticky fingers. "I know I'm not supposed to be here," she holds it up, handing it to the woman, "but I need help. You're the only ones who can tell me about my daughter."

The woman takes the document from Claire's shaking hand and scans it. It takes only a few seconds for her to recognize the form and the implications that go along with it.

Claire covers her mouth, trembling, and watches for a reaction, considering her next move should they decide to kick her out.

The woman's shoulders drop. She looks at Claire as though she's found another unwanted issue in her already too busy day, "Margaret?"

"Mrs. Tony Brooks. Please call me Claire."

"I'm Ann Marie. And yes, I think I can help you."

"You can?" says Claire.

"You're not the only one. There are others." Ann Marie walks over to the water dispenser and fills a Dixie cup and hands it to Claire. "We're beginning to understand the needs of birthmothers more and more. Drink." Ann Marie waits for Claire to drink the water. Claire finishes the cup and Ann Marie takes it from her, refills it, and carries it as she walks down the aisle of cubicles. "Follow me."

Ann Marie pulls out a cassette recorder from the far corner of her desk and invites Claire to sit down.

Claire tentatively sits and looks at the recorder with confusion.

"Things have changed since the time this agreement was used, Claire." Ann Marie sets up the microphone in front of Claire. "Turns out, it's not safer to be silent."

Claire's eyes lift. She's silent about the adoption, but for whose safety? Certainly not her own. Has it made Sarah safer? In the short term maybe, but eventually she'll need answers about her identity. Has the silence kept the adopted parents safe? Probably not. They might need important information, like medial background in order to take the best care of Sarah. So is the silence to keep the agency safe? The state? Safe from what?

"I'd like to record your story," says Ann Marie. "We are finding the testimonies of the birthmother experience to be useful not only in our own agency training and policy making, but also in support of adoption reform legislation." She pushes the record buttons. "Margaret Claire Jordan Brooks, do you agree to recording our conversation today?"

Claire hears the nurses' words in the labor room, "If you ever want to see that baby, not another sound." Could it be that after ten years of silence, her words today would be heard by policy makers? Claire can still smell the rum on her breath. It took Dutch courage to reveal she had a daughter that night at the tiki party with Tony. He said, "I see a woman with secret purpose." Could this be her purpose? As she sits here today, is she brave enough to speak out without the help of a volcano cocktail?

"Claire?" says Ann Marie. "You came here for a reason. Yes?"

"I have to start trusting someone," says Claire, mostly to herself. "Yes. I'll put my trust in you."

"Thank you," says Ann Marie as she pulls out her notebook. "What brought you to Child Horizons today?"

"For me, the adoption process was the most degrading, inhumane, punitive, traumatic experience I've ever faced." Claire looks down at her hands, gripping so tightly her knuckles are white. She looks up at Ann Marie for confirmation.

Ann Marie simply nods with sad eyes. She doesn't seem surprised at all. As though Claire's words confirm what she already knows.

"I was inflicted with shame for an unwed pregnancy and made to feel unworthy as a mother. I was asked to relinquish my child to a system that forbid me any knowledge of her or the right to even know her as an adult." Claire holds her forehead and slowly brushes her brow. "They told me to forget any of it happened." Claire looks directly at Ann Marie, "Impossible. I relinquished my right to parent, not my concern." She touches the yellow bow at her waist. "A part of me is missing. I am," she clasps her hands in her lap and looks up with an exhale, "broken."

Ann Marie looks back into Claire's eyes with empathy. "I'm so sorry."

The unexpected simple apology pulls the air from Claire's lungs as tears burn down her face. She thinks of her parents, who never offered a single word of regret for how they treated her. Not a single gentle inquiry of how she was doing. For them it never happened. An airline stewardess who married a pilot and had a son is the pretty picture they can share with friends. They continue to compliment Claire's fakeness.

Ann Marie grabs the tissue box from the back of her desk and sets it next to Claire. "You are married now. Do you have any children together?"

"Yes," says Claire, sniffing with long exhales. "We have a son, Adam, he's two."

"Congratulations," says Ann Marie with a genuine smile. "I'm so happy for you." Ann Marie sits back in her seat with some satisfaction, like finding a rainbow in a break of the storm. "Many first mothers continue their lives not able to have children. We're just beginning to understand how the distress of relinquishment affects a women's body," says Ann Marie. "Tell me about Adam."

Claire immediately misses having Adam near her. Then she thinks back to what it was like to have Sarah near her, when she was pregnant. "Everyone asked, 'is this your first baby'? I always said yes. It was my first baby with Tony, but I always felt like a fraud letting everyone think my second pregnancy was my first."

"What else are you feeling?" asks Ann Marie.

"The guilt," says Claire, ready to get to the point of her trip. "As I care for Adam, I'm consumed with the idea that he can never measure up to what I imagine my daughter is. Like she's been a sort of sacrifice for my son." Claire looks at Ann Marie, recklessly hoping somehow, she might comprehend an experience no mother should ever be feeling. "I can't stop wondering if my daughter really was better off than she would have been with me, then why shouldn't I relinquish Adam as well?" Claire reaches for the Dixie cup and takes a sip of water to try and help her swallow. "It's harder and harder to hide my . . . weaknesses from Adam." Claire slowly sets the cup back on the desk and rubs her thumb across the yellow and orange daisies. "Please tell me there's something you can share about my baby. Anything to shift her from the phantom existence in my mind to a real, living, joyful being."

Ann Marie does not give a physical indication there is an answer one way or the other. No nod or headshake. No sudden inhale indicating a response will immediately follow. She pushes the stop button on the recording and the little plastic teeth on the reels cease to spin. "Claire, I want to help you." She stands up. "Can you excuse me for a few moments?"

Claire's eyes blink an acknowledgement as she sits back in her chair and watches Ann Marie walk through the maze of cubicles. Claire reaches for the thin leather wallet in her purse to look at the photo she carries of Adam. She took him to Sears that day, dressed in the shirt his Grandma Brooks embroidered. He was fascinated by all the props they offered and posed perfectly with his hands folded on the wooden fence.

Ann Marie returns and plops a small set of papers on the desk in front of Claire. She reaches for a couple of pens and smiles with a sense of accomplishment. "Claire, the adoptive family continues to keep in touch with Child Horizons."

Claire closes her wallet, setting it in her lap, not bothering to put it back in her purse.

Ann Marie references freshly made notes, "The adoptive mother resigned from a career as an educator to become a full-time mother. The baby was adopted at six weeks of age and had a completely normal early development. The most recent notes on file describe her as a talented student in elementary school who enjoys activities in music and dancing."

"You're sure, this is about my baby?" asks Claire, unable to absorb what she is hearing.

"Yes, Claire. The child is healthy, happy, and part of a loving family."

Claire collapses a second time and bursts into tears. Every part of her exhales. Her heart feels the energy of reconnection. Finally, a true image, ghosts are no longer necessary. Sarah dances. Of course she does. Claire imagines her in pink ballet slippers and short netted tutu. Sarah's being raised by an educator. A light of gratitude for the adoptive mother is lit for the very first time. A warmth never before imagined becomes part of Claire's energy. Ann Marie pulls out a Kleenex for Claire and hands it to her with a smile.

Claire sniffs in twice and exhales, several times before she can make words.

Ann Marie is silent and just breathes with Claire.

"Thank you," Claire finally manages to say.

"You're welcome," says Ann Marie. In a slow and patient transition, Ann Marie shifts the mood toward opportunity. "There are some things we can add to the child's file that may help you create a connection with her at a future date." Ann Marie indicates the forms on the table. "These do require signatures. I don't want you to feel rushed or pressured in any way. We can take care of these at any time in the future. Or if you like, we can go over them now."

Claire holds her breath in shock, and realizes she is finally on the right path to Sarah. This time, she can choose to take steps forward that are grounded in reality. Claire sits up straight, blows her nose, and wipes her eyes for a last time. She smooths out her dress and crosses her feet politely under her chair. "I'm ready now." For the first time, Claire looks around the agency. They've updated the flooring with brightly patterned carpeting, like the kind you would see in the children's section of the library. The walls are no longer institution white, but have a pallet of light blue and yellow. One wall is decorated with children's artwork. Things really have changed.

Ann Marie hands Claire a pen and begins sliding forms in front of her with brief descriptions, pointing to where the signature belongs.

_____ You may provide your own medical information
should the adoptive family or the child at any age
contact us and request it.

_____ You may waive your anonymity should the child
once a legal adult, contact us and request your name
and contact information.

_____ You may indicate a desire for reunion.

Each form she initials, dates, and signs without hesitation. Ann Marie explains to Claire, "I want to be straightforward with you, all these things take time. They sit in the file and wait for unprompted action by the adoptive family. That may take decades or may never happen at all."

Claire swallows hard. "I understand." This is so much more than the empty place she was in just hours ago, it's not hard to hold onto even the tiniest modicum of optimism. Claire pulls out the roll of Certs from her purse and offers one to her new friend.

"This," says Ann Marie, accepting a Certs while holding up the final form, "is a new Child Horizons post-adoption service offering. I can contact the family and ask them if they're willing to share recent information with you. Perhaps the child's name or a picture."

Claire's mouth drops open. Her name? Sarah knows herself as the name her adopted mother gave her. Of course she does. A photograph? A photograph could tell Claire so much. Everything. She'd see into how Sarah's been raised, if she's been raised like Claire would have, with never-ending love. The tears begin to flow again. "I can't tell you how much that would mean to me."

"Of course, it's the adoptive parents' call," caveats Ann Marie.

Claire and Ann Marie look into each other's eyes with hope. "I'll type the letter today."

Ann Marie then presents a newsletter to Claire. "And this is for you to do."

"For me to do?"

"Claire, there are many things you can do. Not only for yourself, but for other women like you."

Claire remembers her promise to Lilli. "What I was put through, no person should ever again have to endure."

"There is an organization, Concerned United Birthmothers. CUB. They support birthmothers with legislative involvement and facilitate opening dialog with the adoptive family," says Ann Marie. She flips open the newsletter and circles the phone number at the bottom. "They have support groups that help women move toward eventual reunion."

Reunion. Just this morning that was an impossible dream. Now it has a phone number. Claire is overwhelmed, but in a good way. After ten years, the restraints have loosened.

"Is this the help you needed, Claire?"

For the first time since she found out she was pregnant with Adam, Claire senses a strength within herself she'd forgotten. She feels Adam-can-count-on-me strong. How do you tell someone they didn't just help you, they breathed life back into you? Claire's chin quivers as she can't make words but lowers her head with a bow of gratitude.

"Very good. I'm happy we met, Claire." Ann Marie stands up and collects the documents and heads back to the filing room to type up the request.

Dear Johanka and Wilfried,

We acquired an additional medical information card from Julia's birthmother.

Her birthmother has asked if you'd be willing to share recent information about how Julia is doing. This may include sharing her first name and a recent picture.

Additionally, we have written permission from Julia's birthmother to release her identity should you or Julia want to meet her.

Sincerely,
Ann Marie Joyner,
Post-Adoption Specialist

Chapter 15

Karl and Jules sit on their dirt bikes and discuss hill strategy. Motors off, helmets on. It's not like a break or anything, just a little planning to make sure they both come out of this alive. All the neighborhood kids got together and dug up the vacant lot in front of the Fossil Creek cliffs to make the course. It took the whole last summer to build it. Lots of parents won't allow their kids to use it, saying it's not safe. Life isn't safe, so why miss out on the fun? It's pretty cool how Horsetooth Mountain is in the distance at just the perfect angle for a sundial. When the sun touches the tooth, that means they're late getting home. And that spells trouble.

They've already outgrown the Hondas Grampa Fats gave them a couple years ago. Rumor has it he might be shopping for bigger, more powerful ones. Meanwhile, small bikes and garage sale helmets suit Karl and Jules fine.

"We're too tall and heavy." Jules feels compelled to state the obvious. "There's not enough power to jump the double."

"So we go up and down the double. Duh," says Karl.

"Uh. No." *Seriously, he can't see the physics at play here?* "There's not enough distance between them, we'd never make it up the second hill. We go around the double."

"That's what a girl would do," says Karl.

"That's what a sane person would do."

"Go be a girl." Karl kickstarts his bike and yells over the motor, "You won't have to eat my dust then." He takes off with a reckless fish tale.

Typical. Karl's been wearing his Evel Knievel attitude all day.

When Jules goes to start her bike, it's never a smooth thing. After a couple kicks, she looks up and Karl is already almost to the double. One more try and she gets the motor going. She looks up again and there. he. goes. Leaning up over the handlebar like an Australian cowboy riding a pony up a bluff. *Holy crap, he did it.* Up and down the double just like he said he would. Fine. As Jules picks up speed, she feels her pigtails flapping on her back. First hill, no problem. Should have gone faster down the decline, because now she's wondering if there's enough momentum to make it up the second hill. Going up isn't looking good. Shit, it's too late to back down. She clenches her teeth and guns it. The taste of metal in her mouth compounds with the smell of gas and shredded weeds. Instead of surging forward, she falls backward, the bike flipping out from under her. A bolt of lightning throws her off the bike. As she rockets high above the course, she looks up and wonders why there are stars in the sky. Looking down, she sees a girl in a cheap white helmet thump to the ground flat on her back. Crap! That's got to hurt.

Jules watches from above as Karl races over and skids to a stop. He drops his bike, rips off his helmet, and plops down next to the girl.

"Jules, fuck, you OK?"

Jules can't quite figure out what's going on. *Karl? Are you talking to me?*

The girl just lies there and doesn't respond.

Karl unstraps the girl's helmet but stops himself from removing it. "Is your neck OK?" He grips her shoulders, careful not to shake her. "Jules. Answer me," he shouts.

The panic in Karl's voice yanks Jules back into her body. She tries to orient herself and holds in the urge to cry. Doing a quick body check, she finds herself drenched with sweat, but the only thing that hurts is her pride.

"I'm OK." Jules spits out dirt and attempts to wipe her tongue with the back of her hand.

"Jesus, you can't gun it like that," Karl says, hiding his relief. "Not mid incline, you dumb girl." He rubs his chin, "The flip was kind of cool," like maybe he's considering replicating the feat someday. He looks over at the bike. "If it was still running, it could have messed you up. Good job hitting the kill switch before you lost your ass."

Karl is good at that. Finding ways to compliment Jules when she's messed up. Jules did manage to perfectly follow the kill switch safety protocol Karl invented. Karl's big on safety protocols nowadays. Says he's practicing for when he becomes a jet pilot. Fine. Meanwhile, Jules has to live by his practice drills and checklists.

"How many fingers am I holding up?" Karl obnoxiously waves two fingers in front of her face.

Ya, she's not answering that.

"What's your name? Do you know where you are?" Karl snaps his fingers around her head.

"No. I don't." She slaps Karl's hand away. *I'm the one who wrecked the bike?* Karl's the one always racing around even though Mom tells them not to.

Karl puts out his hand and pulls Jules to her feet, then dusts her off with a few swats.

"Don't tell on me?" she bargains with Karl. If Mom finds out, there's hell to pay. For both of them.

"Ya, ya, you're fine," he says.

"How's the bike?" If there's damage, they'd have to tell Mom. Maybe wait and tell Dad when he gets home.

They both look over at it. "How do we get it back to the house?" Jules says, hoping Karl offers up something heroic, like he'd ride it home for her or even walk it home if it won't start. She doesn't care, just so long as she doesn't have to deal with it.

Karl rights the bike and wheels it over to Jules. "Looks OK. Guess you have to get back on and see."

He's making Jules deal with her own problem. Stellar.

"Let's go home," suggests Karl. "Get a drink and rinse off."

Jules nods and pulls on her helmet. Feeling oddly weak, she climbs on the Honda and after a few tries it starts. Jules and Karl exchange smiles of relief and give each other a thumbs up.

They ride into the neighborhood and are home within a handful of blocks. They park the bikes in the gravel to the side of the driveway. From the dining room window, Mom sees Jules and Karl arrive. She slides it open, "What's wrong?" She always says that when they show up early.

"Fine, Mom. We got thirsty," says Karl.

Mom closes the window with a slam.

Karl picks up the sprinkler in the front lawn and unscrews it from the hose. Jules turns on the water from the outdoor faucet and they sit on the front step taking turns drinking. The day has been hot and long enough they forgo the usual hose-kinking, squirt-in-the-face tricks. Thank God. Jules hates that game. They're both teenagers now, you'd think the appeal of that prank would be gone by now. Scooting over the carpet wearing socks to take turns shocking each other, now *that* game's fine. It's more a mini science experiment than a game.

"Thanks for helping me," says Jules with genuine gratitude.

"I'm always there for you."

That's not entirely true, but Jules goes along with it. Feeling like somehow she's still going to get in trouble for flipping the bike she says, "Like the way you always took the first round of spankings?" They didn't really get spanked much. It's been years since the last time, but on the rare occasions they did, it was a memorable event. And true enough, he always got it first.

"Ev-er-ry time," says Karl. "That time she broke the yardstick on me and you just got the hand. You're welcome."

Jules nods, giving him full credit. "Remember back in Mrs. Garagus's class?"

"Fourth grade. She was quite the hag." Karl is spot on with his assessment.

"Ya, her. She sent a kid to the principal's office for spanking. He said he got hit with a full-on wooden paddle. Maybe Mom learned how to spank kids as part of her teacher training."

"If we lived in Hawaii, it would be illegal. They banned corporal punishment in 1973."

Jules has no idea where Karl reads that stuff or how he remembers all the random facts, but she's given up on making him prove his wild statements. No matter the challenge, he pulls out some encyclopedia, the *Guinness Book of World Records*, or whatever he's been reading and jams the "prove it" right down her throat. One of Karl's teachers said he may have a photographic memory. Mom says that doesn't really exist. Jules started to just believe everything that comes out of Karl's mouth. Dangerous, but shockingly reliable.

"So, in a parallel universe, if I lived with my birth mom and we lived in Hawaii, there'd be no such thing as you getting credit for taking the first round of spankings." They played parallel universe scenarios a lot, usually with a twist of *Star Trek* thrown in. But this time Karl doesn't elaborate on the fantasy like he usually does.

This time he asks, "You think about living with your birth mom?"

Jules isn't entirely sure why she brought that up. "Not really. You?"

"Na. But she's more than a ghost in another dimension." Karl runs the hose up and down his arms and rubs off a layer of dirt. "She's a real living being somewhere in our world right now."

Jules thinks about all the times they sat on Karl's bed and spun the globe with eyes shut, stopping the spin with a finger. Pointing to a place that instantly became their next *World Book Encyclopedia* research project. Could their birthmothers really be *anywhere* in the world? They're probably somewhere less random than that. Like on the same continent. Or same country. Maybe even they live in the state they do.

"I'll probably find out who my birthmother is before you do," says Karl.

No matter the topic, he's always first. "Why's that?"

"I'll be of legal age first. I can do whatever I want before you can."

Jules can't really argue with that. He will always be older. Unless he dies, of course, and then after a couple years, she'd be older. But that's a creepy thought. "If you find out, will you help me find who my birthmother is?"

"When you leave home, you can do anything you want to, you won't need my help," says Karl.

"You mean like when I'm married?" Leaving home just doesn't make sense to Jules at this point. She has a hard time imagining not living with her family and never understood the whole "running away" concept.

"Like when you go to college, you stupid girl."

Oh, ya. Of course. College. They both have their own college saving accounts where they deposit all the checks their grandparents send for birthdays and holidays. Mom helped them setup CD's at 15 percent interest. They're not allowed to use the money for anything but college, so the five years of not having access to it is no big deal. "I just want to be sure I don't accidentally marry my own brother." Now *there's* a creepy thought. Jules got a book on blood diseases from the library a while back. Ever since she found out that hemophilia is more likely due to inbreeding, she can't stop thinking about the many evils of inbreeding.

"Well, as creepy as that is, I guess it's possible," says Karl.

Jules jiggles her whole body to let the willies out.

"Unless . . ." says Karl, stroking his chin. "Right now, I'm the only person you are 100 percent sure isn't blood related to you. So technically, we could get married."

"That's disgusting!" Jules gives Karl a shove and jumps up with the hose, holding her thumb over the end, squirting him.

"Hey!" He kinks it and yanks it out of Jules's hand. Karl fakes her out like he's going to squirt her back but instead goes over to the bikes and cleans them off. "It took balls to approach that steep pitch with this piece of junk."

Jules can't tell if he's patting himself on the back or somehow attempting to give her another so-called compliment.

"You aren't really a stupid girl anymore; you know that, right? When you're brave and try new things, like today on the bike. Well, you're more grown and kind of cool."

Cool. Huh? She's suspicious there's something Karl wants from her because Jules is notoriously nerdy. She's had glasses since first grade and buck teeth that were mostly corrected from wearing a retainer for years. She tap danced at the annual talent show with little audience appreciation, while Karl merely lip-synced and got a standing ovation. She likes ballet and square dancing. Karl knows all the moves to *Saturday Night Fever*. Karl offered to give her "coolness lessons" to help her have at least a chance at getting boyfriends. But seriously, what good are boyfriends anyway? Besides, Karl is plenty nerdy.

"I heard Grampa Fats talking with Dad about getting us the Honda 120 when we come to the farm this summer," says Karl.

"Seriously? This summer?"

"Ya, so he can send us on errands while he stays in the field. You know, pick up the lunch bucket from Grandma Dolly so she can stay in the air conditioning. Stuff like that."

"I bet those errands will include side trips to kiss Jessie, huh, lover boy," Jules teases.

"Hey, she is beautiful . . . and stacked."

Mom slides open the front window again, and Karl jumps thinking maybe he got caught talking about girls' boobs. "Kids! Karl, Jules?! You out front? I hear the water on. Turn that off." She slams the window shut.

Jules turns the faucet off.

Mom's at the front door now. "You two are a mess! Get upstairs and shower before dinner. We're going to the farm a couple weeks early. I need you to pack up tonight. Suitcases are in your rooms."

"Tonight?" asks Karl.

"You heard me."

Jules picked up the receiver in her room yesterday while Mom was on the phone with Grandma Marta. She overheard that Grampa Emi's cancer tests didn't go well and his next round of treatments had been moved up.

"I'll be staying with Grampa Emi while you two help Grandpa Fats cut cane. We leave at 5."

Karl and Jules let out whiney groans—because they have to wake up early, not so much about cutting cane. It was actually pretty fun walking through the soy fields swinging a scythe. Grandpa Fats usually took them to the Barnston pool hall for burgers afterwards. It was really just a bar with an old pool table, but Grandma Dolly says they don't go to bars.

"Dad's coming this time," says Mom, "so you'll both be in the backseat. Take something to keep quiet with. My nerves cannot tolerate any fighting. Understood?"

"Understood," they say in unison.

"Jules, check the box for mail before you come in. Put it on the downstairs desk, I'll look at them when we get back. I don't have time now."

"OK, Mom."

Mom goes back inside, the screen door slamming behind her.

"How much more do you think Grampa Emi can take of those treatments?" Jules asks as she walks over to the mailbox at the curb. She reaches in and pulls out a single letter. It's from Child Horizons. Once they put their family vacation photo in their newsletter. It was in the section called "The Successful Adopted Family." That seemed odd to Jules. Were they trying to sell the idea that adopted families could be successful? Why didn't they just say "The Successful Family"? Anyway, they get letters from Child Horizons all the time. Mom says they're always asking for money. Junk mail. Stellar.

"I dunno. At Thanksgiving, he looked weirdly skinny, like he might die right there on the davenport."

Jules nods. Grampa wasn't himself during the last visit. She decides to toss the Child Horizons letter in the trashcan at the side of the house instead of bringing it in to the desk. Mom has better things to do than look at junk mail. "I heard him ask Uncle Jim to get him some joints." That means he's in pain too. Jules never guessed Grampa'd ever smoke marijuana.

"No fishing again this summer," speculates Karl as he reconnects the hose to the sprinkler.

"Probably not. I'm glad I never got too old for Grampa Emi to put the worms on the hook for me. That's love," says Jules.

"What about the bloody fish guts?" says Karl, hoping to gross her out. "Ripping those out for you, now *that's* love." Karl pushes off the front step, swings open the front screen door, and bolts up the stairs. "Beat ya to the shower . . ."

Chapter 16

Claire soaks in the pleasure of an overly hot shower on a snowy winter morning. Steam fills the room and Claire breathes in the fragrance of her favorite shampoo. She's a devoted Breck girl. Even if her life isn't manageable, at least her hair is. The pulsing massage mode beats hot water down her back, a worthy upside to waking at ridiculously early hours. Tony is sent off for his early flight having had morning sex and a hearty breakfast. This is the perfect way to indulge in a modicum of peace and quiet before Adam is up. The only thing that matters in this moment is the hot water holding out for just a few more minutes of lathering time.

Claire's heartbeat echoes off the shower walls, synchronizing with the pulse of the water on her skin. The shampoo has the same sweet earthy scent of eminent rain. An electric spark sends her a float from her body, and it rises gently within the clouds of steam. She looks down and sees an overly thin woman enjoying a hot shower.

Mother!

Is someone calling her? Or does she *think* she's hearing someone? Claire sees the woman in the shower call out, "Just a minute," as she begins a hasty suds rinse.

Mother! Where are you?

A sense of urgency pulls Claire back into her body as she bends over to turn off the water and freezes to listen. There's just the final drips from the showerhead. Someone slides open the shower door and a rush of cold air sends a chill through her body.

There stands Adam, wearing his Christmas pajamas and a demanding face.

Claire jumps to grab a towel. "Adam. This is Mommy's private time."

"I'm hungry." He runs out of the bathroom stomping the carpet.

Claire wraps the towel around herself, and another one, turban style, on her head.

Where's my brother?

Claire freezes. She heard that, clear as day. "Who's there?" Claire's embarrassed for saying that out loud. It's just her and Adam, of course. Usually, it's just her and Adam. She grabs her orange quilted robe and ties the sash. The voice was close. Maybe from Adam's room. Claire tiptoes across the hallway and looks in his room. No one. She takes a double look and sees wet PJs and underwear on the floor with the bed covers somewhat pulled up, presumably covering wet sheets.

Adam pulls on Claire's robe from behind, which makes her jump, startled, and leak a little pee herself. "Shhh. Sissy's sleeping." He whispers with a finger in front of his lips.

Sissy? Claire catches her breath, bends down, and whispers to Adam, "Who's sleeping?"

Adam playfully pretends to steal her nose and runs off to the living room.

Claire sees the blinking lights from the Christmas tree in the living room cast their dance on the walls of the hallway. It's the third of January, Sarah's thirteenth birthday. Instead of the ghost of Christmas past, could it be Sarah who's visiting? Claire follows Adam to the living room with her toes curled tight within her slippers, holding her breath in anticipation of greeting a spirit.

Adam jumps like a frog on the couch next to his new Amelia Earhart and Babe Ruth Famous American dolls. He offers them Cheerios from his Tupperware snack container, then pops them in his mouth. Claire snorts at the shadows and shakes off her paranoia. She steals her nose back from Adam and puts it on her face, then pulls the knob on the TV and dials in channel nine. "Captain Kangaroo should be on soon." Claire tightens her sash and reminds herself she and Adam are safe. Safe in her own house. Safe in her own body.

Taking the Tupperware and a pillow with him, Adam plops down on the floor in front of the TV. Claire picks up a cup left out on the end table and carries it into the kitchen. Out the window, winter clouds are low and grey, throwing tiny spits of snow. The recurrent dreams of storms and the internal phantom Sarah chatter has faded for the most part. Apparently, that made room for her mind to start hearing voices again. A single crow lands on the bare tree limb in the back yard. She's not going crazy. It's too much *Amityville Horror* is all. She was creeped out for weeks after seeing it with Tony at the drive-in and should have known better than to pick up the book. The book is *always* better. As weird as it is to hear a voice ask her "Where's my brother," at least there's no voice telling her, "Get out!"

Claire pours a cup of coffee at the work desk she set up in the kitchen nook. Simple folding table with a dining room chair pulled up to it, the typewriter awaits to distract her with a bit of correction tape left out. Ever since the day Ann Marie handed her a CUB newsletter, Claire was determined to make a difference for herself and for countless other birthmothers. On any given evening when Tony is flying long-haul and Adam's tucked in bed, Claire types letters to legislators. Her paperwork is meticulously organized. A wire desktop file holder neatly stows labeled manila folders: CUB Newsletters, Courts Letters, Legislature Letters. With consistent pressure on the county courts and legislators, maybe someday she will meet Sarah. Maybe someday Adam will know his sister. Maybe someday the horror of closed adoption will be just a dark moment in history.

She reaches over to the typewriter and whips out her latest work in progress from the roller. After a final proofread, all that's left is to prepare envelopes for mailing. This set goes to several county courts in Iowa, as part of a campaign to reverse the law that seals adoption records and original birth certificates.

> Adoption as it now exists is not working. The growing number of adoptee and birthparent movements says it's not. The young women of today who choose abortion and would rather live with the knowledge of the death of their unborn infant than live with the repercussion and pain of adoption says it is not working. The dwindling number of babies surrendered for adoption says it's not working. Sealed records must be opened. Many agencies realize this and are allowing and even encouraging "open adoption." We who were a part of past adoption practices have the same right to know and should not be punished because of our place in time.

> Present adoption practices divide the birthparents, the adoptee, and the adoptive parents. We are important parts of each other, and we need to be whole. Adoption is a lifelong process of changing needs. Each of us has the right of knowing, the right of feelings and needs, the right to be responsible for these needs. Our rights and responsibilities regarding these needs must be morally and judicially acknowledged.

Claire flicks the letter, watching it drift down onto the table. She puts her hands on her hips and stretches her chin upwards in an attempt to loosen her jaw and stop clenching her teeth. Words, words, words. God knows when this is going to pan out. Legislative action takes years. There has to be another way. If only there was more time in the day. More time to focus on a real search effort. That's impossible with Tony gone most of the time and Adam not starting school until next year. Claire massages her forehead wondering if the emptiness will ever heal.

Won't you help me?

Claire freezes. The voice is so clear now. Right by her ear. She's surprised she's not feeling Sarah's breath on her neck. Claire surveys the room for . . . anything. She feels a clenching in her stomach and her throat tightens. Could a spirit really be trying to contact her? She thinks of her great-grandma Oma, who passed when Claire was a child. Oma often heard voices. Schizophrenic or gifted, no one could really say. Family lore reports many loved ones still receive notes in Oma's handwriting, warning them of future dangers that actually come to pass. Oma's now remembered as the family mystic instead of the family psychotic. In childhood, Claire observed her Oma talk back to the voices. Maybe that . . . works?

Claire whispers out loud, "Sarah? . . . Do you need me? . . . Give me a sign, baby."

"Good Morning, Captain!" Adam's greeting sings out from the other room.

Claire whips her head around and sees Adam talking to the TV. Not the sign she was hoping for. The crow alights from its perch, heading toward the incoming storm clouds. Dark clouds seem to roll in whenever she senses something from Sarah. Claire sips her coffee and waits. Her eyes fixate on the orange rotary wall phone that matches the flowers on the trendy avocado-green wallpaper she picked out and installed herself.

The phone rings twice.

Claire's spine stiffens and her mouth pops opens.

It rings twice again; the echo of the ring reverberates within the workings of the phone.

"Mommy, the phone."

Claire looks toward Adam, then swallows with a gulp as she slowly lifts the receiver. Claire answers in a shaky voice that is barely more than a whisper, "Hello?" She stops breathing, prepared to hear her daughter's voice.

"Sandy?" Claire collapses back in her chair and massages her forehead. It's just her neighbor. *Jesus, Claire, get it together. Sarah is not going to just up and call you.* "Oh . . . I'm fine. Sugar?" *Well, of course. Just a neighbor who needs her morning coffee.* "Yes. I do. You'll send Becky? OK. Bye." Claire hangs up and grabs a cup to dip it into the Merry Mushroom ceramic container of sugar.

Coming from just next door, Becky arrives in a flash. Sandy must really need her coffee. Becky is in the eighth grade—about the same age as Sarah. The Jansens have Becky babysit frequently and they say she's very responsible for her age. Claire looks at Becky now and can't help but imagine her as an example of what it would be like if Sarah were here to be a big sister for Adam.

"I was wondering," asks Becky, looking over at Adam interacting with the TV show characters. "Any chance you need a babysitter?"

Claire is a little taken aback, wondering if Becky has access to her thoughts. Claire's never really had a babysitter for Adam since she's always home with him. She prefers it that way, keeping him close.

"Or maybe a mother's helper?" asks Becky.

Again with the mind reading.

"I'm actually bored with Christmas break this year. Mom keeps finding me 'things to do,' which is kind of annoying to be honest."

Hold on. Is this . . . the sign? Have Becky look out for Adam so Claire can look out for Sarah?

"It's funny you ask," says Claire. "It just dawned on me; I need to make a million phone calls today for my support group and could use some help with Adam."

Becky smiles and is enthusiastic, "When can I start?"

Claire looks over at Adam, who is entranced by Mr. Green Jeans watering a plant. This will be good for him.

"How about now till dinner?"

"Sure," says Becky, heading toward the door with the sugar. "Be right back."

Claire stands at the doorway watching Becky skip back to her house with the sugar. The tiniest bit of blue sky peeks through the shifting clouds. "It's grey and uncomfortable now, Sarah, but everything's going to be just fine. I heard you, and I'm coming."

Claire dressed for the day in her smartest suit, complete with a bright-orange scarf and heels. She thinks better in a suit. Even if she is only in her own breakfast nook, sitting at a folding table, talking on an orange wall phone. Claire glances into the living room, where Becky is sitting next to Adam in front of the TV. Claire puts on lipstick. She needs every ounce of confidence in this endeavor. There's no time to work through the local CUB leader, she's calling the organization's president, long-distance direct. They published her phone number right there on the back of the monthly newsletter, after all. Claire will be seeking advice from the most experienced expert who's willing to work with her. Though there is a fair amount of controversy surrounding the stories, it's been said that Lisa is personally responsible for multiple successful searches.

Why didn't she think of this before? Claire shakes her body like a dog, in an attempt to release the regret for time lost. All Claire has to do is call her up and ask how to begin a search. Easy. Of course, she wouldn't mention she sees her daughter in dark clouds and dreams, hears her voice in the kitchen, and very much intends to physically go see Sarah with her own eyes. Generally, direct physical interaction with an underage child adopted at birth is not recommended. This guideline is for the wellbeing of both the child and the birthmother, not to mention that is straight up illegal unless agreed to by the adopted parents. However, this is a special case. When the spirit of the child calls out to her first mother, that is clearly an exception to the rule, right? Besides, Claire would never do anything to hurt Sarah.

Just sixty seconds into the call, after brief introductions and Claire announcing her intent to begin an active search effort, Lisa not so gently interrupts and asks an unexpected question, "Before we get too far, Claire. Let me ask you this."

Claire becomes all ears and holds her note-taking pen at the ready.

"Can you bold-faced lie?" asks Lisa, very matter-of-factly.

"I'm sorry, say that again?" Claire can feel the sweat from her ear on the receiver, feeling like somehow Lisa knows she's hiding her intent to see Sarah in person.

"I'm talking about manipulating people currently embedded in our social management systems. They're used to withholding information. You want them to give information. Understand?"

Claire writes "Bold-faced lie" on a sheet of typing paper. "Yes, I think I do."

"You'll rely on people's instinctive desire to be helpful. Then you lie, all while being convincing and creative about it. My question is, can you do that?"

This is not the conversation Claire expected.

"While you think about it, I'm going to ask about funding. Are you prepared to grease palms?"

"Bribes?" is the only word that Claire manages to spit out.

This time Lisa doesn't respond.

"You're serious."

"Look, Claire. Telling your story in letters to the legislature and county courts is all well and good, but going by the book takes time. If what you want is to find her *before* she can legally find you, you'll have to break some rules."

Claire hears Lilli's voice ring in Lisa's words. "Yes." Claire's tracking now. Yes, she can in good conscience lie and bribe in order to help her daughter. "Yes, I can. Lisa. I just. Well, thank you. For reassuring me this is possible." Claire can feel her stomach begin to knot with a jolt of excitement as she begins to believe. "I'm wondering, in this process, is there a way I can get a picture of my daughter? The agency said they asked the adoptive parents for a photo, but they haven't heard back. To see her . . . would mean a lot to me."

"The schools, Claire. They all have yearbooks."

Claire pauses. *Well of course they do.*

"Once we have the child's location narrowed in, getting a picture is usually not a problem. Local newspapers are also going to be part of this. You'll be specifically looking for a public notice of adoption, but oftentimes we find published family events and announcements that include photos."

Adam and Becky are laughing together in the living room. For the first time, Claire can imagine both of her children happy.

"I'm obligated to remind you, CUB is not a search organization. We may suggest reliable searchers. We let members know of other search groups in their area. We help searchers be sensitive to others' needs as they plan for contact and reunion."

At this point, Lisa can go ahead and say any caveat she needs to, Claire *will* have a photo of Sarah. She scribbles "year book/newspaper" and underlines it twice.

"You have a pen and paper?"

"I'm ready," says Claire.

"Here's what you'll do . . ."

CHAPTER 17

Back from Kmart, Claire has the supplies needed to convert her CUB support group desk into a Search Desk. Adam ran to hug her legs as soon as she walked in the door. No surprise he had a bout of separation anxiety. But apparently it wasn't too traumatic, because before Claire had a chance to put down her bags and give him a big squeeze, he was already running back to the puzzles he and Becky were playing in the living room.

"That was fast," says Becky.

"Sure was." Claire looks at the grandfather clock in the entryway. Record time. Though it felt a little odd to be out without a child in tow, there's no denying shopping is easier and faster without a toddler.

"It's really worked out well today," says Claire with genuine gratitude. "You two really get along well."

"You're a smart little guy, aren't you?" says Becky giving Adam the credit for their good first day.

"I'm Adam."

"Very true," says Claire. "I'm starting a . . . project. Would you be open to watching Adam on a regular basis?"

"What do you think, Adam? Want to play with me more?" asks Becky.

"Yeah!" Adam jumps up like a frog leaping.

"Sure, Mrs. Brooks," says Becky. "How long will your project last?"

That's a good question. This could take a while. Lisa said to ex-

160

pect years, not months. If that's the case, Becky is going to become like a partner in this endeavor. "If all goes well, several months. But maybe even a year."

"Oh, *big* project," says Becky.

"Big!" says Adam, leaping again.

As Claire was shopping for the search supplies, she quickly realized keeping the purpose of her "project" under some veil of privacy with Becky was senseless. She'd obviously overhear phone conversations and be able to see her search desk. "I'm," starts Claire, "going to find my daughter."

Becky remains politely quiet while attempting to hide her confusion.

"I gave birth to her before I was married. When I was a teenager. She lives with her adopted parents now. She's about your age."

Becky clasps her hands, and her lips disappear as she sucks them in.

"Ribbit," says Adam, leaping and sticking out his tongue, and jumps on all fours back to his bedroom.

"Mr. Brooks is supportive, and Adam will grow to understand." Claire thinks back to Riley, her friend at the Franklin Maternity Home. At the time, she was only a year older than Becky. Than Sarah. "I want you to know, it's OK if you ever want to ask questions."

"OK," is all Becky has to say. On second thought she decides to share, "My older sister's boyfriend's sister got pregnant."

Claire figures almost everyone knows a friend of a friend who's been pregnant before they're married. This is real life, after all.

"She managed to go full term and keep it a secret from everyone all the way up to the day she gave birth. She had the baby on the toilet one night then snuck out and got caught leaving it in a dumpster. She spent a year in prison." Becky looks directly at Claire, not afraid to be judged.

Jesus Christ. Is that what fourteen-year-olds talk about? Where is the love? Claire has no words.

"Anyway, I know it doesn't matter what I think, and there's no way to compare things, but I'm glad your daughter has you."

Claire's eyes begin to water. "Thank you," she whispers. Claire smiles at Becky with genuine gratitude for being open not only to creating a relationship with Adam, but to the idea of creating a relationship with her.

Claire lines everything out across the folding table. A spiral-bound steno pad, a box of colored bulletin board tacks, a package of index cards, a Rolodex, a set of colored markers, security envelopes, more typing paper, fresh pens, and star stickers. Lisa said not to scrimp on the star. Claire digs a hammer out from the garage and nails up the big cork bulletin board above the desk. She pins up the first note, "Break some rules." Claire feels like her quest is somehow official now. All out in the open, broadcast for anyone in her home to see. She is no longer a woman with a secret, but a mother with a mission. She unwraps the package of index cards, uncaps a fresh marker, and begins creating the search framework Lisa described over the phone.

Name Card. Claire writes in bold block letters "Sarah." She stops herself. No, this is for the name her adoptive parents have given her. Claire rips up the card and starts over. The name card simply says "Name" and the rest is blank. This realization sends a chill running up her spine. She doesn't know her own daughter's name. Soon.

Date of Birth Card. Claire fills it out: DOB 1/3/66. It's more than a date of birth. It wasn't the first wound of adoption that Claire experienced, but it is the day of the first injury for Sarah. An injury, because she didn't have a mother there to hold her, to nurse her. Claire tries not to think about how lonely that steel hospital bassinet must have felt. She realizes she's holding her breath and beginning to sweat. *Don't freak out. Focus on the love.* Claire imagines the "Filled with Love" envelope she contributes to faithfully every year and glances over at the Hallmark card she picked up along with the other supplies. Before she goes to bed tonight, she will write the thirteenth letter for that envelope.

Agency Card. Child Horizons. Claire puts Ann Marie's name and number on the card, the post-adoption counselor that was so helpful. If she hadn't brought in the new policies and procedure to Child Horizons, none of this would even be happening. It's a good time to call her back and see how that letter to the birth parents was going. This card is already in action, so Claire puts a star on the card. Huh. Stars really do raise confidence.

Court of Jurisdiction. Claire was already sending letters to county courts. But she hadn't previously considered focusing on counties likely to have a relationship with Child Horizons. Lisa mentioned that would likely be proximity based or religion based. Claire gets up and goes over to the *World Book Encyclopedia* the salesman sold her as something Adam would need to be successful. Tony was visibly upset with this purchase and made Claire swear not to buy things from door-to-door salesmen anymore. Claire pulls out the "N" volume. Today that set is already worth it. She isn't quite sure what to do with this information just yet but she can list the counties nearest to Child Horizons: Lancaster, Douglas, Seward, Saline, Gage, or Sarpy. Six. How hard could that be?

Place of Birth Card. Nebraska University Medical Hospital. She writes "Lilli" on the card. Last she knew, Lilli still works with the University. Claire pens in Lilli's phone number and pins this card to the board, then sits back to evaluate her most valuable resources—friends. She has more friends on her side than she realized. Claire takes another card and draws a chain of stick people on it. Each a different color. She labels the figures: Lilli was first, then Bonnie. Tony,

Ann Marie, CUB members, Lisa, and now Becky. All these people believe it's worth their time and energy to bring a mother and her child together. She's not in this alone. Claire puts a star on the card and pins it to the board.

She steps back to consider the board as a whole. This is the hand she was dealt. Claire smiles to herself and adds a sense of accomplishment to the rollercoaster of emotions she's experienced today. Lisa was right. The cards would get things moving; however, the movement of stuffed-down emotions wasn't quite what she expected. Claire sits back down acknowledging the overwhelm washing over her. There are several leads. Phone numbers and addresses she can reach out to. A chain of people supporting her, rooting for her. The impossible is becoming possible.

It's a special occasion when she and Lilli connect. They don't talk often but when they do, Lilli always manages to create a place of safety for Claire. She relaxes at her desk and kicks her heels off while they catch up.

"I see," says Lilli. "So you're busy breaking rules."

This compliment puts a smile on Claire's face. "Did the university hospital records ever get converted to microfilm?"

"Umm." Lilli hesitates. "What you need might not be considered a patient record," says Lilli.

The energy of her original optimism drains. "Yaaa." Finding where the hospital sent Sarah's original birth record now sounds harder than originally imagined.

"We need Rachel," says Lilli, instilling confidence. "We go straight to the University Medical Center Archives and pull everything."

"Rachel?"

"Rachel is a student I brought in for work study," explains Lilli.

Of course she is. That's just what Lilli does.

"Smart cookie that one. If anyone can find it, she can."

Claire creates a Records Card and puts Rachel's name and number on it.

"About the local newspapers," continues Lilli. "Public notice of adoption wouldn't be indexed."

Claire figured as much, but thought it'd be worth asking.

"We could send copies of the entire newspaper." Lilli begins brainstorming, "Six counties spanning a few months after the date of relinquishment. My goodness, Claire," Lilli takes a deep breath. "That's going to be reams and reams of paper. Are you up for that?"

Claire creates a Newspaper Card. "Let's do it." At this point she is all in. All in.

"We're going to need a donation to cover the printing and mailing," says Lilli.

Claire pens dollar signs on both the cards.

Lilli thinks out loud, "I'll put Erika on this. She's doing work study in microform."

"Like I was." Nostalgia warms Claire's heart. Her days setting up the microform department were some of the hardest of her life, but every minute of it, she was with Sarah.

"This warrants a generous textbook scholarship for both Erika and Rachel. Don't you agree?"

Claire puts another dollar sign on the cards and pins them to the board. Lisa was right. Money to finance the search is already adding up, and this is just the beginning. "That's my Lilli," says Claire. "Always looking out for others."

"We women need to stick together."

"Thanks a million, Lilli. Again."

Tony stands in front of the search board sipping his coffee while Claire prepares his favorite early-morning-before-a-long-haul breakfast: sausage gravy over biscuits with two eggs and a glass of orange juice. Claire could never eat at 4 a.m., but she's always gotten up and sent Tony on his way well fed. "Looks like you are making progress. More cards have dollar symbols on them," Tony half teased.

So far, Tony has been supportive of the extra money going toward finding Sarah. He only tracks the expenses at the end of the month when he reviews how Claire balanced the checkbook. He hasn't imposed a budget yet. So as long as Claire doesn't need to use his credit card, the financial part of the effort has been for the most part a non-topic.

"The newspaper copies have been coming in every other day. I've started going straight to the post office each morning." Claire peeks in the oven. Biscuits are rising nicely. Stacks of paper are in strategic piles on the search desk, waiting for Claire's methodical review.

"Anything promising yet?" Tony sits at the table and Claire serves him the steaming plate. She sits to keep him company while he eats.

"No. Not yet," she sighs. "Lancaster County was a miss. One county down, potentially five more to go." It's not hopeless, but after a full batch of nothing, it's clear now the idea that this was going to go quickly was overly optimistic.

Tony comments on Claire's slumped posture and attitude this morning, "You look tired, sweetie. Maybe schedule time to take a break?"

Claire nods while looking down in an attempt to hide the dark circles under her eyes. She politely smiles, accepting his suggestion, but knows darn well she's not going to ease up now. This is just the beginning. "What I need is a little luck," says Claire. "Fingers crossed Douglas County is the one with the notice of adoption."

"Becky seems to be good for Adam," says Tony. "I noticed he's using new words."

Claire's noticed that too. Becky spends a lot of time reading with

Adam. She's been able to come every Wednesday after school, fix Adam dinner, and put him to bed. Jealousy grips Claire's stomach momentarily, as though Tony is praising Becky for something Claire wished she was acknowledged for. Jealousy fades into guilt, which Claire swallows down with her coffee.

Claire walks in with the latest stack of mail to find a dance party in her living room, *Electric Company* blasting on the TV. Adam manages to tear himself away from his dance partner long enough to hug Claire's legs. In a flash he runs back to Becky and grabs her hand.

"You have a message—on the Code-a-Phone," says Becky as she spins Adam. "I think you're going to like it."

She'd like it if it's Child Horizons. Claire called in enough times asking about a response to the inquiry Ann Marie sent the adoptive parents, that they essentially told her to stop calling.

Claire drops the mail on her desk, the call light blinking. She presses down the rewind button and then plays the message from the beginning.

This message is for Claire Jordan Brooks from Rachel Manny with University Medical Records. First of all, I want to thank you for the textbook scholarship. Lilli has so many beautiful things to say about you, it's my privilege to contribute to your search before I transition out of the Records department. Per your request, I mailed the entire original file and created copies to put back in the archives. What I discovered in your record, Mrs. Brooks, is remarkable. I called right way, so you have the information before the file arrives in the mail. Child Horizons requested your daughter's hospital birth record sent to the Saline County court. Also, the contract between the hospital's foster care services and Child Horizons included an exhibit that outlined they only took adoption applicants from the D.O.C. That's the Disciples of Christ network. I took the liberty of calling them up, and at that time they had contracts in five cities: Omaha, Lincoln, Beatrice, Nebraska City, and Wilber. So, ma'am, since only Wilber is in Saline County, you can narrow your investigations to one city—the Czech Capital of Nebraska. I went to that festival just last summer. Love the koláče. The whole town shows up. Who knows, maybe I saw your daughter and didn't realize it. Anyway, I already notified Erika in microform. She was very relieved to hear this as I am sure you are. Her next and hopefully final batch will include only their local newspaper, The Wilber Republican. There is one more thing that is absolutely incredible, I've never seen it before and probably never will again. A sealed envelope is in the file. The nurses' notes indicate this was an

—the tape reaches its end, and the machine clicks off.

Claire bursts in, "It came." She waves about a large manila envelope from the University of Nebraska Medical Center. They've been waiting for it ever since the Code-a-phone tape cut off Rachel's message, which seemed like an eon ago. Adam and Becky look up from their puzzle play and drop what they're doing to meet at the search desk. Claire slips her commemorative bicentennial letter opener into the corner of the envelope and tears it open in a single motion. She pulls out the medical record folder and inside there is the usual set of papers secured by a metal fastener on the right and one sealed regular letter-sized envelope scotch taped on the left. Claire carefully peels off the envelope from the folder and inspects it. No writing on the envelope. It's sealed and whatever's in there is not completely flat, but it doesn't have any significant weight. She touches the fastened papers, thinking maybe she should read up first.

"Just open it," says Becky.

Adam nods in agreement and jumps up and down.

Claire taps the envelope on the table before she inserts the letter opener, then slowly tears it open and looks inside. "It's dried . . . tissue?" She holds the envelope open to Becky and Adam so they can see inside.

Becky jumps back and cringes, "Eww. Maybe better read." She stands over Claire's shoulder as they both take a moment to silently read the top page of the record.

En caul birth at 37 weeks. Female. Active response, pink, with a vigorous cry. Contact Dr. Greene's personal attorney Ike Cerny in the event of placement issues through Child Horizons. Amniotic membrane prepared for archive.

"Amniotic membrane?" says Claire, looking at Becky.

"What's an en caul birth?" asks Becky, looking at Claire.

Claire snaps her fingers and waves, "*World Book*." Becky hustles off to the encyclopedia set on the hallway bookcase.

"What's that?" asks Adam.

"I don't know," says Claire, still peeking at the contents of the envelope without touching it.

"It's magic," calls out Becky from the living room, reading as she brings the book. "An en caul birth is a rare event where a baby is born still inside an intact amniotic sac."

"Sweet Jesus," says Claire. She can't even picture that in her mind. "Is there a picture?"

Becky shakes her head, "Nope, but according to ancient Slavic legend, an en caul birth effectively extends the protective qualities of the maternal membrane beyond the womb."

"Slavic? Like Czechoslovakian?" she asks, envisioning what maternal protective qualities might entail.

"Just says Slavic," says Becky. She continues, "Children born en caul often possess powers of clairvoyance, gifts of healing, and qualities of dexterity that provide immunity from death by drowning."

Claire pauses, absorbing the idea that her daughter may be like Oma. According to family legend, the traits could be passed on. This membrane is in her hands now, a physical reality. A gift. Claire ponders the stormy visions, seeing events from outside her body, and voices she hears that no one else can. *Maybe my mind isn't creating these. What if Sarah is . . . sending me messages?* Claire whispers out loud, "I'm just receiving them."

Becky raises an eyebrow, wondering what in the world Claire is talking about. Claire shakes her head indicating it's nothing. "Keep reading."

"The caul additionally locates the supernatural powers within the object itself, allowing magical benefits to be transferred through changes in ownership. Southern Slavs sew the caul into a pouch to be worn as a good luck charm or kind of companion spirit. The caul is placed under the owner's head on their deathbed to ease their passing."

Claire takes the caul out of the envelope. It's carefully preserved by being dried and film wrapped to a small rectangle of lining paper. She presses it to her chest and closes her eyes, as though she's hugging her daughter. "My companion spirit."

"Your good luck charm," says Becky.

"Magic," says Adam.

CHAPTER 18

There's nothing different about this drive to Nebraska to see their grandmas and grandpas. For a full hour, Karl and Jules sing along with the *John Denver's Greatest Hits* 8-track tape. "Sunshine on My Shoulders" is a favorite.

Karl sings, "If I had a day that I could give you, I'd give to you a day just like today."

Jules sings, "If I had a tale that I could tell you, I'd tell a tale sure to make you smile."

They sing the chorus together. "Sunshine, almost always makes me high." Karl pretends to inhale a joint at this point in the lyrics, which is ridiculous, though some people think it looks cool. Joints and other drugs are readily available and even passed during class at school, Karl and Jules vowed to each other to always stay clean. Only losers do drugs.

Though it's obvious Karl has a better singing voice than Jules, he never criticizes, which is weird because he teases her about everything else. This makes Jules pretty sure that she must really suck at singing. Even Mom says, "Jules, I think you'd be better off signing up for band than choir in school." So Karl and Jules reserve their singing sessions for family car rides, and the occasional Saturday afternoon while listening to records in Karl's room.

Halfway there, they visit the rest stop, use the restrooms, jog around the path, and eat the fried chicken Mom packed. The public picnic tables are always too dirty to use, though other people don't seem to think so. They eat in the car. After that, Jules sleeps the rest of the way to Grandpa Emi's house.

It was surprising to arrive and see Grandpa Fats at Grandpa Emi's house. Grandpa Fats is always at the farm. It feels like he doesn't belong here. But this time Grandpa Fats is here to take Karl to the farm so he can help out in the soy fields while Mom and Dad and Jules stay to help Grandpa Emi with his chemo treatments.

Jules asks to go with Karl, but Grandma Dolly doesn't think it's a good idea, because . . . and Jules can hardly believe the ludicrous basis for this decision . . . because Jules started her period. Why Mom even told Grandma Dolly about Jules's bodily functions in the first place is beyond reason. Jules's embarrassment doesn't seem to interest anyone. Grandma Dolly says, "You must be restful when it's your time. Keep your feet out of cold water and stay in the house."

What the hell does that even mean? Is she really worried for Jules's health? Is she worried that . . . God only knows . . . she might get pregnant out in the fields? That she might end up infertile like her mother? Maybe it's something to do with Grandpa Fats—maybe he doesn't allow women on their period in the fields so the work crew doesn't have to take bathroom breaks or something like that. This makes zero sense. Arguing with Grandma or Grandpa is absolutely never allowed, and it takes every ounce of discipline not to argue. This advice comes from a woman who is one of twelve children! Grandma Dolly's own mother came to Nebraska in a covered wagon, for Christ's sake. Those women never stayed in the house and rested during their period.

So, Karl gets to go do the fun and interesting things, again. Grandpa Fats said he had that new Honda waiting in the garage for Karl. Figures.

*   *   *

The very next day, Dad and Jules are out doing yard work that Grandpa Emi hasn't been able to take care of. That's when the phone call comes. Jules is never told what's said on that phone call, but Mom's face is pale as she stands at the screen door. "Will!" she shouts, her voice cracking as she tries to hold in panic.

Dad stops chopping and her voice goes oddly robotic, "Karl's had a motorcycle accident. We need to go. He's at Lincoln Memorial."

Jules sits in the family side of the emergency waiting room, trying to distract herself from eavesdropping on the other family's devastation. A thirty-three-year-old father is here for emergency brain surgery because during the church's Sunday family softball game, he and a teammate hit heads while going for a pop fly. His wife sits with their toddler on her lap waiting to hear if Daddy's still alive.

They don't know Jules is sitting here because her sixteen-year-old brother with a broken collarbone, broken ankle, and punctured lung, is indefinitely unconscious from a swelling brain. All because he somehow managed to run his motorcycle into a semi-truck filled with pigs on their way to slaughter. She doesn't want to be here when the doctor comes back with news for the young mother because some sick part of her has already imagined that young church-going woman as a widow.

Even though Jules promised to stay put until Mom and Dad get back from another secret conference with Karl's doctor, she heads out of the emergency waiting room to retreat to her hiding spot. Sitting with Mom and Dad's worry and constant speculation is just not something Jules can do, so in the thirty-six hours she's been there, she's explored every corridor of the hospital. It was pretty clear there wasn't much Mom or Dad could do to tend to her needs, so she went ahead and took care of herself. Last night Jules asked Dad for change for tampons, by saying she needed change for the snack machine.

Mom doesn't allow them to get food out of vending machines, but he didn't think twice about it and just gave her everything he had in his pockets, $2.95. The machine on the third floor is the only one with the little chocolate donuts she knows Dad likes. It also has orange peanut butter crackers. Mom never lets Jules have those, saying it's a ridiculous price for just a few crackers and a dab of peanut butter, but that's been her dinner and breakfast since they arrived. They'd never eat at the cafeteria, because they couldn't afford it, but Jules figured she could eat off Dad's pocket change for another day or so.

Jules hunkers down in her hiding spot, which is the stairwell between the fourth and fifth floors that seems to be generally unused. It's the only private place she's found. It's also pleasantly not air-conditioned. The rest of the hospital is freezing cold, which makes the cramps feel so much worse. She opens up a half-eaten package of orange crackers. They have good intentions trying to protect her from bad news. She tried to explain to them that her comprehension of what the doctors say is way better than the crap she can make up inside her head.

Listening to Mom try and translate the doctor's information is a painful experience all on its own. There's a lot she doesn't want to say. She doesn't even try to find sufficient euphemisms. She just leaves shit out. *Mother, where are you?* Her anxiety is so out of hand, she probably can't even hear her own words. She feels like if she doesn't say it out loud, it's somehow not real. Dad's busy seeing to the decisions the doctors and hospital staff need. Meanwhile, Jules has been finding out the truth about Karl's condition from the ICU nurses and the medical journals in the staff library on the fourth floor.

Jules is pretty sure she's seen Karl more than her parents. She asked the nurses how often she could come see him since the visiting hours sign is ridiculous if you are living in the hospital waiting room twenty-four hours a day. They allow her to go in for ten minutes every couple of hours, so she developed a little routine. She visits Karl. Asks the nurse on duty for a cup of water and any information on Karl she's willing to give. Then Jules goes to the library and looks up the conditions the nurse mentioned in the medical journals. Next Jules checks in with Mom and Dad, who are always glued to the waiting room in case a doctor shows up to talk with them. After that, Jules goes to her hiding place in the stairwell, to warm up and try to relax out some cramps while eating an orange cracker and taking a little nap. Then it's about time to repeat the whole cycle.

Jules stands at the ICU room entrance and patiently waits. She doesn't see Karl in the spot he's usually in. The nurse on duty finally comes over. "Where's my brother?" she asks as the sick side of her wonders if he died, but at the same time the optimistic side of her considers maybe he got moved out of the ICU into a regular hospital room.

"The doctor had us reposition his bed to the coolest space. Over there." She points to the dark corner in the back of the room. Jules tries not to look at the other patients in the room as she steps over to Karl's bedside. He's hooked up to all the machines, on the bed with nothing covering his broken body but a folded sheet across his mid-section.

"Excuse me, can I cover him? The air-conditioning is really cold."

"No, dear, he is running a temperature. We want to keep him cool."

Jules studies the various displays and tries to find body temperature. 103 degrees. A journal in the library said it's not unusual for a dying person to have an elevated temperature as they draw closer to death. Jules puts her hand on Karl's forehead. His skin is strangely sticky and clammy. The side of her hand brushes against his hair, matted with blood. Disgusting. Boy, if he was awake, he'd flip out about it.

"Can I rinse the blood out of his hair?" Jules asks.

Nodding, the nurse fills a kidney-shaped basin with water and puts a washcloth in it. "You can wipe the hair around his face and ears, but best not turn his head. As soon as he's stable, we'll shave the hair."

Holding the basin in one hand and squeezing out the washcloth with the other is awkward. Jules wipes his forehead. Karl does not react. She suddenly feels nauseous; her mouth tastes metallic, and her guts feel like they're being sucked into her throat. Jules closes her eyes and exhales. She feels her pulse throb up her neck and the pounding of her heart is so loud and erratic she's sure it must be echoing off the sterile white walls. A spark of electricity unzips her from her body. She looks up, and beyond the ICU ceiling, she sees a dark sky filled with stars. Curious and without concern for how to return, she allows herself to leave the hospital and explore the darkness. What could be worse than the ICU? She looks down, and she sees Karl, standing on the side of a highway. Jules knows exactly where he is, where 162nd crosses Highway 8. Not far from Grandpa Fats' farm. How she and Karl got here, however, is a mystery.

Karl is wearing his favorite blue satin shirt, brown corduroy pants, and jacket. He bought the clothes at the mall with his girlfriend, apparently inspired by *Saturday Night Fever*. Mom was livid that he spent so much money on it. He does look really good, though. Jules descends from her hawk-like vantage point to see what Karl's up to.

"They said you'd come," says Karl.

"Who said?"

"I don't know, angels I guess," says Karl, with no issue giving a child's response. "They said you had a gift."

Jules looks up the road just twenty yards and sees Grandma Dolly standing there, in the shade of a hog trailer that's stopped in the middle of the road. She's standing next to Grandpa Fats. They are looking at Karl's broken body lying on the highway in front of them. Grandma's eyes are sad but she's not crying. She is pinching her lips, her hand shaking as she tries to make sense of what she sees. "Is that his brains?" she asks Grandpa Fats.

"That's the pears he had for lunch," says Grandpa.

"A gift?" Jules says, to the version of Karl standing next to her. "What, that I can magically show up when people are about to die?"

"I doubt that's it. Do I look dead to you?" says Karl.

"Well, your body over there looks pretty close to dead."

Karl walks over to the motorcycle wreckage and gives it a kick. "Too bad. Brand new bike." He tries to pick it up, but it's so mangled it's no use.

"What are you doing?" Jules asks.

He drops the pile of twisted metal and squats down next to it, looking defeated.

"What are *you* doing?" says Karl. He doesn't bother looking up at Jules.

"I guess I'm just here . . . hanging out with you." Jules reaches over to brush his hair off his forehead.

Karl whips his head away, "Watch the hair."

She backs off and changes the subject. "Grandma looks pretty upset. Should we try to help her?"

"They don't seem to see or hear us," says Karl.

Jules looks at Karl. He seems as real as he was just yesterday, singing with her in the car as they drove to Nebraska. "Jesus, Karl, are you an angel?"

"Fuck no."

"But you're still in the hospital," Jules tries to explain to Angel Karl.

"So are you, you dumb girl. As far as I can tell, you brought us here. We must be in a parallel universe or something," says Karl.

"Parallel universe?"

"Multiverse. Alternative reality. Light cones. Learn physics, will you? Schrodinger, Hawking. Did you even read the "P" encyclopedia? Physics, Jules. Look it up." He sounds annoyed and impatient for an angel.

"Fine." What's the point in arguing in an alternative reality? "If there's multiple universes, can we go somewhere . . . more beautiful than highway wreckage that smells like hogs?"

"As far as I know, you're in charge of this encounter, so by all means, make it more beautiful."

Jules closes her eyes. *How can I make this more beautiful?*

She grabs Karl's hand and breathes in the earthy smell of hogs mixed with fresh-cut hay. A shock of electricity passes through her hand into Karl's, like when they rub their socked feet on the carpet in winter and touch their pinkies to the screw in the light switch. She looks up and sees stars beyond the blue sky. She looks down onto Grandpa Fats' farm and sees it like the aerial photo that hangs in their farmhouse mudroom. Jules focuses on the west storage garage down the main house's driveway. She sees Karl is already there, leaning against the garage. He's standing just around the corner from where Grandma planted the fuchsia four o'clocks on the north side of the building. They are wide now, open for the evening. The barn cats and old Skipper are lined up around the rusted tin trough lapping up the dinner scraps, pellets, and dry milk mixture Grandma stirs up for them every night. Robins and doves are singing their goodnight songs. Jules and Karl look to the west, and watch the sun go down over the alfalfa fields.

"Better," says Karl, complimenting Jules's pick of a beautiful place.

"You know, Mom's going to have a meltdown over this."

"What, knowing you can meet people across multiple realities? Just don't tell her."

"No. Not that," says Jules, pushing his shoulder. "This is just a hallucination brought on by menstrual blood loss and eating orange peanut butter crackers as my sole sustenance for almost two days . . . I'm talking about you leaving. Living this angel life as a John Travolta wannabe is bound to get boring after a while. I want you to come back and be my brother."

"Look, you saw my body. You read the medical journals. It's not going to be the same if I come back. I don't know if I can still protect you." He rubs his chin, thinking. "Hey! Any chance you can drop me in a different parallel universe?"

"What?"

"You know, if I can't be normal again in our universe with Mom and Dad, maybe I could go to another one. Maybe where my birth mom decides to keep me."

"Do you really think that would be more normal?" Jules asks. Like any of this is normal.

"I don't know about normal, but it does seem more natural," says Karl.

Can't argue there. A universe where people work together so mothers can keep their own babies if they want to does seem like an improvement. "I like where you're going with that, but I don't think it's something I can do. Not by myself anyways. Besides, in that universe you wouldn't be my brother."

"Fine," he says, picking up a rock and throwing it out into the field. "But meeting people across multiple realities seems pointless if you can't actually do anything with it. You're going to have to work on that Jules."

"Come on," says Jules, ready to go before Karl thinks of more things she could do. "Just keep Mom busy. Let her focus on you. She's starting to put effort into making me 'ladylike,' which is just another word for subservient. Rehabbing your ass will keep her distracted."

"Look," Karl waves his head toward the sunset, its last light glowing as it dips below the horizon. The crickets and frogs begin their evening song. "You really did make my transition more beautiful. Thanks for being here with me."

"So you'll come back?"

"I'm your friend no matter what universe we're in. I'll be there to take care of Mom and Dad, and I'll be here to take care of you."

Karl stands up and brushes off his suit. He straightens up his collar and cracks his neck. "But before I get to all that, you know what I wanna do?"

"What?"

"Strut."

Jules laughs as she watches him strut into the sunset singing "Stayin' Alive" in falsetto.

As she stands up and brushes the dust from the seat of her pants, Jules realizes she's been sweating like crazy, and the armpit stains are downright embarrassing. She flaps her shirt to air it out and is surprised to find herself back in the ICU at Karl's bedside. The machines goes off, and she looks up to see his temperature blip down to 101.

CHAPTER 19

Becky is at the stove flipping grilled cheese sandwiches and turns off the burner to the tomato soup. Adam stomps into the kitchen and grabs her leg. "I'm hungry."

"Of course you are. Go and wash your hands, it's almost ready. How about you, Claire, want a sandwich?"

From the search board, Claire pulls down the card labeled "Public notice of petition for adoption." I'm going to find you, Mr. Public Notice.

"No thanks." She flicks on her desk light and spreads out the mimeographed pages of the *Wilber Republican* across her desk.

Trotting back to the kitchen with dripping hands, Adam grabs a triangle slice of his sandwich off the plate and comes over to Claire. "This is good!" He holds it up for her to take a bite.

Claire takes a bite. "Umm. Good." Claire lifts Adam up onto her lap and gives him a big squeeze as she kisses his neck. He giggles and wiggles out of her arms, climbing up into his chair and joining Becky at the dinner table.

Flipping through the pages, Claire scans the Public Notices section and realizes how tedious newspapers are. Ev-er-ry-week: obituaries, weddings, and graduations including people who don't even live in Wilber but are friends and relatives of people who do. The same local business ads again and again. Repetitive mention of preparations for the annual festival. Without fail there's an opinion from the Pythian Sisters to "help others grow through the principles of Purity, Love, Equality, and Fidelity." Blah, blah, blah. Claire rubs her eyes and stands up for a cup of coffee.

By this time, the kitchen is already clean and Becky has Adam in PJ's. She gives his back a tap. "Go give your mom a kiss goodnight." Claire squats down, and Adam holds onto each side of her face and they flutter their eyelashes together, exchanging butterfly kisses. She breathes in the warmth of this joyful exchange and feels grateful to have him near her.

Becky tucks Adam in, turns out the lights in the house, and lets herself out. As she calls out goodnight from the front door, everything seems peaceful and as it should be.

Claire adjusts the lamp over her desk, ready for the final push on this stack of reading. She holds her hand over her heart to feel the little silk pouch she sewed for the caul, which she keeps pinned to her bra. Could use a little magic about now. She flips to the Announcements section, which is always an interesting grab bag of small-town trivia. What will she find today?

Kindergarten Teacher Resigns: 75 guests welcome baby girl.

A retirement/baby shower of that size must be a main event in a small town. Wait a minute. Claire bites her lip. That last trip she took to Child Horizons, Ann Marie mentioned the adoptive mother resigned from a ten-year career as an educator. Claire pulls the paper closer to read every word carefully.

Shower gifts and guests covered every square inch of the church basement, including an overflowing donation basket for Child Horizons Adoption Agency.

Claire's breathing stops. She can barely believe her eyes. She circles the words "Child Horizons" and feels frozen in time, staring in front of her into nothingness. She seems to lift out of her body. This is *my baby's* baby shower? Claire presses the caul against her heart. She looks down at the mimeograph, no longer aware of her orientation to the breakfast nook or her existence in this moment. She is in the basement of Shepard of the Hills Lutheran Church in Wilber, Nebraska.

The whole community celebrates the arrival of Jo's beautiful daughter, Jules.

Jo's daughter. Jules. Claire's body sits in stillness, not aware of time passing. Eventually, she hears the ticking of the grandfather clock in the entryway, and her body returns to the search desk. She stands up and methodically pulls the pin from the name card on the bulletin board and sets the card on the desk, snapping it on the table's hard surface. She picks the thick black marker from the holder and smells the sting of chemical solvent, reminding her of the cleaning fluids used in Child Horizons's adoption unit. She writes in squeaky bold block letters "Jules Tischler." She carefully pins the card to the board, then reaches for the desk lamp switch and turns out the light.

"What's next now that you know her name?" It's a sunny morning, and Becky is standing over Claire's shoulder drinking hot chocolate and reorganizing the cards pinned on the bulletin board, making the relationships more visually clear.

"Well, for starters this moved up the plan for how Tony and I talk with Adam," says Claire.

"Should I know?" asks Becky.

"The relationship you and Adam have now makes this so easy for him to grasp," says Claire, feeling the power of her good luck charm at work. "Tony and I talked with him at dinner the other night. We said there's a girl, Jules, who's his sister. She lives with another family, is about the same age as Becky. And someday you both may choose to be friends." Claire glances over at Adam sitting at the kitchen table playing with his scrambled eggs. "He seems satisfied with that. It's easy for him because he loves you. And trusts you. He's open to someone who might be like you. Someone like you who is both a friend and part of the family." Claire touches Becky's shoulder and smiles with gratitude shining from her eyes.

Becky smiles back and redirects their energy to the search board. "So what's next?"

Claire has spread out the next batch of *Wilber Republican* copies on the table. "I've never seen a group of people who identified themselves so deeply by saying they are from another country." Claire taps her pen at a picture looking down Main Street. The signage is frequently in Czechoslovakian, a sign saying "Vítáme Vás" is in the foreground. "In Wilber, everyone's name sounds like they are all originally from the same Slovakian village: Jelinek, Zajicek, Dvorak, Travnicek . . . They call themselves Bohemians."

"Isn't that somebody who lives in an attic and starves for art?" asks Becky.

Claire looks at Becky and blinks, teasing her, "Sweetie, the entire *World Book* set is right over there. You're welcome to educate yourself at any time."

Becky crosses her arms and snorts.

"The agency said they would place my baby with a family whose nationality and heritage matched mine, including similar physical traits. I'm sure these people have many positive qualities, but they're certainly not Nordic. Why am I surprised. It was just another lie."

Becky returns with the "B" book from the encyclopedia and sets it down on the search desk and pulls up a chair.

"Someone in the family was very diligent about submitting notices to the paper about many of the children's events. Usually listing all the relatives who traveled into town." Claire lines up all the various pages she's marked with circles and stars. Trick or treating, visiting Santa, Jules's birthday, big brother Karl's birthday, Easter egg hunt. "As if a small town wasn't small enough."

"Convenient for anyone who may be watching them," says Becky, trying to rationalize why anyone would publish a child's birthday party in the newspaper. "It's almost like they want you to know."

"Yes." Claire flips through several more papers she has marked as pertaining to Jules or her family. "It goes on like that for a few years. But then . . . nothing."

"Maybe they got tired of living in a place where it was hard to spell everyone's name, so they moved."

Claire looks over at Becky with a smug grin, but then bites her upper lip. "Yes . . . they moved."

Becky rocks on her toes, proud of her insight. Then she sips the last of her hot chocolate and goes into the kitchen to clean up from breakfast.

They moved. That makes things more difficult. Surely there must be some kind of a going away event. A walk around the block and three coffees later, Claire finally sees it. An advertisement for Freddy's Tavern. It just looks like the usual happy hour beer special, but then in small italics:

Toast Tischlers' Move to the Mountains—Gone fishing at Horsetooth Reservoir.

Claire circles Horsetooth and a chill runs up her spine. She's gotten everything she can from the newspaper. With names and a location, it's time for Directory Assistance.

Claire picks up her orange phone and dials 4-1-1. "Can you connect me with Information near the Horsetooth Reservoir."

"State, please."

Right. Well, there are mountains in three nearby states—South Dakota, Colorado, and Wyoming. Where would you move to raise kids? she wonders. "Colorado?"

"One moment." *Click-click-click.*

"Directory assistance, what city?" asks a new voice.

"Horsetooth Reservoir," says Claire. *Well, that's all I got.*

"Ma'am, there is no number for Horsetooth Reservoir."

Claire just remains silent, hoping this operator chooses to be helpful today.

"I can connect you with Larimer County, or Ft. Collins directory assistance."

"Thank you!" Claire scribbles Larimer County on a card. "Ft. Collins, please."

"One moment." *Click-click-click.*

"Directory assistance. How may I connect you?" says lucky voice number three.

"Jo Tischler, please." The direct approach seems a good idea. But then again, what to say? Claire feels panic arising in her throat as she prepares to hang up.

"There's no listing for Jo Tischler. Would you like another number?"

Claire can feel herself breathe again as she flips through her steno pad to the instructions that Lisa gave her. That's enough winging it for one day. Claire hears Lisa's voice in her head, "The schools all have yearbooks." Claire puts her hand to her heart, touching Jules's companion spirit. *Here we go.* "May I speak with your most successful real estate agent?"

"Ma'am, I can connect you with the RE/MAX office, though they operate out of Denver."

A big city doesn't seem right.

"Or . . ." The operator hesitates like one does when they know they're breaking the rules but does it anyway knowing everyone involved may benefit from it. "My neighbor, Beverly. She's with Foothills Investments, right here in Ft. Collins. She helped me find my home."

Claire sighs, thanking her lucky spirit daughter. "That's perfect. May I tell Beverly who provided the referral? Ms . . ."

"Jackson."

"Thank you so much," says Claire. *More than you know, Ms. Jackson.*

"You're welcome. Just one moment while I connect you." *Click-click-click.*

"Foothills Investments, this is Beverly," says voice number four.

"Hello, Beverly, Ms. Jackson gave me your number." That is very true. "We'll be coming to the area soon and I'd like to know more about homes near schools for grades 7, 8, and 9." Also true. *This isn't hard at all.*

"Oh, that's wonderful. Yes, I'd be happy to answer your questions about the area . . . Ms . . . ?"

"Jordan." Claire feels her heart pounding and her face flush. Using her maiden name is almost like using an untraceable alias. She stands up to pace as far as the phone cord will allow. She reminds herself that this is a perfectly normal conversation.

"We are part of the Poudre R-1 School District and we have five fine junior high schools: Cache La Poudre, Lincoln, Lesher, Boltz, and Blevins."

Claire scribbles down the names of the schools. "Could you repeat the name of the school district?"

"It's French. *Poudre*—after the Cache la Poudre River, the heart of the National Heritage Area . . ."

Claire's thoughts move on while Beverly continues her historical tour of the area. A National Heritage Area will certainly be in the *World Book* set, that will be another thing to read up on. For now, assuming the family did choose to live in the city nearest Horsetooth Reservoir, *and* assuming they didn't move from there yet, theoretically she has everything needed to find out what school Jules is attending and finally see a photo of her. That's an enormous amount of optimism, even for Claire. "Could you give me the phone numbers of the junior high schools? I'd like to call them today and get a better understanding of the curriculum and special programs they support."

"Of course," says Beverly as she pulls out her school's information sheet. "Do you have a pencil ready?"

Claire presses the caul to her heart, feeling a pulse in her fingertips. The schools, they all have yearbooks. And Jules has already given her picture to one of them.

"Tonight, there's a special dessert," says Claire just as Tony finishes his last bite of dinner.

"Yeah! Dessert!" says Adam.

Claire stands up and brings a pie to the table, "It's an Impossible Pie." Next to the pie, Claire also places a large envelope that she picked up from the Post Office just this morning. The sending address reads Lincoln Junior High. It's the first yearbook order to arrive and it about killed Claire to leave it unopened all day. Pictures seem to make things real, and Claire wanted Tony to believe in Jules and that the impossible was possible. It's been fifteen months since her decision to pursue the technically illegal search for her daughter. During that time, Tony's been truly supportive, but ever since it became clear that the adoptive family moved from Nebraska, Claire could tell that Tony became skeptical that Jules could really be found. He started asking deeper questions about the checks being written and took particular interest in the five junior high school yearbook orders. Claire had no problem getting the schools to agree to send the yearbook to a person out of state with no relation to a named student: Claire simply said she'd like to donate to the schools' music and arts programs and could she also purchase the current yearbook. As a result, that day she wrote ten checks: $50 dollars in donations and $20 dollars in yearbook orders. When Tony reviewed the month's checking balance book, he let it slip that he thought that was a little steep for a wild goose chase. This of course created some tension between them. Which Claire intended to fully alleviate with tonight's special dinner.

"Finish your carrots before dessert, Adam."

Claire has good feeling about this first one to arrive. She's been wearing the caul close to her heart every day, and was just positive that tonight, she and Tony would see the face of Claire's first child.

Tony picks up the envelope and considers the sender. "You want me to open it?"

"Honestly, I want to," admits Claire, taking the envelope from him, "but I want you and Adam to be with me the first time I, we, see her face."

Tony digs into his piece of pie, "Yum . . . coconut."

Claire takes the book out of the envelope and flips through the pages until it gets to the rows and rows of the student portraits, labeled in alphabetical order. "We're looking for Tischler," she says. "Jules Tischler."

Tony and Adam watch Claire's progress while they eat pie. She thumbs through to where the "T" names begin. Her right hand methodically moves down the page, guiding her eyes so as not to miss anything. Taylor, Thomas, Townsend. Claire holds her breath, and her hand begins to tremble. Sanders, Schmidt, Simpson . . . wait . . . she might have just missed it. She goes back to the T's. Then she flips through the book a bit further. "Oh!" she says with relief, smiling at Tony and then at Adam. "That's just the ninth grade. There's also eighth and seventh grades in Colorado junior highs." Claire goes through the eighth grade and still doesn't find Tischler. Tony gets up and takes his and Adam's plates to the sink. Claire continues searching through the seventh grade.

"Time for PJ's," says Tony to Adam.

Adam puts on his best whiney voice, "But Becky does bath first."

"Well, Becky isn't here tonight. Scoot." Tony takes the book from under Claire's hands as she's still trying to find what isn't there. He sets it aside, then holds her hands in his and kisses them. She looks up at him, still bewildered. "Look, Claire, it's been over a year now. I think it's time to stop putting your time into this."

He didn't say it, but Claire has a feeling Tony thinks it's time to stop putting money toward the search as well. "But . . ."

"Hear me out." Having reached his limit, Tony interrupts her pushback, "Dr. Thomas said to acknowledge the voices, but tell them you are not going to focus on them."

Hold on a minute. What in the world is going on with Dr. Thomas? Claire's been seeing him for years. But now? Now's the time he calls Tony? Now that she's so close to finding Jules. What the hell? "He told you about that?"

"Yes, he called me about your recent appointment. Thought it was important you completely shift away from the Diazepam. For good."

The diversity of medications that Claire has been on and off and on again ever since Jules was taken, has been honestly somewhat staggering. But it takes a lot of experimentation to find what really works. And most of the time she takes nothing. Did Dr. Thomas mention that? And though she told Tony about hearing Jules's voice calling out to her in the beginning, Claire's been keeping all the subsequent episodes to herself for some time now. She didn't want Tony to think that was a factor in her search effort. Everyone knows taking action based on hearing voices is what crazy people do. But thanks, Dr. Thomas, here we are.

"It's time to make arrangements with Becky and agree on the last day she babysits while you're at home."

"She's been helping me. More than just playing with Adam."

Tony nods, but continues with his direction, "Two more weeks is reasonable. Gives you and Adam both time to adjust."

"But we're so close." *Can't he see? We can't possibly stop now.*

"You've said yourself you'd like to spend more time with him before he starts school in the fall."

Claire did previously share with Tony that she's had moments of guilt around trying to balance attending to Adam with attending to Jules. "Tony, I just know something is wrong. She needs me to find her."

Tony is clearly not sympathetic to any reason associated with woman's intuition. He's flat out said it's just a thing women say to get their way more often.

Tony stands firm, "It's best to shut this down for now."

Walking away from the conversation, Claire slaps the yearbook down on her search desk.

Claire enters the front door juggling her purse, grocery bag, and the latest package from the Post Office. Adam and Becky are in the front room looking through books and coloring. Adam doesn't run up to greet her and hug her legs anymore. That's a good thing, right? With his going to kindergarten in just a handful of months.

"Need help?" asks Becky.

"I got it," says Claire. She waves the large envelope, "It's the last yearbook!"

The week has been heavy with the mood of disappointments. After the complete flop with the first yearbook hopeful, the next day Claire woke up and tossed out the rest of the Impossible Pie, which did make her feel momentarily better. When she went to the Post Office, three more yearbooks had arrived. She sat in the car and scanned through those so the disappointment was at least more contained.

She asked Becky to double check them for her while they were discussing the approach of her last day. It would be next Wednesday, which works out well since Tony would be out of town for five days on a long haul. Becky asked Adam all the things he wanted to do with their last play days. Adam thoughtfully outlined all of his favorite activities and visibly anticipated their time together. Claire started having stormy dreams again and quit eating dinner. She knew that if Jules wasn't in this last yearbook—well, it would be a lot like starting over again, but now with an extra helping of guilt.

"Fingers crossed," says Becky, holding up her hands to show her set of crossed fingers.

"Fingers crossed," says Adam, attempting to mimic his best friend but not quite getting both hands doing the symbol of luck at the same time.

Claire kicks off her shoes, drops her purse, then shoves the whole unpacked grocery bag straight into the fridge. And takes her mail to the desk. She opens the envelope and pulls out the Boltz Junior High School yearbook. "Welp, Jules, the last one . . ." Claire holds her hand to her heart, pressing the silk pouch against her skin. At least she will always have the connection the caul provides. Claire takes that energy and runs her hand over the cover of the Boltz book, as if she could magically will it to have Jules's picture. She thumbs through to where the "T" names begin. Her right hand methodically moves down the page, guiding her eyes so as not to miss anything. Taylor, Thomas, then—Tischler, Jules.

Claire holds her breath, and her eyes go out of focus as they tear up. Her hand trembles as she slides her finger across the portraits to the last one on the row. The girl in the black-and-white photo smiles back at her. "I've found her!"

Becky and Adam come running.

"Are you sure?" asks Becky.

Claire's chin quivers, "Ye-es." She points at the photo.

Becky scoots over the book and follows the name across with her finger. "This girl . . ." she begins.

"Is my daughter," Claire finishes, pulling Adam close to her and squeezing him tight. "I'm more relieved than I've felt in my entire life." Claire clings to Adam as she sobs.

"Well," says Becky. "She looks happy and healthy, and geez I don't know, maybe a lot like her father?" Claire starts laughing. "Check out the curly hair and freckles!"

"Freckles?" says Adam, not completely sure what that is.

Now everyone's laughing. Claire remembers Zach's wavy hair.

Claire circles the photo and is immediately obsessed with trying to imprint it in her mind and heart. Oddly, she senses a kind of resistance within her. This just isn't how she's imagined Sarah. She's been longing to see this face for so many years now. Who could ever predict the emotions that would arise? It's reasonable to assume not all the emotions would be pure joy. Claire whispers as if to convince herself, "This is my daughter."

She can still hear Jules's voice in her mind. It was her calling that started this active search, brought her the caul, and brought her this photographic evidence of not only her daughter's wellbeing but her very location. Any given day Jules can be found at Boltz Junior High School. Claire's never been there for her daughter before, but my God, this time will be different. She is *never* letting her daughter be taken from her again. Not by an agency, not by family or social pressure, not even by her own uncomfortable emotional reactions. This is just the beginning of her relationship with Jules Tischler. Claire whispers again to the photo, "Jules, I am your first mother, and I am coming to help you."

"Are you really going to go?" asks Becky. "To Colorado?"

Claire knows that on any given day Jules is at Boltz Junior High

School. Is it even an option to *not* go? Ha! Claire has every intention of seeing Jules with her own eyes. Hopefully even talking with her. Maybe even touching her. Whatever Jules agrees to. Their friendship will begin on Jules's terms, on her turf. "Yes. I am."

"I can take care of Adam." Adam climbs up on Becky's lap and gives her a huge sloppy kiss on the check. "Mom said I could stay overnight here if you ever needed to travel for your search while Tony's away working."

"She said that?"

"Well ya. We're all rooting for you, Claire."

Claire just nods and chokes a bit on the lump in her throat. They say reunion is just pure emotion, but they don't tell you what emotion. Relief, gratitude, joy . . . fear. This particular moment's emotion is a whirlwind of determination.

"I've found her," says Claire, twisting the phone cord around her finger. "I followed everything you said, Lisa. I'm looking at her yearbook picture right now." Claire doesn't know whether she is proud of herself or scared. "What I don't have is her home address. I could just go to her school and ask Jules for it, straight up." Claire is beginning to create a mental checklist of what to pack for the trip.

"Wait. Hold on, Claire. You know the ethical dilemma you're messing with here, right? You, a complete stranger, walking up to a child and announcing you're their first mother could be very damaging, to you both. You have no idea if she even knows she's adopted."

Claire knew Lisa would provide a solid reality check, but she wasn't expecting that Lisa would try and talk her out of this. "Of course. I know, you're right . . . It's just, if I can't be her mother, I'd like to be her . . . friend. By her choice, her friend."

"Look. Besides the very real emotional trauma that an unsupervised, surprise encounter like that could incur, the child cannot realistically give you consent under those conditions. You know that, Claire."

Claire taps her pen on the steno pad. Yes, she's been made aware of these things many times by the various CUB publications and meetings. But this is different. Jules was already the first to reach out.

"Have you tried working with the agency? Many agencies are altering their communication protocols. Ask them to contact the parents. Who knows, maybe they're open to releasing additional information, or even allowing an in-person introduction visit."

"I've done all that." Claire realizes that therein lies the real issue. If the parents won't reply to a letter from the agency, why would they reply to a letter from her? If she's really going to answer Jules's call for help, she's just going to have to go directly to Jules, in person. There's really no other way. "The adoptive parents aren't responding. Lisa, there is urgency here. I just *know* something is wrong in Jules's life. She needs help."

"How do you know?"

Well, I hear her voice calling out to me, for God's sake. Asking . . . begging for my help. How does a rational person describe that? "I just know. Lisa, her information came to me for a reason. How rare is it that searches come around this quickly?"

"It is rare," admits Lisa. "Your search effort has been remarkable. Which is all the more reason *not* to do something impulsive at this point. The kind of interaction you're talking about could destroy any possibility of a future relationship."

"I think the adoptive family *wants* me to find them. They announced showers and birthday parties in the town newspaper, for Christ's sake." Claire's neck is starting to ache from the tension in her shoulders from clenching the phone. It's all so obvious. "Lisa, I think this is all coming together for a reason. I feel I am *supposed* to go to her."

Lisa lays down a bargaining chip, "With the information you have, there is a way to get the adoptive parents' home address. You don't have to go anywhere."

Now, this is exactly the kind of support Claire expected from this conversation. Finally.

"We've developed a network within the DMV. You just send what you know so far concerning the family names and locations and enclose $30. If the information you have is reliable, they find a match and send your PO box a copy of the adoptive parents' DMV records."

After Claire writes down the DMV contact's name and address, she starts to outline her *own* plans. This is how it's going to go. Becky stays overnight Friday and Saturday night to take care of Adam. Claire mails the family information and $30 cash in an overnight delivery package and enclose a pre-paid overnight response envelope. Meanwhile, she can use her *own* credit card to book a flight to Colorado. Once there, she can orient herself to Jules's neighborhood based on the information she's already received from Beverly the real estate agent. She'll call Becky and get the Tischlers' home address over the phone. Then she'll see Jules's beautiful face in person and be back before Tony returns to town, completely avoiding the need to ask anyone's permission to see her own daughter. This can work.

"I recommend your first contact with them is via letter," says Lisa, being very insistent. "Do you understand, Claire? Write the parents and introduce yourself."

"Understood," says Claire, to the person who taught her to bold-faced lie. She presses the caul to her heart, almost there.

PART 3

The Colorado morning air is crisp, the sky clear. The hotel is just a mile away, so even though school starts at 8 a.m., it was easy to get here early, well before the teachers and kids arrived. Claire's already driven around the campus a couple times, gone to a coffee shop, and now is back. The parking lot was essentially empty when she first arrived, so Claire parked at the curb across the street from Boltz Junior High, hoping to just blend in as one of the locals. Claire's coffee balances on the dash of the rental car, steaming up her view through the windshield.

Even though her nerves are fried with excitement and fear, Claire likes the feeling of being here, on her own, taking charge. She feels stronger and more capable than she has in a long time. After mentally envisioning this encounter thousands of times, in just a few minutes Claire will see Jules with her own two eyes.

There's just enough time for one more review of her notes. Claire opens her steno pad and reads through the name and address information Becky gave her over the phone this morning as she read from the DMV record copies. Just to be safe, Claire memorized the adoptive parents' names, phone number, and address, in case someone decides to ask for proof of relationship. The yearbook sits on the passenger seat, open to the page of Jules's circled photo. Claire has studied the staff photos enough she can pretty much recognize the teachers as they come in for work. Coach Stafford is standing at the side of the building next to the game field. Kids in gym clothes are gathering around him. Various pods of kids around the grounds begin to form as they wait for the doors to open. It won't be long now. Claire ponders if it's too late to turn back. She gives herself a brief but effective pep-talk in the rearview mirror, "Jules is counting on you. Hold it together."

She pulls out the one-sheet Beverly sent her of a house for sale in the Tischlers' neighborhood that Beverly sent her. Stapled to it is a copy from the county records office of the property lots for the whole neighborhood. Bev really is the best realtor in town. Claire penned a circle around Jules's house lot but was still undecided about just showing up unannounced to their home. She hopes Jules would invite her there.

The school doors open and the line of busses streams kids into the building as the first bell rings. Claire tightens her ponytail scarf and straightens her blouse. She fixes her lipstick in the rearview mirror, then rolls on a little perfume. All set to pose as just another person coming into the school that morning, Claire drives across the street and parks in a visitor's spot.

One more bell, and the kids will be in their homeroom class. That's when Claire is going to call Jules to the office, and that's where they'll meet. In the safety of her own school, surrounded by her teachers and friends. There is absolutely nothing threatening about this. It will be just fine. Claire pulls a $10 bill from her purse and bookmarks it in the yearbook. The grounds become quiet, and the homeroom bell rings. It's time.

Upon entering the building, Claire immediately sees the Main Office sign and walks in the door. There is a mother at the counter that looks like she's waiting for something. Her toddler is hanging onto her leg and looks directly at Claire with curiosity. Claire sits down in the plastic molded school chair next to the counter to wait her turn. She opens the yearbook to the circled page and looks through the office windows with anxious expectation. It's possible she might see Jules walking past in the hallway. However possible that may be, the hallways have already cleared for the most part. Homeroom announcements begin over the PA system.

Claire redirects her attention inside the office and notices a student helper is handing a yearbook to the mother who's been waiting. Hold on. Claire squints her eye to zero in on the student who is barely tall enough to see fully over the counter. Could that be . . . Jules? Right here, right now? Claire's heart leaps into her throat. Her eyes wide, she flips opens her yearbook to the circled picture and compares. She looks up to the student behind the counter and down to the book several times. Yes. Oh my God yes. It's her. They're in the same room together. Breathing the same air.

Just then, the mother of the toddler says, "Thank you, Sue. I don't know how he lost the first one."

"You're welcome, Mrs. Hardy. It's no big deal. We order extras."

Claire involuntarily springs up to standing and blurts, "Sue?"

The toddler, his mother, and the other office workers look over at Claire.

Sue purses her lips with a bit of a smirk and shifts her eyes between the toddler and Claire. "I'm Sue."

An administrator sitting in the back office stands up and walks over.

Claire looks at the administrator, Mrs. Hardy, down at the staring toddler, then back at the yearbook in her hand. She points to the picture and calls out the obvious, "This picture says you're Jules Tischler."

Everyone exhales with dismissal and goes back to what they were doing while Sue explains.

"Ya. Me and Jules's pictures got swapped again." Clearly this is not news to anyone else and Sue isn't upset at all, in fact she seems pretty entertained. Sue acknowledges Claire's disbelief. "It isn't the first time," she continues with the backstory. "Me and Jules," she says with her fingers crossed indicating their close friendship, "we've been confusing teachers and students ever since the first day of kindergarten."

Claire's mouth is still open as she remains stunned and confused.

"Tisch*l*er and Tisch*n*er?" Sue emphasizes the pronunciation to make the issue crystal clear. "I'm the shortest in class, she's the tallest." She makes the letter "L" with her hand, and speaks in a low whisper, like this is the secret tip, "The 'L' is for the ta*ll* gir*l*." Sue now wears an ear-to-ear grin across her freckled face. "We just tell everyone we're twins." The administrator smiles. Mrs. Hardy smiles. Even the shy toddler smiles, fingers in his mouth.

Claire closes her mouth and darts out of the office without another word.

Somehow, and she honestly can't remember how, Claire finds herself parked at the back of a Sears parking lot. She turns the rearview mirror inward and gives herself a talking to.

"What the hell were you thinking?! Go to the school? Sweet Jesus, Claire. You were inches away from touching that girl's arm. A breath away from saying you were her mother." Claire looks into the eyes of her reflection, "You could have ruined yet another family." Claire rests her elbow on the steering wheel and holds her head and covers her face in shame.

Claire opens the yearbook to the page of who she knows now is Sue. *How did you miss this?* One of those ridiculous family congratulations ads was the worst distraction. It made an odd break on the page so that Sue's picture and Jules's picture were on separate pages. Probably why the editor missed it as well. Sue was so easygoing about it, who knows, maybe the girls planned it as some kind of cute prank. "Why the hell did you never turn the page?"

Claire pulls a pen out of her purse and circles the correct picture on the other side of the page—the one labeled Sue Tischner that is really Jules Tischler.

And then it happens. All the sensations and awareness Claire knew she would pick up from a photograph of her daughter flood into her heart. Jules's eyes are slanted at the exact same angle as her father's. In Claire's own minds eye, she can see Zach's face morph into Jules. The slope of Jules's nose is exactly like Aunt Georgia's nose. Her hair is long, straight, and blond, just like Claire's. And though she presents a polite smile, and her jawline gives the impression she has it all together, Jules's gaze is dimmed. A young woman who sees the world through the grey clouds of grief. It's the same gaze Claire has seen in the mirror these last thirteen years. Claire knows with every fiber of her being, this is her daughter and it's been her voice calling out for help.

Claire looks in the rearview mirror again to remind herself, "Never, they said, never directly contact the child." That doesn't mean she's not going to be there for Jules. This time, she will answer her baby girl's cry for help.

Claire bites her lip, looks around in all directions, wondering how she's going to do that. Finding herself in the rearview mirror she knows, "You *have* to face the parents."

Chapter 21

It's ten o'clock and Jo is still in the floral housecoat she ordered from last season's Sears catalogue. She sits on the kitchen stool balancing the phone receiver on her shoulder while tugging at the cord reaching across the counter, flicking it to get a little more slack. "Yes, Sharon, it's in his backpack." Her toast pops up, and she dips her knife into the margarine tub, spreading heavily. "I can't thank you enough for driving Karl to therapy today." A glint of sun reflecting off the hood of a dove-grey Chrysler Cordoba catches Jo's eye as she sips the last of her coffee and watches the car drive by. "Sleeping in is exactly what I needed."

They just got back last night from her dad's funeral. Jo's mother didn't hide the sense of relief she and everyone in the family were feeling, knowing Emi's grueling years-long battle with stomach cancer had finally ended. The Pythian Sisters provided sandwiches and lemonade for family and friends after the burial. The conversation often cited the idea that he hung on so long just to see Karl's recovery. Jo's brother stayed to look after Mom for a couple weeks, so the Tischlers decided to head home right away for what feels like a new beginning since Karl's motorcycle accident.

Will is getting his men back on track with the latest house remodel job. Jules announced she's dropping scouting and wants to focus on an experiment for the state science fair. And even though Karl still isn't talking, well other than curse words, he is walking reliably without the walker and is ready for the next stage of therapy. Finally, today Jo can truly take a rest.

She can't remember the last time she had the house to herself. It seems so quiet. Jules isn't in the upstairs shower, Karl isn't watching game shows on TV in the living room, Will isn't drilling or hammering something in the family room. Laundry's not tumbling. Hanging out barefoot in a nightgown for a morning feels like a luxury. Jo breathes a long, releasing exhale as she realizes how beautiful and well-manicured the front yard is. Her eyes well up thinking about how fortunate she is to have such supportive neighbors. Everything has been taken care of while the family was gone: the yard is spotless, the mail separated, and a couple different casseroles are in the fridge. She noticed there was a lasagna, something she's never made before. That will be interesting to try out on Karl. Maybe she'll bake Will's favorite: chocolate chip cookies.

Jo walks around the counter to hang up the receiver, "See you at four." Ready to get dressed and move on with the day, she grabs the coffee pot and pours herself a second cup to bring with her upstairs. No one else in the house is allowed to bring any form of food or drink up to their bedrooms. Mother's privilege. Mostly because she's the only one who reliably cleans up after herself. Up the first flight of stairs, Jo stops at the landing to find the front door wide open. Well, of course, Will *was* born in a barn. Out the front screen door there's the grey Chrysler again, this time going in the opposite direction, the young woman driver looks around at the houses and back down at a paper in her hand. Jo shrugs off the lost woman and closes the door to the outside problems of the day.

Jo catches her big toe with the door, triggering a childhood memory of being scolded for not having shoes on while in their dingy old garage. She brought coffee out to her dad, who was at his workbench tinkering with electronics. "Dammit, Jo, you'll step on something and get lockjaw," the dreaded disease that could be brought on by almost any Cerny household incident. A strange awareness comes over Jo as she realizes memories of her dad now that he's passed have somehow become sad memories, where before they were just . . . memories.

Jo sets her cup on the windowsill as she begins to make the bed and sees the grey Chrysler is now parked directly in front of her house. A young woman dressed in a beautiful but loud yellow dress walks across the yard and rings the doorbell.

New Avon lady? She's not carrying her blue case. Amy did mention last time she was here to deliver Jo's Skin So Soft order, that she was retiring and there would soon be a new girl covering the neighborhood. Jo looks at herself in the dresser mirror, she hasn't even combed her hair. She will not be tempted by those darned adorable cologne figurines. Will already has quite a collection, but really only wears the scent from the green glass golfer. Besides, there just isn't money for those things anymore, not with Karl's medical bills. No browsing today, not even samplers. But the sales magazine to look at later, would be OK. Jo goes back down the stairs and opens the door, and talks through the closed screen door, "Yes?"

Claire was in this neighborhood yesterday morning checking out the house for sale. She had no idea she was just down the street from the Tischler household. When she called Becky that morning, the overnight envelope with the DMV information hadn't arrived yet. Claire decided to spend the day checking out what kind of city her daughter has been growing up in. Beverly, her real estate agent friend, provided information on the one home for sale that was zoned for Boltz Junior High. She mentioned the seller's wife had been the local Girl Scout Troop leader for the past five years. Claire was tempted to ask for a tour of the home but decided to just drive by the property instead.

Last night when Claire called home to give phone kisses to Adam, Becky was excited to announce she did receive the DMV records. Thank God for the perfect timing Claire willed into existance! Wilfried Karl Tischler and Johanka Černý Tischler, apparently with no middle name. Jules of course didn't have a DMV record, so maybe today she would learn Jules's full name.

Claire puts her hand on her heart over the little silk pouch, amazed that here she is on the very street where Wilfried, Johanka, Jules, and Karl live. Claire finally parks up along the front curb of the house and looks in the mirror. She sees herself look back with terror in her eyes. "Only drove around the block three times." Walking up to the front door felt like walking in a funhouse, but without railings to hold onto. Claire is impressed by the well-kept yard. Once on the doorstep, she watches her hand as if it's moving in slow motion, raising up to push the doorbell.

The person inside stomps down the stairs. The door opens and a woman in her forties stands behind the storm door. "Yes?" she says as a greeting.

Claire winces, feeling the sting of what seems to be an immediate rejection, as she wasn't expecting to be spoken to through a screen. She wonders if she should respond now or wait for the screen door to open. The woman just stands there and snaps shut the top snap on her housecoat. "Mrs. Wilfried Karl Tischler? Johanka?"

"I'm Jo."

She's short, with red hair and blue eyes, matching the DMV description Becky gave. She has bedhead and not a stitch of makeup on. Oddly, she looks like she could be Sue Tischner's mother. But this is Jules's adopted mother, and she's just . . . a regular mom. Claire realizes her gaze is causing some discomfort for Jo but she can't seem to remember the opening words that she rehearsed in the hotel.

"You are . . ."

Claire swallows and looks down at herself, smooths out her sunshine yellow dress. She bends her knees and shrugs down a bit to accommodate for the good seven- or eight-inch difference in their height.

"I'm Jules's birthmother."

Clearly these are words that Jo never thought she'd hear. Claire watches shock and horror wash over Jo, as her body stiffens, and she steps back with one foot, apparently losing her balance. Jo's eyes widen and her mouth drops open. It's as though the worst person in the world appeared at her door. "My name is Claire. Mrs. Anthony Brooks. I know this is a shock."

Jo grips the front door handle behind her with white knuckles. "You have no business here." She's never in her life closed the front door on someone.

Claire recognizes she is one swift moment from being shut out. "Mrs. Tischler, I . . . I asked Child Horizons to contact you. I . . . they . . . never heard back."

"If Child Horizons asked me for something, I'd see to it."

"I came here in person to respectfully request your response to their inquiry."

"Claire, is it? I don't know how you know a single thing about us. Stay away from my daughter and our family." Jo steps back to close the front door.

Claire cries in desperation, "Mrs. Tischler. Please!" Claire puts her hand on the screen door handle as though she would open it.

Both women look down at her hand. Would she really try to force her way in?

Claire takes her hand back and speaks with as calm a tone as she can manage. "I've come so far. I just need to know if she's all right."

Jo pauses from her intention to slam the door shut.

"It's crazy, but there are days when I feel what Jules feels. Lately, it feels like . . . grief."

Claire and Jo look directly at each other. Both see furrowed brows, dark circles from lack of sleep, shoulders high with tension. As though looking into a mirror, each woman recognizes the emotional exhaustion that comes with motherly concern.

"Mrs. Tischler, my heart's held this question for thirteen years. I only ask for what's right according to . . . human decency. Please won't you tell me, is Jules safe?"

Jo answers cautiously, nodding, "We loves Jules. The whole family does. Of course she's safe."

Claire can't hold back her tears of relief and gratitude. Her hand tries to steady her quivering chin, "Thank you."

Jo opens the screen door indicating an offer for Claire to come in.

Claire tucks her chin and bravely walks in. She stands in the entry; her shoulders settle down as she releases a long exhale of relief. Relief to hear firsthand that Jules is alive and loved. Relief that this woman, her mother, is protective, but also open and strong enough to respond with compassion to what appears at her front door. Claire reaches into her purse and, attempting to regain composure, pulls out a Kleenex.

Jo considers Claire's shaking body and offers more detail in an effort to further calm her. "Jules has many friends and does well in school."

Claire breaths out a long exhale of relief as she corrects her posture to regain composure.

Jo leads Claire down the stairs. "I'm calling my husband," says Jo.

"Of course." Claire intentionally tries to notice everything she can about Jules's home. They go past the front room, which is designed for regular informal concerts with a piano prominently placed across from a velvet upholstered sofa in a room without competition of a TV. They continue on into the back addition, set up as a family recreation room. Claire looks at the treadmill rigged up with a safety harness and a folded wheelchair next to it. Shoved up against the opposite wall is a standard-sized ping-pong table, unusable in that position.

"The kids love that thing. They did, until . . . the motorcycle accident. I've been thinking of putting it in the garage, but maybe they'll play again. We're still hopeful." Jo indicates with her hand for Claire to have a seat in their most comfortable chair.

Jo opens the door to the end table to reveal a stack of family photo albums. She wiggles out the large white faux leather–bound one near the bottom of the stack. "You can look through this while I make the call."

Claire accepts the photo album with a nod and a polite smile. Her heart pounds with disbelief, that somehow in under a minute from entering their home, she has in her hands the very thing she's ached for. It's as though Jo prepared the story of Jules's life just for this moment.

Jo stumbles a bit as she leaves the room—her body wanting to move more quickly than her feet can keep up.

Jo runs into the kitchen and dials the number to Will's office, her finger flicking the rotary with each number. The phone rings twice. *Pick up!* It rings twice more.

"Tischler Remodeling." Will answers the phone in a professional tone.

"Will?"

"Who'd you expect?" says Will, sounding slightly annoyed.

"Your secretary?"

"Do you need to speak to her? She's on her 'break,' " says Will in a sarcastic voice. Pat won't answer the phone when she's on her officially designated "twenty-minute break" even though most of the time her so-called break is just her sitting at the desk smoking like she does all the time anyway.

"Will, come home. Now." Jo is talking in an intense kind of whisper, not at all like her typical loud voice.

"What is it? Is Karl OK?"

"He's fine. Sharon took him to therapy."

Will pulls out a cigarette, lights it.

"Will, *she's* here . . . in our house."

"Who's in the house?"

"Jules's birthmother." There is silence on the other end. "Did you hear me?"

"Are you sure that's who it is?"

"I don't know how she found us." Jo takes in a deep breath and looks around the room as if Claire might be sneaking up on her as they speak. "She knows my full name. She knows our address. She just walked right up to our front door. And now, she's in the rec room."

"Jesus, Jo, you let her in? She's probably crazy or . . . on drugs. Dammit, where's your common sense?"

"Actually, she's just . . . young."

"I'm on my way."

Will slams the phone. Now what? Jo opens the fridge as a knee-jerk impulse to nervous eat. She closes the fridge. She opens it again and pulls out the Tupperware of molasses cookies she keeps on hand for unexpected visitors. If there was ever an unexpected visitor, this is it. Will seems to think it was a bad idea to have her in the house. As Jo prepares a tray to serve coffee and cookies to . . . Jules's birthmother . . . she wonders why she invited her in. It's just asking for trouble. But if you'd given up a tiny infant, it would be worth the risk of trouble, wouldn't it? To know the child was being properly taken care of. Christ, not knowing that for thirteen years would be nothing short of pure torture. Hopefully this visit will satisfy her, and she'll leave before Jules gets home.

As Jo walks toward the rec room, she can imagine that Claire will have a lot of questions. But what questions does Jo have? Jo doesn't honestly care to hear her story, of why she gave up Jules, she doesn't need any more sad stories. Jo just wants reassurance she doesn't intend to try and take Jules back.

As soon as Jo leaves the room, Claire stands up, hugging the photo album with both arms, and looks around the home that Jules lives in. Updated carpet, cleanly painted walls, skylights, a custom brick fireplace, all the features one might expect in a home owned by a master craftsman. But more than the pleasing esthetics, this home is comfortable, organized, and functional. It feels safe here. Claire feels safe with Jo. She's not so sure how she's going to feel when Wilfred arrives.

Claire walks over to the fireplace—the centerpiece of the room, with frames across the handmade mantle. There's a picture from what she assumes to be last summer. Jules and her brother Karl are in baseball caps with their field gloves on. With the physique and posture of confident athletes, they seem to be playfully elbowing each other while trying to hold still for the shot. Jules has long blond pigtails hanging around her shoulders and squints as she faces the sun. She's almost as tall as her brother and stands next to him like a competent equal. Her smile is toothy and genuine. Her checks full, like you just want to squeeze them—just like Adam's. Karl's complexion is completely different from Jules. His skin is bronze, and he has wavy jet-black hair and thick eyebrows that meet in the middle. He has the spark of mischief in his eyes and a crooked grin. They look like they belong together.

What seems to be the most recent photo is without a frame, leaning up against the ballpark photo. It's from Christmastime as a decorated tree is next to the piano in the front room. Karl and Jules are sitting on the bench together, but Karl is just a shadow of the young man at the ballpark. Jules is attempting to conceal her grimace with a polite smile. She has her arm around Karl, steadying him, as he has barely enough strength to sit up. He is slumped over, collarbones protruding, head shaved, and looking through glasses with empty eyes. The crooked grin is all that remains the same. The contrast in the two photos leaves no doubt about the depth of the tragedy. The motorcycle accident. "No wonder you're looking for your brother," whispers Claire. She sighs with relief knowing Jules wasn't harmed. Her sense of ease is short lived though, as the sadness of their family situation sinks in.

Claire goes back to the chair Jo designated and carefully opens the photo album on her lap. As she opens the large cover, the collection of memories diffuses golden rays of love combined with the bouquet of family history. Claire closes her eyes and breathes it in, a calmness coming over her.

Claire recognizes the photos that match the announcements she read in the *Wilber Republican*. The huge baby shower, Jules in her christening gown, Karl in his little white christening jumper, Halloween costumes, Czech festivals with the whole family in traditional dress, family Thanksgiving gatherings—with several long tables lined with smiling people in front of settings of fine china, and crystal and oh so much food.

There's no shame here. These were not bastard children with a lack of identity. Jules and Karl are cherished members of the family. Their faces glow with confidence in knowing exactly where they belong. These children never second guessed their safety and are simply experiencing the beauty of childhood. She reaches into the side table and pulls out several more albums.

The organization of the photos is meticulous. Each album labeled by the years the photos spanned. Claire is impressed with Jo's long-term dedication to carefully capture every precious occasion. There were dancing recital costumes, with both Karl and Jules in tap shoes. Grandma pushing them in the carriage on an old-fashioned swing set. Grandpa pulling the kids seated one in front of the other in a Radio Flyer wagon. There were birthday parties. Always beautifully themed, with at least a dozen cheerful guests. One year a circus, another year all the kids are eating cake while dripping wet in swimsuits. Would Claire love to have been there? Of course, but this wasn't her family and their traditions. Claire feels . . . happy for Jules. There were camping trips, with the kids crossing streams, starting fires, and climbing rocks. Exhausted faces peeking out from their sleeping bags all nestled up in a camper loft. Jules and Karl were both in scouting, proudly wearing badges and beads. There were science fair projects with Karl pointing to a series of plants growing in a homemade desktop planter and Jules in front of her display describing how cigarettes affect lung health. Christmas always involved a decorated tree and mountains of gifts. There were a couple of pitiful photos of the kids with chicken pox. They looked so miserable, it made Claire laugh a little. Karl and Jules were in matching pajamas with pox all over their faces, surrounded by various *World Book Encyclopedias* for entertainment. The very same *World Book* set Claire has in her home.

Claire pauses. How long has the worry sat in the pit her stomach, poisoning her body and mind? Jules has been safe and loved the whole time—learning, moving, always growing. Jules has two dedicated parents who are not only there every step of the way but clearly in this for the long haul. Claire puts her hand on her heart and feels the silk pouch that holds the membrane her body created for Sarah—the name she'd given her unborn child. Only Claire and Sarah were frozen in the trauma. Jules has been living.

Jo's love for Jules is so obvious. She's put everything she has into motherhood. And Jules receives Jo's love without hesitation. "Thank you," Claire whispers as she feels the warmth of loving gratitude arise in her throat. Claire hugs the album. She pulls out another tissue from her purse, wipes her eyes, blows her nose, and then hugs the album again before she carefully places it back into the side table.

Jo, still in her housecoat and bedhead, carries a tray with two of cups of coffee, spoons, milk and sugar containers, and a plate of perfectly shaped molasses cookies.

Claire politely takes a cookie and a coffee from the tray. "Thank you. Jo. For everything. I just . . ." A lump in Claire's throat cuts off her ability to speak.

Jo stands up and briefly touches Claire on the shoulder to acknowledge she is OK, then walks over to the fireplace mantel and retrieves a framed photo of her father standing on a dock showing off a large fish he caught.

"Fishing with their Grandpa Cerny was a favorite activity for both Karl and Jules." She looks at the photo and grins. "He always had a can of tobacco in his pocket. When Jules was little and asked him for some, he told her tobacco was really mashed worms. And that was the end of Jules's interest in chewing tobacco."

Claire shares a polite smile with Jo.

"He passed away two weeks ago. A long struggle with cancer. He willed himself to stay alive until he saw Karl recover."

"I am so sorry for your loss."

Jo's eyes tear up, and she pulls a wadded-up Kleenex from her housecoat pocket and honk-blows her nose.

"There was an accident?" asks Claire.

Jo nods. "Motorcycle accident. They said Karl had a 50 percent chance of surviving. He was in a coma for seven weeks. They said he'd never talk or walk again."

Jo's hands shake as she brings the coffee cup to her lips and takes an unsteady and audible sip. "Karl was so strong and athletic. They think that's why he was able to recover as well as he did. When he wasn't chasing girls, he and Jules were always up to something, including plenty of scrapping. If they weren't down at fossil creek or climbing trees, they were reading the encyclopedia—constantly quizzing each other. But since the accident . . ." Jo looks down and shakes her head. "He's had to start over. Relearning everything, like a baby."

Claire takes a moment to consider all the recent loss in Jo's family. Her father suffers from cancer and dies, her son's promising future turns into a prayer that he may someday learn enough to regain independence. It's unfortunate timing to additionally have her daughter's first mother come knocking at the door. "I think that's the pain I felt," says Claire.

Jo tilts her head, not following.

"The feeling that brought me here . . . I think it was Jules missing her brother."

They both sit in silence as Jo's gaze drifts away—not able to imagine a connection between Jules and Claire.

"I have a son too," offers Claire.

Jo seems surprised and leans forward with interest.

Claire pulls her wallet out of her purse. "I'm married now, and we have a little boy of our own. His name is Adam." She opens it to show Jo the photo of Adam.

Jo smiles as she inspects the photo. "He's beautiful."

"Every time I look at him I can't help but wonder about the well-being of his *sister*."

Jo looks up at Claire with the light of a new awareness on her face. Jules has another sibling.

"He's going to start kindergarten in the fall. He doesn't understand much, but he knows I'm here to find his sister."

Jo is silent, processing.

Claire shifts her knees toward Jo and leans in, "They lied to me about you."

Jo shifts her lips to one side.

Claire continues, "They said they placed Jules with a mother and father she would physically resemble, and Jo, you really don't look anything like her."

"Me?" Jo let's out a little snort, "Short and red-headed with freckles on every inch of my body?" She purses her lips and shakes her head, "No. Jules is tall with those long legs, thin . . ." She opens her hand toward Claire, "like you."

"Jo," says Claire, awkwardly putting down her cookie on the side of the tray. "There's something I want you . . . and Jules . . . to know."

Jo looks up with caution.

Heat from her heart floods Claire's face as she attempts to form words.

Jo puts down her coffee, her expression shifting to concern.

Claire whispers, "I didn't give her up."

The whisper echoes in Jo's head as her toes grip the carpet and her hands clench around the coffee cup. She anticipates Claire's next words will be demands to take Jules back.

Claire continues, seemingly confirming Jo's fear, "There wasn't a shred of consent in the surrender."

Jo feels her defenses begin to build. Why is Claire really here? Is there really any way to bring fairness to such a reprehensible, coercive event that occurred over a decade ago? "We always told Jules you loved her so much, you wanted her to be with a family that could take the best care of her. I believe that's still true, don't you?"

Claire often wondered if she could have given Jules a similar quality of life had she raised her. As Tony's wife, absolutely, yes, they would be the family that could take best care of her daughter. But before she got married, well, that situation was temporary. But Jo is missing the point. For the Tischlers' beautiful family to form, a previous family had to be broken apart, denied the chance to be together, and Claire suffered as part of that destruction. "Child Horizons and the whole world. Everyone convinced me I wasn't capable of raising a child without a husband. They told me to do the impossible—to forget I even had a daughter." Claire pauses and looks down, thinking of her time as an airline stewardess when she actually tried to forget. "Jo, who could do that?"

Jo has no words. She looks at the pictures of Jules and Karl on the fireplace and bites at her nails. Of course, no one could. "The kids mean everything to us. Everything." After struggling with infertility for a decade, Child Horizons was a godsend for Will and Jo. The children brought a depth of purpose and meaning into their lives far beyond what they ever thought was possible. Jo pauses until she has eye contact with Claire. "Without you," acknowledges Jo, "we would never have known that kind of love."

There's something that happens when you discover the truth about someone—it changes everything.

"I'm no threat to your family, Jo. I would never interfere with the lives of people I care so much about."

The storm door creaks. The front door is thrown open with such force it bangs against the entry wall. The women look at each other as they listen to the sounds of a man entering his household. Thunderous stomping down the stairs takes over the beat of Claire's heart and she stiffens in her chair. The hall closet door opens. Then slams with the sound of something banging against the wall and falling to the floor.

Will bursts into the back room and grabs onto his belt with both hands, feet apart, ready to fight for everything he loves, "Why are you in my home?" His words reverberate in the skylights.

Claire grabs her purse and jumps up to her feet, assessing the best way to run past him if she had to.

Jo stands up and positions herself between Will and Claire.

"Will, this is Claire. She's here from . . ." Jo looks to Claire to fill in this detail which she has managed to overlook until now.

Claire's voice is barely audible, "Idaho?"

"Idaho." Jo looks at Will like that should make everything immediately better.

Will's rage quickly turns to confusion as he evaluates the scene before him. "And against all common sense, Jo let you in, and," he looks over at the coffee table, "offered you cookies." Will turns to Jo in disbelief.

Jo raises an eyebrow.

Will stares again at Claire, but asks in a slightly more controlled tone, "What do you want?"

Claire realizes Will is here to settle the problem. It's time to say exactly what she came for. "I want a continuing flow of information regarding Jules, so I know how she's doing."

There is silence as everyone absorbs her demand.

Claire clears her throat and holds her chin up, now remembering the words she'd practiced, "I'm grateful to have such a loving family raising Jules. I came all this way because I can't go on pretending she's not part of my life."

Jo and Will look at each other. They knew that Jules never felt part of her birthmother's life, she was such a tiny baby when they brought her home. They never even thought her birthmother considered Jules part of *her* life.

"The secrets need to stop. I want my husband and my son to learn the whole and honest truth about their family. Truth is where love begins, no one can convince me otherwise."

The three of them look at each other and share the unexpected bond of a common philosophy.

"Truth is important," agrees Will, coming up with a solution. "Jo writes an annual Christmas letter." He looks to Jo.

"Yes. I send a picture of the kids and an update letter every year." She looks at Claire, "I'm happy to add you to the mailing list."

Claire gives Jo a brief smile of gratitude.

"OK then," says Will, ready to wrap this up. "Jo, can you get Claire a pen and paper? Let's get her address."

Jo walks over to the desk in the corner of the room and grabs a notepad as directed and hands it to Claire with a nod.

Will and Jo watch silently as Claire writes her address. "I appreciate this more than you know, but . . . I was hoping Jules might update me herself."

"No," says Will.

Claire holds her mouth with both hands and looks to Jo. "I'd like us to have the chance to become friends someday."

"Now is not the time for Jules," says Will again. Jo softens with empathy for Claire but supports her husband's perspective.

"Claire, you understand Jules is going through a lot right now," says Jo.

"If she hasn't already, Jules *will* reach a point where she needs to know her full identity," says Claire. "Including the opportunity to know her brother."

Will looks over at the picture of Jules and Karl on the fireplace, digesting the idea of relationships available to Jules.

"I came here to help Jules. To make sure she was safe," says Claire. "I found a beautiful loving family, who understands all the complexities of what making a child feel safe really means, and . . ."

"When she turns eighteen," interrupts Will. "The right time for us to give your information to Jules is when she's eighteen."

"But that's . . . five more years." Claire's voice drips off in despair. She covers her mouth, still trying to take in Will's decision.

"Jules must choose, Claire," says Jo.

Claire knows Jo is right. For their friendship to have a chance, Jules must be in a position to make the first steps. But five more years? She stands there, looking to her shoes, feeling like pouting, and doing everything she can to not burst into tears with a full-on tantrum.

"We almost lost our son," says Will as he wipes a tear under his glasses with his thumb. "We are all still recovering from that. I won't allow Jules to be put in a position for something she's not ready for." Will steps back and clears his throat. "I won't have it, Claire," says Will in a tone that borderlines as a threat. "We'll give Jules your information when she turns eighteen and Jo will send the annual letter."

Jo turns to Claire, indicating that that's as far as this negotiation is going to go.

Claire snaps her purse shut, acknowledging it's time for her to leave. She stands up chest to chest with Will. "Your anger . . ." She gulps for a bit of air. "I would've been disappointed with anything less."

Will is caught off guard by this expression of love and devotion for his daughter. He looks to Jo for validation of his comprehension of Claire's intentions. Jo nods with a bittersweet smile. Will looks down as he summons the discipline to do what he knows he has to do.

"I can only imagine how hard this is for you," says Will, "but to be clear. You will not come to our home again."

Claire looks at Will, and then at Jo, and drops her head in submissive agreement.

Jo reaches out and touches Claire's arm, to support her on the way out. She opens the storm door and walks out onto the doorstep with Claire. Claire pledges to Jo, "I've waited this long, and I will continue to wait . . . for the day Jules chooses to contact me."

* * *

Jo and Will watch the defeated young woman walk back to her car and drive away. Jo is relieved this encounter is over and wonders if it ended well.

"Did we do the right thing?" says Jo. "She is the one who gave us our baby girl." When it comes to family, you can't make decisions based on fear, you have to make them based on hope and love. Was the decision to turn away Jules's birthmother based on fear? Jo considers the idea of telling Jules about Claire sooner than later. Jules would see her birthmother is loving, capable, beautiful, young. There are many things Claire can teach Jules that Jo just can't relate to. Like what's involved in having sex before marriage. Or what it's like to be pregnant and give birth. Jules has inquired about these topics before, and Jo realizes her responses were shallow and lack wisdom that comes from experience. If Jules knew Claire, it's possible she could gain meaningful information and advice. Would Jules want to go live with Claire? Would Jules love her? Jo shakes off this whole train of thought. It doesn't really matter. They've already reached an agreement about waiting until Jules is eighteen. So that's that.

Sensation is finally coming back into Jo's body, as she feels the cold of the cement front step beneath her bare feet and the gentle breeze of springtime on her skin. She holds the neck of her housecoat closed.

But Jules has another brother. Is it right to keep information about her blood relatives a secret? Jo and Will understand fully the bond between siblings: full-blood, half-blood, zero-blood relation—none of that matters between brothers and sisters. It never did between Jules and Karl; they wouldn't have it any other way.

"What if she comes back?" asks Jo. "Do you think she'll keep her word?"

Will opens the storm door to the house and holds it open for Jo, "I think she's satisfied."

*   *   *

Claire unpins the cards from her search board and hands them to Adam, who slam dunks each one at a time into the trash can. *Mr. Rogers* is playing on the TV in the front room and Adam sings along to it. "I'm learning to shout," he sings in an overly loud voice. "I'm getting it out." Claire sings the last bit with him, "I'm learning to know the truth. I'm learning to tell the truth. Discovering the truth will make. me. free."

The trolly rings: "The Neighborhood of Make Believe!" Adam runs into the living room to plop himself down on the couch.

Claire raises her eyebrows, impressed he strung all those syllables together beautifully. She dumps the junior high yearbooks into the trash and jams in all the microform copies of newspapers. Did all this really help Jules? Did her time with Jules's parents make a difference? Time will tell. Meanwhile, the voices that interrupted her connection with Adam have left her alone. Maybe Mr. Rogers is right. Where would the sadness and anger go if they were never let out?

The front door bursts open, "Claire, Claire, turn on the TV!" Becky rushes into the breakfast nook. She assesses the empty wall and overflowing trash can. "Wow. Taking it all down."

"Don't need it anymore," says Claire. And that was that.

"I guess not," says Becky. "Check this out." Becky goes to the TV and turns the channel to *Donahue*. "Sorry, buddy," she says to Adam, who crosses his arms and presses out his lower lip.

"You know I don't watch talk shows," says Claire.

"Look. He's interviewing birthmothers."

Sure enough, the stage was lined with brave women describing their experience in surrendering their children. Claire has heard stories similar to hers at the local CUB meetings, but this is national TV. Donahue speaks softly into the microphone he has perched on his torso, "Even if subconsciously, an agency might lean on a pregnant teenager to surrender a baby, especially a white baby, because of the tremendous demand for those babies . . . there is money involved in this."

"Wow," says Claire as she adjusts her favorite orange head scarf. "So we're saying it all out loud now."

"So you *do* still have something for your wall," says Becky. "The adoption reform work."

Claire picks up a drawing Adam made her for a welcome home gift. It's of their family—a stick figure boy inside the house holds a circle cookie, a stick figure woman dressed in a yellow triangle is carrying an oval with a face that is a baby, and a big "x" in the sky has a face and a four-fingered hand waving. "Adam? How about we pin your art on the wall?"

Adam nods and jumps up to go help hang it up.

"The letters for adoptees' access to sibling information?" says Claire. "That's doing just fine in the typewriter."

Chapter 22

Five years later

"Jules, can you come down here, please? We have to talk," Jo calls up the stairwell.

She looks toward the kitchen to Will, who's sitting next to Karl helping him out with breakfast. "Will, I think we should both talk with her. In the living room." Jo has a red embossed envelope in her hand, and she waves it in the direction of the living room.

Will nods, turns on the TV for Karl, and joins Jo. They sit in their designated recliners, awkwardly silent, the envelope on the end table lying between them. Will looks at his watch and lights a cigarette. Jo is in her housecoat and misses her mouth as she goes to sip her coffee, spilling it all down her front.

"Damn it." She pulls out a wadded Kleenex from her pocket and pats at the drips. "Just look at me." Jo holds out her hand so Will can see it shaking.

Will isn't the least bit concerned.

"Do you think she'll want to leave us, to live with her?"

Will exhales the smoke out the corner of his mouth and looks at her. "Jo, we've been through this." He flicks ashes into the tray, "She's a grown woman. When Jules is ready to move out, we'll help her pack."

Jules leaps down the stairs in her cheerleading uniform, does a cartwheel, and lands in a full lotus right in front of her parents' feet. She throws her arms out and sings, "Ta dah."

Jo and Will both look at her with blank faces. Typical Jules behavior. Jo never did manage to train her to be ladylike, too busy taking care of Karl.

"I heard you," says Jules. "You said I was a grown woman. I'm ready for my extra privileges now."

Jo raises her eyebrows at that comment. Jules has been doing whatever she wants for quite some time. Oh, she's responsible and considerate for sure, but if there were more privileges to give, Jo couldn't think of any.

"Like my very adult, eighteenth birthday outfit?" Jules looks back and forth between her mom and dad. Will usually has something to say about modesty and short skirts. But today there's no commentary about her outfit or makeup. Will didn't even give his typical warning about leaving the curling iron on in the bathroom—the most common cause of house fires.

Jules looks at them and their silence with confused suspicion. She squints and attempts to read their serious faces. "I . . . are we OK? Everything good with Karl?" She turns her head to look into the kitchen and sees Karl slurping down cereal while engrossed in the morning cartoons. She looks at them both, now taking on their serious demeanor. "Did someone die?"

Jo looks for Will to start "the talk," but he remains quiet. "Jules, you're eighteen, and there's something we want to tell you." Jo looks over at Will again, waiting for him to chime in. He doesn't.

"OK."

Jo picks up the red envelope and hands it to Jules without explanation.

Jules takes the card and looks at her mom and then her dad. "This *talk* is about a birthday card?"

"Yes," says Jo. "It's from your birthmother." Finally, the words came out. Jo's entire body melts into the recliner.

Jules notices Jo's reaction, "You're OK about this?"

Jo quickly nods. Keeping that red envelope unopened in her desk for the last two days was no easy thing. Her instinct was to read it and make sure there was nothing threatening, or intimidating. But Will is right. Jules is grown up. That's the whole reason they waited this long to tell her. Jo and Will are no longer in the position to protect her from a relationship with her birthmother or any subsequent siblings she may learn of. What she does with this information is completely for Jules to decide. *That* is the gift Claire, Jo, and Will are giving Jules today.

Jules looks at the card and then to her dad for his confirmation. Will nods, spits off whatever bit of tobacco is on his lip, and takes another drag from his cigarette.

Jo slurps her coffee and looks at Jules over the rim. "Do you have any questions? Anything you want to say?"

"Oh. Right." Jules taps the card on her leg a few times, "Thank you." She offers it back to Jo. "It's OK if you want to read it."

Will finally speaks, "No." He brushes the back of his hand toward Jules, indicating she should keep it.

Jo shakes her head, "It's for you."

Jules bites the corner of her cheek. She stands up, grabs her letter jacket from the hall closet. "You realize this isn't a surprise to me, right?" She jams the card into the pocket. "You've told me all my life I was adopted. I knew someday I'd know her."

"How did you know?" asks Jo.

"I just do." Jules looks for her keys in the front pocket of her backpack and turns with an eyebrow raised, "How did *you* know? This. From my birthmother?"

"Well . . ." Jo looks at Will for any help.

He offers nothing.

Jo is *done* with secrets. "She came here once, a long time ago."

"Huh," says Jules, biting her upper lip. "Why didn't you tell me? She asked you not to?"

"No," says Jo. "It wasn't like that. She wanted to meet you right away. But it was right after Karl got home from the hospital and we thought . . . it would be too much."

"Too much," says Jules, repeating.

"Too much for *us*," continues Jo as she looks over at Will. "It was too much for all of us at the time. So we asked her to wait. Until now. And she did."

The three of them sit together in that moment of vulnerability, witnessing what it's like to have honesty, love, and trust as part of their lives. No one knows quite what to say or do. But somehow that's OK. Maybe even the way it should be.

"Well, you better get going," says Jo finally. "You'll be late."

"Any plans?" asks Will. "For your birthday."

"Oh it's going to be good," says Jules, "I'm taking the girls directly to U-Pump-It for a full tank of gas and to legally buy a six-pack from Old Man Eddie, which I will keep legally hidden in my trunk. Me and Maggy will drive to TCBY for lunch, order soft serve with sprinkles, and get slightly drunk in their parking lot. Don't worry. Just slightly. I'll get back to school in time for fifth-period Calculus, where I can prove to the nerdy boys that even a drunk cheerleader can solve integrals faster than they can."

Jo shakes her head, "For Christ's sake, Jules."

Will stamps out his cigarette and gives Jules a snort and a half-grin.

Jules throws her backpack over her shoulder, "Hey, Mom—can we have pork chops and plum dumplings tonight for my birthday dinner? With butter and cinnamon?" Jo was prepared for this request, since Jules asks for it every year. The recipe is best with fresh plums, but the store had canned and that will do.

Jules leaps up the stairs and opens the front door to see her car idling in the driveway, the windows scraped. "Thanks for warming up the car, Dad! Love you, bye!"

Jo stands up and starts up the stairs to close the door, which will inevitably be left open. "Drive safe."

Will stands up and adjusts his pants, tightening his belt a notch. "Well, that's a relief." He looks at Jo and gives her a kiss on the cheek, "Good job, Mom."

Jo watches him walk down the driveway and climb into his work van. She exhales with a slight moan and closes the door on the cold January breeze.

"Yo birthday girl, we still picking up the beer?" says Rita as she swings opens the door of Jules's 1966 green Chevy Impala, they named "The Tank". She's the last one in and tosses her backpack in the back seat next to Fran. Maggie's sitting in front next to Jules, eating a pancake off a paper plate.

"I'm on it," says Jules. "Dad gave me the gas card. Aunt Tylene gave me the beer money and a stick of gum."

"Any gifts from your mom?" asks Maggie, licking her fork.

"Funny you ask. I got this." Jules pulls the red embossed card from her pocket. "It's from my birthmother."

"Your what?" says Fran.

"You guys know, I'm adopted."

"Ya, but that never really meant anything," says Fran.

"It means I've never known the woman whose womb I occupied for nine months . . . until now."

Maggie snatches the card from her hand. "What's it say?"

"I don't know. I haven't read it yet."

"How did you not rip it right open the second it was in your hand?" says Fran.

"Claire Brooks . . . Idaho," reads Maggie.

"I don't know. I guess I didn't want to hurt my mom's feelings by being overly eager. What's weird is she already knew it was from my birth mom. She's been keeping it a secret."

"She was probably just protecting you," says Rita. Rita is usually spot on with the maternal perspective. Which makes sense since she nannies part time for the Richardsons. It's just babysitting like usual but with the occasional overnight stays. She also goes on vacation with them, which is great because they go to places like Hawaii and Puerto Vallarta. Apparently, she and Mr. Richardson, Jim, sleep together too. But how does that even make sense with his wife around? Rita's never very clear on the details, but she said Jim wanted her to go on the pill so they didn't have to use condoms anymore.

Jules was glad Rita shared as much as she did. It got Jules thinking about her and Devon. Since he started college and lives in the university dorms now, they spend a lot of their free time just hanging out naked together. Exploring. Relaxing. Listening to music. All under the guise of doing research at the university library for AP English and science fair projects. The idea of not having to mess with condoms is why she decided to go Planned Parenthood and ask for the pill. There was a basketball game that night, so Jules just went in her cheer uniform during lunch hour. They asked only one question, if Jules was employed, because they charge on a sliding scale. Jules paid two dollars for the required wellness exam based on the fact that she did make some money babysitting for the Hanson's when they went to Marriage Encounter every Wednesday. They gave her the monthly pill packs for free.

"Protecting me from what exactly?" says Jules.

"I watched a *Donahue* show once years ago where they had birth moms who claim they were forced to relinquish their babies and how that messed them up. Do you think she was forced to give you up?" says Fran.

"Never heard from her till now," says Jules.

"Do you think she may be messed up?" says Maggie.

"All this I don't know. To be honest, that's part of the reason why I'm not sure about opening that letter. What if she is messed up? Do I really want that in my life?" Jules pulls up next to the gas pump and parks.

"I'll pump," offers Rita, "You go," she waves her hand. "Buy beer."

Picking out the beer is easy, because there are only two kinds of three-two beer and everyone knows to go with Coors. As she is paying and telling Old Man Eddie it's her birthday, Jules watches Maggie climb over the seat to be in the back with Fran. Typical Maggie behavior.

By the time Jules gets back into the driver seat, all the windows are completely fogged up and everyone is hunched over in the backseat. "What's going on?"

"You seemed nervous about it, so we screened the card for you, while you and Old Man Eddie were flirting," says Fran.

"So, is she messed up?" Jules asks, ignoring the BS about flirting. It's common knowledge she doesn't know how to flirt. During the senior survey, apparently someone wrote in a category where she received a vote for most likely to be virgin. Jules tried to figure out who would go to the trouble to document such a ridiculous thing. Roy, the lead in the brass section said if they had a category for biggest prude, he would have voted for her. Whatever. What they didn't know is a lot.

"The question is, are *you* messed up," says Rita.

"What?"

"In my Family Sciences class, they said babies need to have skin-to-skin contact to help with the transition from the womb to the outside world. Without that, the baby may never bond with her mother.

So, being adopted as in infant, and not having skin-to-skin, there's probably a problem with you."

"I'm not messed up," says Jules. Clearly.

"Denial," says Maggie.

"Well, the letter is totally normal," says Fran, giving her full assessment, "A single bit of advice, key information, an open invitation with no obligations, and a message of love. The perfect letter according to *Cosmo*."

"That postscript though," says Rita, "that's something else."

"And this is a fucking biohazard," say Maggie, holding up a white silk pouch, pinching just the corner, trying to not really touch it.

"A biohazard? What the hell?" Jules yanks the card from Rita's hand and the silk pouch that Maggie's dangling.

Dear Jules,

Happy 18th birthday. I've waited so long for this. Know that I love you dearly and I look forward to hearing from you whenever and however you're comfortable reaching out. I hope we can become friends. Remember now that you're of legal age, you may contact Child Horizons and request your records. The truth is where love begins.

Your first mother,
Claire

P.S. Enclosed is the membrane from your en caul birth. This is part of who you are. It's part of me too. I wore it as a charm when I was searching for you—and here we are reconnected. I feel you should have it. You were born imbued with maternal protection. I hope you walk in confidence knowing that. My Oma could speak with angels and continues to leave messages to family. I often wonder what gifts may have passed on to you. I look forward to hearing your stories.

Jules thinks back to her conversation with Angel Karl when he was in the hospital. Apparently, she does have something in common with Claire's Oma. "OK," she says, tying the white silk pouch to the rearview mirror. "I'm ready for advice."

"Definitely get your records," says Fran.

"Right." She definitely wants to know as much as she can about Claire before reaching out to her. Getting the records should be easy enough. Jules contacted Child Horizons once to get her time of birth. It was part of a school assignment to create an astrology birth chart mapping out the position of the planets the day you were born. It was the only time she could remember feeling "other than" due to being adopted. She could either cheat on the schoolwork and fake a time or ask someone who knew, and that someone wasn't Mom or Dad. She wrote the agency a letter and asked. A few weeks later she received a response. 12:04 p.m. Jules always wondered if the Child Horizons secretary just made it up. It's not like they sent a copy of her actual birth record.

"Well, if you lived in Salem, Massachusetts in the 1600s," says Maggie, "you'd have burned at the stake."

"Seriously?"

"That's all I know about en caul birth. Found that doing a book report in Mr. Olson's history class," says Maggie.

"I got nothing except some throw-up in my mouth," says Rita.

"OK. Change of plans." Frozen yogurt and beer day is just going to have to wait. "Maggie, can you sign in for me and tell Mrs. Beesly I'm doing independent study at the university library today and forgot to tell her?"

"Yep."

"Hey, you guys can just up and ditch like that?" says Fran.

"AP English, baby," says Maggie. "It pays to be nerdy." Though Maggie was also a self-proclaimed nerd, she had a knack with how to twist the image into social and practical advantage. Jules always thought Maggie gave her the 'coolness lessons' that Karl never could.

"We're still doing the sleepover tonight, right?" says Rita. "I've been craving your mom's butter popcorn."

"Yes, yes, of course. I can tell you all the creepy things I find out about this little artifact," says Jules as she taps the silk pouch that swings on the rearview mirror. She starts The Tank and pauses. "Hey, let's keep this birthmother, caul thing within our sacred cone of silence for now." She holds her hands up, fingertips touching and creating a triangle in front of her face.

"Got it," says Maggie. "The cone." All the girls make a triangle in front of their faces.

"You get sports time out of school for cheering?" asks Fran.

"Yep. And band competition." Band trips are way more fun than cheer trips.

"And science fairs," says Rita with disgust.

"Have you even been in class at all this year?" asks Fran.

"Of course," says Jules. Being in two places at once was just a matter of who you tell where you are. She shifts into drive pondering if being in two places at once would qualify her as a witch.

"Karl, you asleep?"

Big fart.

Jules sits on the bed and lays her head on his chest. Karl puts his arm around her, it feels like old times. "Mom and Dad gave me my birth mom's name and address today. And her phone number. And an enchanted amniotic membrane. Wanna touch it?"

Belch.

"Gross. I could feel the hot air on my head."

"Heh," says Karl, clearly proud of himself.

"Mom looked worried this morning. I don't know. I thought they were going to tell me someone died."

"Psht."

"All I could think about was how it might hurt her if I was too excited about it. I didn't want to be too eager, like she wasn't enough of a mom or something. You know?"

"Fuck."

"Well, Dad made it clear this is my relationship to manage, not theirs. Wish they'd treat my romances like that."

"Huh." Karl rolls over, like he's going to sleep now.

"Hey, I have romance."

Fart with a disgusting squeal at the end.

Jules sits up and slaps his butt. "Just so you're aware—I got to know who my birth mom is, *first*."

She goes back to her own room and flops on the bed. The "who gets things first game" is absolutely no fun when you know darn well the other person is always and forever going to be last. And there are times when a girl needs a little more than just friends' advice. When Karl was in the hospital, Angel Karl said he'd always be there when Jules needed him. She wishes that was true. "Now would be a good time, Karl."

Jules holds the white silk pouch. Claire thinks this is part of who they are. At the library she discovered there's a name for it, she's a caul bearer. As if being adopted wasn't weird enough. If she played the parallel universe game with Karl and was born in Tibet, as a caul bearer she could become a Dalai Lama. And if she was born in Egypt, she'd be considered a mystic.

Jules imagines Claire wearing the caul as a talisman. The idea seemed weird at first, but it turns out Roman midwives were known to sell cauls to lawyers. One could argue Claire had a legal victory of sorts, in finding her child's adoptive family. Then there's the myth that babies born en caul never drown—and Mom's a lifeguard, even saved her life once when she was little. The list of superstitions and folklore goes on and on but the one Jules can't stop thinking about is the notion that the membranes protect the baby from birth trauma.

Birth trauma. Are Rita and Maggie right to think she's probably messed up? If she did have trauma, did the caul really protect her? Maybe she could go to the supposed moment of trauma and find out. She went to Karl's trauma, there on Highway 8 that day of the motorcycle accident. Angel Karl said she helped make his transition more beautiful. What if she could do that again? Some believe caul bearers have special powers. Does she?

Jules closes her eyes and holds the white silk pouch to her chest. *What's this protection from trauma all about?* A metallic taste hits her tongue, and the smell of rain before a storm fills her nostrils. Her heart pounds as she feels a soft vibration start in her legs that crescendos into an electric pulse that snaps her from her body. Jules looks up; beyond the ceiling of her bedroom, she sees darkness lit up by a million stars. One shines brighter than the others, guiding her. Looking down, Jules sees a young woman in her high school cheer uniform standing in a white-tiled hospital hallway. Jules joins herself in the hallway, standing just outside of Room 11.

Inside, a woman is giving birth. The small, sterile room looks more like it's meant for torture than birthing. The woman's legs are strapped to stirrups and her arms restrained. Her whole body convulses while a nurse manually forces the baby out of her seizing body. Jules stays outside the doorway, shocked by the brutality and unsure of what to do. Soon the newborn lay outside of her mother's body, peaceful while safe inside the fluid-filled sac. When the membrane is removed, the baby's cry awakens the mother.

"Let me see my baby," pleads the woman.

A young nurse puts the baby into a bassinet and wheels it into the hallway next to Jules. "Should we put this one in the Baby Showcase?"

For a moment, Jules thinks maybe the bitchy nurse is asking her.

"Yes," says the older one, "until the agency foster nanny comes for pickup. It's the perfect one for display hour."

Jules peers into the bassinet. The caul is sitting in a kidney tray near the baby's feet. Under the tray is a piece of paper with the instructions "Prepare for archive."

"This baby is me," Jules says out loud to the nurses. They don't acknowledge her. "Hey," says Jules, louder now, "Shouldn't she . . . I . . . be lying on my mother's chest while I learn how to breathe air?" Everyone knows the baby should be in her mother's arms, where she can feel her warmth, and be soothed by the sound of a trusted, steady heartbeat.

"Mom didn't get you for six weeks," says Karl.

Jules looks over at Angel Karl, now standing next to Jules, dressed in his light-blue satin shirt and brown corduroy suit. He never could resist joining in on the parallel universe game.

"What about the name card?" asks the young nurse.

"Just write Baby Girl," says the older nurse.

Jules looks at Karl, reaches into the bassinet, and brushes the newborn hair with her fingertips. With a tiny baby-sized electric spark, Jules scoops her up in her arms, "OK, Baby Girl, you're coming with me."

"My mom calls me Sarah." The baby speaks with confidence to Jules's heart.

Jules looks at Karl, to see if he heard Sarah's voice too.

"You heard her," says Karl.

"OK then, Sarah. Let's get out of here."

Jules takes the three of them to the west garage on Grandpa Fats' farm, where the fuchsia four o'clocks are opened, the robins and doves are singing, and the sun is setting over the alfalfa fields. Karl and Jules sit with their backs leaned against the garage, making cute cooing noises while cuddling Sarah.

Jules unbuttons her shirt.

"Hey, what are you doing?" says Karl.

"Skin-to-skin," says Jules.

Jules holds Sarah close, "We don't want you to be messed up, do we?" she says in a sweet talking-to-her-baby-self voice.

The top 40 countdown is playing on the radio. Jules is on her bed rereading for the ninetieth time the birthday card from Claire. She looks at the phone sitting at the head of the bed. This could be as easy as dialing her number and saying hello. It'll show up as a long-distance bill, but she can warn Mom about it before the bill comes in the mail. It'll be fine. Dad said, "Use your judgement." Jules pulls on the cord and drags the phone over to her, then press the lit squares with Claire's number. The connection clicks. She hears the first ring, panics, and hangs up. Nope. Not ready yet.

Jules kicks up her feet and bounces up from the bed, plopping in front of her child-sized desk and digging through the lap drawer. There it is, the letter she received from Child Horizons that says she was born at 12:04 p.m. Their phone number is on the letterhead. She plops back down on the bed and presses the lit squares with the Child Horizons number.

"Child Horizons, how may I help you?"

"This is Julia Fae Tischler. I was adopted through this agency. I understand now that I'm eighteen, I can have my records mailed to me."

"Hello, Miss Tischler. Yes, we can help you with that. Just one moment."

Jules twists the cord around her finger.

"I see there's a note on your record to forward your requests to our senior post-adoption specialist Bonnie Cox. Please hold while I transfer you."

Jules listens to the hold music in one ear, and the Casey Kasem show in the other ear, which is now playing a long-distance dedication. "Like a Virgin." Seriously?

"Julia Fae Tischler?"

"Yes."

"Well hello honey, my name is Bonnie. I'm so glad you called. I understand you're requesting your file?"

"That's possible now that I'm eighteen, right?"

"Yes. However, the state of Nebraska doesn't allow me to send the adoption records."

"Oh." Didn't she just see on some *60 Minutes* episode that states have opened adoption records? "I can't access files that contain information about my own life?"

"Well, hon, many people, including your birthmother, have been advocating for adoptee access to county and agency records. The laws are decided state by state and unfortunately, the open record policy does not apply to adoptions processed in Nebraska."

Why even bother? After all, she has Claire's contact information, so whatever it is that people feel they need to hide, the cat's already out of the bag.

"Is there someone I can contact about getting my original birth certificate?" asks Jules.

"Well, no one, hon."

Really? Jules already knows the name of her birthmother. She sent a piece of the amniotic sac, for God's sake, and yet she's not allowed to possess her own birth certificate. How is that even considered legal?

"The state isn't always clear on that," continues Bonnie. "They'll take your request money and send you the birth certificate that was rewritten with your adopted parents' information."

"Agencies can just rewrite people's birth certificates?"

"Pretty much like that."

So if birth certificates can be rewritten, what good are they? "What *can* you send me?"

"You do have documents explicitly released to you by your birthmother."

"I do?" How in the world would Jules ever know to ask for them if Claire didn't tell her in the birthday card? It's not like Child Horizons sent a card and said anything. Where is the common sense in all this? Weren't these people ever told that truth is where love begins?

"Yes. Carefully filed over the years, just waiting for your request."

At least they have good filing practices. Jules tries not to sound sarcastic with Bonnie. She seems nice, and she didn't make the rules. "OK. Will you please send everything you can, then?"

"Of course, honey. Now let's see, do you have a different address from your parent's? It is an . . . *unusual* file. I want to be sure it goes to the right place."

"Wait . . . you personally *know* my file? What's unusual about it?"

"Well, it's just that . . ." Bonnie looks at the large overstuffed manila envelope, labeled eighteen years ago in her own handwriting. "It's just filled with so much love."

Jules hangs up and feels . . . happy. Joyful even. She bounces on her bed with anticipation for the day she receives the apparently notorious file filled with love.

She picks the phone up again and presses the lit squares. Now, she's ready. The connection clicks, the phone ringing in Claire's house. Jules stops breathing, prepared to hear her birthmother's voice.

"Hello?"

EPILOGUE

LIZA R. SILLER
STATE SENATOR
Twentieth District
—
HOME ADDRESS
Rural Route 5
MARSHALLTOWN, IOWA 50158

COMMITTEES

Natural Resources, *Chairperson*
Agriculture
State Government
Natural Resources Appropriations
Subcommittee

The Senate

STATE OF IOWA

Sixty-Eighth General Assembly

STATEHOUSE

Des Moines, Iowa 50319

April 9, 1979

Mrs. Claire Brooks
25 Virginian Hidden Springs
Idaho 83714

Dear Mrs. Brooks:

Thanks for your wonderful letter telling of your
decision and how it affected your life.

A bill concerning one's birth rights was passed
in the Senate this morning. Enclosed is a copy
of this bill as it stands today. Of course it
must still pass the House, or could be reconsid-
ered and would also have to be signed by the Gov-
ernor.

Very sincerely

Liza R. Siller

AFTERWORD

This is a story of two women entangled by the patriarchy of the 1960s. They faced circumstances created by choices made for them according to social constructs designed to protect reputations of men. It was a time in American history when over two million birthmothers were affected by coerced relinquishment.

Those in the shadows of power recognized emotionally charged problems like unplanned pregnancies and infertility create lucrative opportunity. Legal infrastructure formed with the purpose of destroying one family in order to create a socially superior other, all under closed records. Women who didn't want to be mothers were not allowed access to effective birth control or medically directed abortion. A broadcast sociopolitical message created the common belief that taking children from unwed pregnant women and placing them into the arms of infertile married couples is *what's best for everyone.*

At that time, the birthmother was not given guidance in how to cope with the separation from her firstborn. All she was given was a secret to hold, wrapped in guilt and shame. We know now that women who relinquish their parental rights experience grief, mourning, and emotional trauma that can last a lifetime: a wound so deep that 30 percent of women who experienced this are physically unable to have children again. And that has not changed even as the context of adoption practice has changed over the years.

During that time, the adoptive mother knew she couldn't control her community's acceptance of the adopted child that some would consider illegitimate. She understood the child will never know their own full identity; however, she was not given guidance in how to cope with the child's reaction to that reality. The adoptive mother was not given any visibility to the birthmother's response to the adoption. She was given the responsibility to unfold the potential of a child while wrapped in a shroud of uncertainty.

Current events make it clear it's time to raise awareness of past mistakes and remind each other there is a variety of healthy and beautiful ways families form. Difficult decisions that affect the development of a family should always come from a foundation of love and concern for the wellbeing of individuals.

FAMILY RECIPES

2 pkg yeast (dry)
2 cups warm water
½ c sugar
1 large can evaporated milk
2 tsp salt
2 eggs
1 c vegetable oil
7–8 c flour

Combine in large bowl, cover with a damp dishtowel and let rise

Push down dough, folding in sides, and let rise again

With floured hands, create balls from dough and place 12 on a cookie sheet

Poke the middles of the balls creating a center for filling and let rise

Poke the middles of the balls again, creating a center for filling

Fill with canned cherry filling (don't put more than 3 cherries, otherwise it'll run all over)

Beat 2 eggs and gently apply egg wash with goose feather pastry brush

Cut soft butter with sugar and flour just enough to be stable, creating a flaky sprinkle

Put a pinch of sprinkle on the top center of the cherry filling on each pastry

Bake in 350 degrees oven until golden brown

Cool on rack

Peanut Brittle for Candy Plate Gifts

1 c sugar
1 c white Karo syrup
½ tsp salt
1 tsp baking soda (set aside for quick use later)

Prepare buttered cookie sheet

Place all ingredients except baking soda in a heavy frying pan and mix well. Cook over medium flame, stirring constantly until it reaches 290 degrees on a candy thermometer and is amber in color. Remove from flame, immediately stir in the baking soda and pour out on buttered sheet spreading out quickly but gently and let cool.

Cream Cheese Mints
for Special Visitors or Formal Occasions

For 50 molded mints

    3-oz package cream cheese, softened
    3cups powdered sugar
    1/4 teaspoon mint or peppermint extract
    Green or red food color, if desired
    Granulated sugar for coating the mints

Combine cream cheese and sugar until smooth. Keep adding powdered sugar until the dough is not sticky. Add mint extract and food color and knead until evenly tinted. Roll into a rope, pinch off marble sized pieces, roll in sugar and press into rose- or leaf-shaped rubber molds. Remove mint by inverting the mold. Store in refrigerator until ready to serve. Freezes well.

Volcano For Tiki Cocktail Parties

3 jiggers Golden Rum, 1 jigger Dark Rum, and ¼ jigger 151
    Rum in top of volcano
6 dashes Absinthe, 6 dashes Angostura Bitters
Equal parts Pink Grapefruit Juice, Orange Juice, Pineapple Juice,
    Lime Juice
½ jigger Falernum, ½ jigger Grenadine Syrup

Add all ingredients (except 151 proof rum) into a large mixing glass filled with ice. Stir with a bar spoon for 15 seconds. Pour into a volcano bowl. Top with crushed ice. Pour 151 proof rum in top of volcano and set light. Garnish with your cocktail cherries and cinnamon sprinkle.

Emi's Dill Gravy for Family Gatherings

Cook a little hamburger. Set aside.

Boil eggs, peel and leave them whole. Set aside.

Boil new potatoes until soft. Keep the potato water.

Add salt

Add canned (or cooked) green or yellow beans

Add a carton of half and half

Add 3 T vinegar

Thicken with flour

Add the boiled eggs, cooked hamburger

Season with dill to taste

May be peppered

Karla's Girl Scout Graham Cracker Sandwich When Playing with Fire

16 graham crackers
8 bars of plain chocolate
16 marshmallows

Roast the marshmallows over hot coals slowly to avoid catching them on fire

Will's Milk Toast When Mom's Not Cooking

Heat a cup of milk and a pat of butter and sugar

Toast white bread slices

Pour heated milk mixture over toast

Option to sprinkle on cinnamon

Claire's Sausage Gravy Over Biscuits Breakfast Before Long Hauls

Prepare Bisquick biscuits according to the box

Brown a package of Jimmy Dean Maple Sausage

3 tablespoons butter (not margarine)
3 cups whole milk

Remove sausage leaving the drippings in the pan. Stir butter into the pan until melted. Add flour and stir until smooth. Reduce heat to medium and cook until light brown. Gradually whisk in milk and cook until thickened. Season with salt and pepper.

Add cooked sausage back to the skillet. Reduce heat and simmer for 12 to 15 minutes. If gravy becomes too thick, stir in a little more milk.

Serve with eggs cooked how he likes them and a glass of orange juice.

Impossible Pie for Breaking Hard to Believe News

1 cup flaked or shredded coconut
3/4 cup sugar
1/2 cup Bisquick mix
1/4 cup butter or margarine, softened
2 cups milk
1 1/2 teaspoons vanilla
4 eggs

Heat oven to 350°F. Grease 9-inch pie plate with shortening or cooking spray. In medium bowl, stir all ingredients until blended. Pour into pie plate. Bake 50 to 55 minutes or until golden brown and knife inserted in the center comes out clean. Cover and refrigerate any remaining pie.

Molasses Sugar Cookies
Keep on Hand for Unexpected Visitors

¾ c Crisco
1 c sugar
¼ c molasses
1 egg
2 tsp baking soda
2 c sifted flour
1 tsp cinnamon
1tsp cloves
1 tsp ginger
½ tsp salt

Combine Crisco and sugar, add molasses and egg, and beat well. Sift dry ingredients together and add to mixture. Chill. Form in 1 inch balls, roll in sugar and place on greased cookie sheet 2 inches apart. Bake in 375 degrees oven for 8–10 minutes.

Jules's Plum Dumplings
Serve with Pork for Birthday Meal

1 egg
1 c milk
1 tsp baking powder
1 tsp salt
Flour until the dough is not sticky.

Combine all ingredients until you can mold into ball that fits in the palm of your hand.

Indent the middle of the ball and press in a clean, fresh purple plum

Close the plum in completely, pinching the dough around it.

Put into boiling water. Test by tearing with two forks, cook until not doughy inside.

Drop into boiling water

Boil until not doughy inside

Put butter, cinnamon and sugar on it

Girlfriend Butter Popcorn
Makes a Huge Bowl for Sleepover Parties

Use a pan with a copper bottom

Add Crisco oil to cover bottom of pan

Put 2 kernels in the oil—when those two pop, take them out

Add 2/3 cup raw popcorn seeds

Cover pan

Once you hear the corn pop, shake the pan with the lid on top continuously

When the popcorn reaches the top of the pan, dump those out and keep cooking the rest of the unpopped kernels

Add salt to taste

Melted butter is optional however not recommended, just the Crisco oil is enough

ACKNOWLEDGEMENTS

I want to thank the Facebook moderator for kicking me out of your adoptee support group. Thanks to your rejection, I began to look deeper into my heart. Thank you, Mom and Dad, Bert and Gene Shriner, for supporting me in every endeavor in my life, including my desire to maintain a relationship with my first mother. I am so grateful for you Carol Bugni, always strong and brave, never backing away from my difficult questions and allowing me to explore this topic freely. Thank you to Evell Thomas, the post-adoption specialist at Child Savings Institute, who graciously assisted with research, offering compassion and insight. Thank you, Natalie Serber, for your expert writing instruction and warm encouragement. Thank you Annie Scott, Katie Post, Jackie Briggs, Sandra Morris, Joan Presley, Mary Marquiss, Cathleen Johnson, Julia Nico Reed, and Elizabeth Nix for your thoughtful review and positive vibes. Thank you, Mila Milic, for the cover design, Brooks Becker, copy editor, and Jaye Manus for your excellence in book production. Sharing this project with all of you has been a miraculous series of beautiful moments.

Thanks Gene, for taking a break from your angel duties to hang out with me while I write.

www.ingramcontent.com/pod-product-compliance
Lightning Source LLC
Chambersburg PA
CBHW071433200726
48294CB00002B/621